GW00597279

Drawing
from
Life

SCEPTRE

Drawing
from
Life

FRANCES NUGENT

SCEPTRE

Copyright © 1996 Frances Nugent

First published in 1996 by Hodder and Stoughton
A division of Hodder Headline PLC
A Sceptre Book

The right of Frances Nugent to be identified as the Author of
the Work has been asserted by her in accordance with the
Copyright, Designs and Patents Act 1988.

10 9 8 7 6 5 4 3 2 1

All rights reserved. No part of this publication may be
reproduced, stored in a retrieval system or transmitted
in any form or by any means without the prior written
permission of the publisher, nor be otherwise circulated
in any form of binding or cover other than that in which
it is published and without a similar condition being
imposed on the subsequent purchaser.

All characters in this publication are fictitious and any
resemblance to real persons, living or dead, is purely coincidental.

British Library Cataloguing in Publication Data

A CIP catalogue record for this book is
available from the British Library

ISBN 0 340 67256 0

Typeset by Palimpsest Book Production Limited,
Polmont, Stirlingshire
Printed and bound in Great Britain by
Mackays of Chatham PLC, Chatham, Kent

Hodder and Stoughton
A division of Hodder Headline PLC
338 Euston Road
London NW1 3BH

In memory of Christine

Acknowledgements

'Emmenez-moi'
Words and music by Charles Aznavour
© 1968 Djanik Music SA
All rights reserved. Copyright controlled.
Lyrics reproduced by courtesy of Djanik Music SA

1

Kicker always wrote on the bottom of her Christmas card: WHAT ARE YOU DOING WITH THE REST OF YOUR LIFE? in felt-tip block capitals. And because it always came at the very last minute, usually second post on Christmas Eve, Helen didn't have time to think about the message. She just laughed and put it in the middle of the mantelpiece (it was always the biggest card they received). By the time the cards were down and in the recycling box she'd forgotten all about it.

Sometimes during the year, though, it came to her – Kicker's message. Was there supposed to be an answer?

It was about twenty minutes until the end of the school day. The calm before the storm. Helen reached for the kettle, a teabag and the royal wedding mug which sat on a plastic tray in front of the window.

Outside on the playing field two dozen children, blue dots against the fresh spring grass, were running round the track. It was May, and athletics had replaced football for the summer term. The rituals of the school year rolled inexorably by.

It would be Kicker's birthday in a couple of weeks. She must phone; they could have a gossip and a giggle. Kicker always helped put everything into perspective, whatever it was. And at the moment, God knows, there was plenty.

Her eyes drifted to the white wall opposite her desk where, between the door and the dusty leaves of a Swiss cheese plant, hung a Picasso – the *Woman in a Blue Dress*, the dress a spotted azure, fresh and bright, the background dark purple, the hair and eyes like those of some ancient Pharaoh.

It was not the real thing. If you looked closely you could

see that this Picasso was executed on paper, not canvas, by a
seven-year-old in Year 3 with school poster paints. Since it had
been decreed that some knowledge of the great painters was to
be incorporated into the National Curriculum, the school had
blossomed with mini Van Goghs and Monets. Up and down the
corridor were pinned vases of bronze sunflowers and purple
irises, poppy-bespattered meadows. The real ones were worth
a fortune; these junior copies, uncannily accurate, would be
taken down at the end of term to be thrown away, or to turn
yellow and dog-eared, forgotten in a drawer at home.

The telephone at Helen's elbow rang.

'Hello? Parkfield Primary, Helen Croft speaking.'

She listened, looking at her watch.

'You want to look round the school today? Er, yes, that
should be convenient. The children come out at three thirty.
How about three forty-five? By that time things ought to be
quietening down a bit . . . No, there isn't a uniform, just a
sweatshirt with the school's emblem . . . The toilets?' She
glowered into the handset. 'Perhaps it would be better if you
judged for yourself . . .'

They always seemed to care more about the uniform and the
toilets than they did about the teaching. So long as everything
looked nice on the surface, the rest didn't matter. She felt like
screaming down the phone at them sometimes; what about all
the dedication, day in day out, thankless?

'The boys' toilets do have rather a pong,' remarked one of
the nursery nurses as Helen put the phone down. She had
come in during the conversation to collect some mail from her
pigeonhole.

'Boys' toilets have ponged since time immemorial, but it
doesn't mean to say there's an imminent danger of typhoid
breaking out.'

The girl glanced at her with admiration. 'How do you manage it?'

'Manage what?'

'To stay so calm. Nothing ever seems to floor you. If I had
your job I'd be tearing my hair out. This is my third term and
I wonder how I'll ever cope – I mean really cope, not just get
through the day on a wing and a prayer.'

'I've got through my whole life on a wing and a prayer, Tamsin, believe me!'

'I don't believe it,' Tamsin said. 'Look at you – it's Friday afternoon but your blouse isn't a bit grubby and your skirt isn't even creased.'

How she came to look so tranquil she didn't know. Dave always said that even her name – Helen – had something of the serene about it. But outward impressions could be deceptive. Deftly, Helen changed the subject.

'Been buying yourself something nice?' she asked brightly, seeing the name of one of the city's best-known jewellers on the packet sticking out of Tamsin's handbag. She didn't really care, but it was something to say.

'Oh, this? It's for my mother's birthday. I hope she'll like it. It's a brooch in the shape of an E. Her name's Elizabeth,' she explained. 'She was born on Coronation Day. Helen, will you look at it for me? See what you think. She must be about your age.'

'Flatterer!' said Helen, pursing up her lips.

Tamsin looked vacant.

'I wasn't exactly a baby on Coronation Day,' Helen admitted. 'I had a toy coronation coach and horses and I learnt to sing *Here's a Health unto Her Majesty*. On the actual day I was supposed to be going to a fancy dress parade as a fairy – I had the wings and everything – but then it poured with rain and my parents made me wear my mac and wellies and call myself "Flaming June". I never forgave them.'

Tamsin looked even more vacant, as though she was recalling some Stone Age ceremony. Helen forced a laugh. 'I remember handjive and hula-hoops and Cuban heels as well, but don't spread it around, will you?'

She examined the brooch which was gold and had probably cost a lot of money. But she disliked it. Somehow it smacked of sugary sentimentality – the sort of present the young thought suitable for the old. Or at least the middle-aged. Why didn't she buy her mother some silk underwear or a few sessions on a sunbed? Something modern.

Helen looked up. Tamsin's skin was golden, perfectly smooth and firm. From her perspective, middle age was probably about twenty-four. Handing the brooch back, she said, 'It's very nice. I expect she'll like it,' and hoped perversely that she wouldn't.

Tamsin didn't seem to feel her icy tone. 'Has your husband heard about his new job yet?' she asked.

'The Chair? Not yet.'

What Helen was thinking was: *Ianthe must be about the same age as her.*

She drained her mug and paused for a moment, her thumb on the bell, the signal for the end of afternoon school. Then she pushed it firmly, and within ten seconds the corridor had come alive with shouts and bustle, doors banging, children jostling each other. Some of them waved cheerfully to her through the glass panel. She picked up some papers and went outside, pressing herself against the wall to let the whirlwind pass.

Crossing the hall, she found someone waiting outside the head's study, a thin-faced woman in a business suit, a dark pageboy cut and large silver earrings. The real thing, all right, as were the diamonds in her oversized engagement ring.

'I rang not long ago, and I thought I might as well come straight round. I've another appointment at five, so it would be nice if we could talk straightaway.'

'Ah, yes, Mrs ... I'm sorry, I don't think I caught your name.'

'Turner. Jo Turner. We've just moved into Kingston Drive. I've two children: a boy of four and a girl of two. We shall be educating them privately later on, of course, but this is so handy. It would be a shame not to at least have a look.'

Helen took out a key and opened the door. The room was hot and dusty, dirty cups languishing on the table, a limp spider plant spilling down the side of the filing cabinet, posters for the Summer Fayre strewn across the desk. Helen swept them away apologetically.

'Why don't you take a seat? I'm sorry about the clutter. You know how it is.'

She was sure that Mrs Turner hadn't the least idea how it was.

The visitor, smoothing down her skirt with immaculately manicured hands, took in the smell of instant coffee, chalk and sweaty plimsolls. 'May I ask how long you've been head here?' she asked.

Helen smiled sweetly. 'I'm not the head, Mrs Turner. I'm only the secretary.'

'Oh!'

The monosyllable said it all. It was condescending, suddenly aloof. And why had she said 'only'? So she was the secretary. So she was middle-aged. Why should she apologise for it? She had met them countless times, these stuck-up women. They were the sort you met at school reunions, the sort who only got a couple of O levels and who had been trying to make up for it ever since, with their mannish clothes and their loud voices, boasting about their high-pressure jobs, their nannies, their five-bedroomed executive homes with mock Tudor gables or Grecian pillars. They had it all, or they liked you to think they had.

She reflected that all her status came from Dave – Dave who was going to get the Chair, or wasn't going to get it, as the case might be.

'The head has been organising games, but she'll be along in a minute. Would you like a cup of tea while you wait?'

She said it cheerfully, but with a covert wish that they kept rat poison in the stock cupboard. The woman seemed to shudder and refused the offer so Helen withdrew, taking the posters with her. She had promised to have them pinned up in some of the local shops at the weekend.

When she arrived back in the general office, Mrs Rose, the head teacher, was signing the day's letters.

'Are those the Summer Fayre posters? I'll take one if I may. It can go on the church noticeboard. I'm hoping that we'll make even more this year. You're doing your cats again, aren't you? They're always a good line. Bring in a fair bit.'

It was on the tip of Helen's tongue to say no. The snooty Mrs Turner had rattled her nerves. She put a lot of effort into painting her cats; sinuous black ones with emerald eyes against a jungle background, supercilious Siamese ones perched on tasselled velvet cushions. They were sleek, stylised creatures; Helen hated fluffiness. But they were very popular and she sold them for £19.99 each in aid of the Parent–Teacher Association, the profits going towards keeping the school minibus on the road and replacing worn out musical instruments. It was a derisory sum but the market wouldn't stand any more. This was a trestle table in the school hall, squeezed between the cake stall and the tombola, not a classy boutique in the Cotswolds.

She always came back from the Summer Fayre feeling depressed, despite the praise. ('You painted them yourself, dear? So clever! It'll do nicely for my daughter's birthday. She likes things like that.') People wanted the same over and over again. The same cats as last year and the year before; the spontaneity had drained away.

'I'm doing something a bit different this year,' she said. 'A unicorn, and another of a zebra.' ('Nature's barcode,' Oliver had called it affectionately.)

'Oh, are you?' Mrs Rose's voice tailed off. She wasn't sure about a zebra.

Helen folded the signed letters and put them in their envelopes with a grimace. If Mrs Rose didn't like it, she could get someone else to earn a hundred pounds or so for the school fund.

'There's a Mrs Turner waiting in your room. She wants to have a look round. Thinks this place might suit her little darlings until they come to the top of the list for St Chads or the High.'

'Boy's toilets first on the list, I suppose?'

'You guessed it. Have a good weekend. See you Monday.'

A quietness had descended. Helen tidied her desk, rinsed her cup, watered a pink geranium and the Swiss cheese plant. The usual Friday routine. The job was undemanding and it would never cross her mind again until 8.45 on Monday morning. At one time she had liked it that way.

She put on her jacket and picked up the post, locking the door behind her.

Her younger son, Tim, was waiting near the car, kicking a pebble half-heartedly up and down the school drive. Helen often wondered if it bothered him having his mother on the premises, but he never gave any indication that he minded. He was only eight, patient and a little dreamy, with Dave's deep-set eyes fringed with dark lashes. Their afterthought. When he was born it used to ruffle her when people asked if he was a mistake. She would laugh and say 'Best mistake I ever made' and mean it.

But he still hadn't reached that bolshie stage when the hormones start to go berserk. Perhaps then she might change her mind.

'I've got to pop round to Gran's,' she said. 'Want to come?'

He nodded with a crooked grin. Gran would give him sweets and make a fuss of him. At home he was only just tolerated by the two older ones and Dave seemed to be late home more often than not. Even then all he could do was shout.

Helen unlocked the nine-year-old Mini, which was older than her son, and Tim threw his sports bag in the back.

'Had a nice day?' she asked.

'OK. Friday's all right. It's nearly Saturday. Like waiting for the traffic lights to go to green.'

'So Friday's a red and orange day, is that it?'

Tim nodded. 'Sort of.'

'And Monday's back to red?'

'I don't like red. Football and mental arithmetic.'

After stopping at the corner to push the pile of envelopes into the letterbox, Helen swung out into the main road. If she was lucky she would just beat the Friday evening rush-hour traffic leaving the city.

Her mother lived just off the ring road in a sheltered housing complex, with a warden and an emergency telephone. There were no stairs, though her mother could still climb stairs quite easily. But one day she might not be able to. You had to think about these things, the doctor had said, and Helen had agreed. Her mother, being cautious and brought up in an era when you did as the doctor told you, had acquiesced.

Had she ever been guilty of giving her mother a brooch she wouldn't have been seen dead wearing herself? Probably. When did it happen, that moment when your parents stopped fretting about you, and you started fretting about them? When they stopped treating you like children and you started treating them like children? She had always felt protective towards her mother, but she would hate it if her children started fussing over her in the same way.

On the hill, Helen put her foot down, but the car nearly died, and she changed down into third. Dave talked about a new car, but he never did anything about it. When it's all settled, he would say. He didn't really care about cars. They were lumps of metal to get you from A to B.

When it's all settled. Damn you, Dave. Their life was on hold, until everything was settled.

'Have you got any old clothes, Mummy? We're doing the Victorians. We have to go in Victorian costume.'

'Have you? When?'

'Dunno. One day,' he answered vaguely.

'Your grandfather was a Victorian. Just.'

'What, Grandad Butcher, that's dead?'

'Yes. He was born right at the end of 1900 a few weeks before Queen Victoria died.'

'Do you remember him?'

'Of course! He didn't die until about twenty years ago.'

'Did he wear old-fashioned clothes?'

'Gran will show you a photo, if you like.'

Suddenly Helen wished she hadn't brought the subject up. When she thought about her father she was about twelve again, trying to please, never quite succeeding. In her head she saw him still: stern mouth, highly polished shoes, long hair at the side of his head smoothed over his bald patch. Outward things. What he was like inside she had no idea. They had never really had a conversation as adults, certainly not as equals.

But Tim didn't ask any more. Children at that age had no sense of what was in the past. Dinosaurs and Spitfires were on an even footing: they were only stories.

'But they weren't Victorian clothes,' she added as an after-thought, remembering that, in French, the word for story and for history was the same.

They came to a halt in the tiny visitors' car park. The residents weren't expected to have cars. Like children they were deemed not safe on the roads, once they entered the sanctuary of Rivergreen House. There was no river, and precious little green, except for some scrawny cotoneasters on either side of the main entrance, though there was a small municipal park over the road with a couple of ducks on a pond and some rhododendrons. The children's play area in the corner was vandalised and covered in graffiti.

'It's nice in the daytime before the teenagers congregate,' the warden told her comfortingly, as though the residents weren't allowed out after dark. And perhaps they weren't.

They all had names like that, the places they had visited before her mother had moved here: either with rural connotations like Hollybank and Hazel Hill or hints of the aristocratic, like Lea Hurst and Claremont. Gleefully she had been searching for one called Parkhurst – a horrible *faux pas*, a stately home and a jail all in one.

Helen gazed at the neat little maisonettes in yellow brick topped with red slates. In the middle was the main door, with windows either side, like a child's drawing. It might not be so very long before they would all be putting her into one of them – Emma, Oliver and Tim. Realistically, more than half of her life must be over. By then there would be sixties' nights instead of old-time dancing. They would sit round the piano and sing 'All you need is love' instead of 'We'll meet again'. They would do it knowing that in truth you needed a hell of a lot more than love. The songs of youth. Not lies, exactly, just illusions.

'Your mother's upstairs. Having tea with Mr Vernon,' the warden told them. 'They're getting very friendly these days, Mrs Butcher and Mr Vernon.' She gave a little snigger. 'Shall I call her on the intercom?'

There was no privacy in the place. The warden always knew. She ought to have looked like one of those hefty, hard-faced Russian women they used to have in spoof spy films, but she didn't. She had soft, greying hair and a lacy pink jumper, with her spectacles hanging round her neck on a chain.

'I don't want to disturb them . . .'

'Oh, I'm sure you wouldn't be doing that.'

Could she read their minds? They were, after all, old enough to do as they pleased. Helen had met Mr Vernon. He was a little bent, but he was always whistling and he wore his trilby at a rakish angle. They might be in bed, for all the warden knew.

It was an amusing thought, but Helen didn't laugh. She resented this woman who was looking after her mother when she should have been doing it herself. Guiltily, she also resented her mother for not being available when she ought to have been.

But she nodded, weakly giving in. They always came on Fridays after school. Her mother should have remembered that.

The little flat was full to bursting with furniture that was too big for it: a dresser touching the ceiling, a squat china cabinet. The children always kicked the cabinet as they went past, and Helen always said 'Be careful' and her mother always said 'I'll have to get Dave to move it for me.' But he never did. There was nowhere else for it to go.

'I didn't know you were coming, dear,' Marion Butcher said. 'Do you want some squash, Tim? Oh, isn't it hot?'

'He can get it himself, Mother.'

But she knew he wouldn't be allowed to. Women of Marion's age never allowed visitors in the kitchen. The squash was brought, and a packet of chocolate biscuits. Tim tucked in. Helen thought of the garden at home and longed for a gin and tonic on the sun-lounger, a salad later on. If Dave and the children wanted something cooked tonight, they could make it themselves, or go for a takeaway.

She wished her mother had somewhere to sit in the sun, apart from the park. They hadn't thought of that, last November. It had all been so rushed, after Marion had had that turn and been admitted to hospital. Now Helen wondered ruefully if they had made a mistake persuading her to give up her own home, though she had never complained. Passively, she had gone along with everything they suggested.

'I've brought your prescription, Mother, and I wondered if you wanted me to bring you anything from town. I'm going in the morning to buy something to wear for the vice-chancellor's dinner party tomorrow night. I've got to do my dutiful wife bit.'

'What's that for? Dave's promotion?'

'Sort of. The other candidates for the Chair will be there. With their wives. I've got to look decent.'

'You always look decent, dear. That's one thing about you. You look nice in your clothes. Sort of artistic. You used to be artistic, didn't you? She used to be artistic you know, Tim. Those plates with the flowers and leaves on them. You see them on television.'

'Not the sort I made, you don't,' Helen said.

It seemed like another century now, those two years or so

when she had teamed up with a friend in Yorkshire. Daisy had made the pots and she had painted them in orange, bitter chocolate, purple – the colours of the early seventies. They had lived on stuffed peppers and wheatgerm, floating about in cheesecloth smocks, before they had gone broke and the landlord had thrown them out and turned the place into a holiday let. That was the whole of her artistic life. Now she painted cats and zebras in the utility room, for sale at the Summer Fayre.

'Well I hope it goes all right for Dave. It's good for a man to feel he's got the job he wants at his age. That's what hit your father. He never got to be head of his section. He ought to have been, but they started to bring in young men with degrees. It was different when he started out, after the war. Nobody had letters after their names.'

'That reminds me, Tim wanted to see a photo of his grandad. Can I show him?'

'You know where they are. But wash your fingers, Tim, there's a good boy.'

She brought a dishcloth from the kitchen to wipe his chocolatey hands and Helen went to the sideboard to look for the old cigar box where her mother kept her most precious photographs. There was one of herself in a christening robe and bonnet, lying on a hand-crocheted shawl, another showing her mother in the austere costume of a post-war wedding. Her father was wearing white gloves. Helen thought it looked bizarre. When did people stop wearing white gloves at weddings? Her mother seemed to simper, her father stared at the camera blankly.

In reality, Helen knew very little about her father. History, with a sweeping generality, has done the Victorians a great injustice, tarring them all with the same brush of gloom and respectability but, from what she could gather, James Butcher had been brought up by parents who conformed to the stereotype and it had rubbed off. He and his older brother had worked in the family grocery shop in a dismal little village on the Welsh borders, without ever travelling much further afield than Shrewsbury. During the depression of the thirties the business dwindled away almost to nothing. Even if they had wanted to escape there was no money to marry, no other job to go to. Their father still ruled them, even as grown men, from behind his bacon slicer. They were trapped in a disappearing way of life, like wasps in a jam pot. Not even as lucky, since wasps meet death happily, drowned in sweetness.

It was the war that made the difference. The war had been the best years of his life, James Butcher always said, fighting in the desert with Monty, landing on the French beaches on D-Day. And all without so much as a scratch, as far as Helen knew. Later in life, all the books he ever bought were war books; or those magazines with titles like *World War II in Depth – the Path to Glory* which came out in weekly parts, the first two for the price of one, so that he could live through it all over again.

The army had been his liberation, not his prison, the only time he ever found real comradeship, a true purpose. Civilian life could never match it and he didn't expect it to. After it was over, he sank back into the respectability that was expected of him, morose and with a tendency to grumble which grew worse as he got older.

After the war he had a clerical position at the town hall, where Marion, more than twenty years his junior, worked in the typing pool. He had never had much time for women, but he recognised that married life was more comfortable than a single existence, coming home to a dark flat and tinned food. For a few months he lived on bread and margarine and corned beef. Then he plucked up the courage to propose.

As far as Helen knew, nothing else had ever happened to him, certainly nothing of importance. He had always seemed so old to her. And now she could never think of him as anything else but a blackmailer.

Marion Butcher looked over her shoulder, pointing.

'Look at that hat! I saved up for weeks to buy it. Nobody had anything then really, not compared with today. But you didn't realise. You didn't miss it.'

She too was plunged into thought. After they were married they bought a semi-detached house and belonged to the chapel. Her husband ran the local Scout troop; she made pin money by icing wedding cakes. They had a bottle of sherry at Christmas and spent a week at the seaside in the summer. While James went to Scout camp in the Peak District or on the Lincolnshire coast at Whitsun, Marion stayed with her sister in Chesterfield. Neither of them had ever been inside an art gallery; that was why Helen had come as such a shock.

Helen was their only child. There had been some problem at the birth and the doctor had advised against any more pregnancies, but James was already approaching fifty and it was no wrench. In fact Marion thought he was rather relieved; sex had always seemed more of a duty than a pleasure. They never discussed it, of course, but at the beginning of the fifties, when he was promoted to assistant head of his department, he suggested they bought a couple of those new divans. He even agreed to pink candlewick bedspreads, just to butter her up, but all the year round she knew he dreamed of his two weeks under canvas. That was where he felt at home.

Helen said: 'People only take photos of good times, never bad. Have you ever noticed that?' She had never seen a photograph taken at a funeral.

They left Tim, flicking through the cigar box, looking for a photograph of himself, or of Emma or Oliver in their prams or in a paddling pool, to prove to himself that once they had been smaller than he was now.

'Talking of good times,' Marion said, 'do you know who I saw in the supermarket on Thursday?'

Helen shook her head.

'Mrs Valentine. You remember, Paul's mother. He's the head of a chain of estate agents now, apparently. Lives in one of those great big houses in Howard Park. They've been burgled twice in the last six months.'

'Mother, really!' It was as if she measured success by the number of times someone had been robbed.

'Stole all sorts. You ought to have stuck with him, my girl. He was always generous. Look at that engagement ring he gave you.'

'I lost it,' she confessed. She hadn't thought about Paul for years, nor about the engagement ring. It had been a diamond solitaire, too big for her finger.

'Did you? You never said. No wonder he dropped you.'

'I dropped him.'

'Not clever enough for you, I suppose, once you'd been to university?'

'Actually, it was because he was a lousy lover.'

Whatever made her say that? You didn't say things like that to your mother, at least women her age didn't.

But her mother didn't seem shocked. 'In my day,' she replied, almost wistfully, 'you didn't think of that.'

Tim had lost interest in the cigar box and picked up a battered exercise book that lay beside it in the cupboard.

'What's this?'

'Don't, Tim,' Helen began. 'Those are Gran's private things.'

'Oh, it's all right,' Marion said. 'Actually I've been going to give it to you. It's your father's old diary. The one he kept during the war. It's yours by right.'

'I didn't know he kept a diary.'

She had never seen her father write so much as a letter by hand, though he used to have an old manual typewriter to compose complaints to the bank or to the Inland Revenue when he thought he'd been hard done by.

'Have you read it?' she asked.

Her mother shook her head, taking the exercise book from Tim and handing it to her daughter. 'No. I didn't like to. Doesn't that sound funny?'

Hesitantly she tried to explain. 'It's all too near to me still – the war and everything. He could never talk about it, you know. You take it. Oliver might be interested.'

Helen opened the book but hardly glanced at the yellowing pages. She didn't want it, but she couldn't hurt her mother's feelings. After all, she didn't have to read it.

Tim began picking out a ragged tune on the piano. Helen didn't know how the removal men had managed to get it into the room, but they had.

'Gran, what was Beethoven doing, lying in his coffin and crossing out all the notes he'd written?'

Marion turned to her daughter, puzzled. 'What's he talking about?'

'It's a joke, Mother.' Working in a primary school she knew almost all of them by now. Round and round they went, new to every generation of children.

'I don't know, dear. What was he doing?'

'Decomposing!'

Marion thought for a moment. 'Oh, yes, I see. Decomposing. That's very good, Tim. I'll tell it to Frank – Mr Vernon. He likes jokes about death.'

'Does he?' Helen asked, rather doubtfully.

'When you get to our age, people don't like to talk about death in your presence. It shocks them and he likes that.'

'You seem to be quite friendly with this Mr Vernon,' Helen said, slipping the diary into her bag.

Only after she had spoken did she realise she had used the same teasing tone as the warden. Her mother had sleek white hair, and though amply covered with flesh was not fat. Men probably thought she was quite cuddly. Helen had never imagined her with a boyfriend before, but perhaps she should have done. Suddenly she was terrified of being like Tamsin, when she had probably been like that all her life.

'Your father didn't have a sense of humour,' said Marion Butcher. It was the worst she had ever accused him of, in spite of his domineering ways, but women of that generation accepted so much more than they ever did now.

'I hope you find something to wear tomorrow, dear. There's nothing I need in town, not just at the moment. But I'm going to treat myself soon. I've decided to get rid of the piano and buy one of those keyboards. Frank says you can make them sound like an organ, or a saxophone, or anything you like.'

Helen was too amazed to say anything at all about that.

As they stepped into the hall at home, the house seemed to throb with the heavy rhythmic noise of Oliver's ghetto blaster.

'Run up and tell him to turn down the decibels or use his headphones, will you Tim?' Helen asked.

Oliver was supposed to be studying for exams but there wasn't much chance of getting anything into his head with that row going on. He thought school was a waste of time; if he scraped a C in computer studies it would be a miracle. And Dave never stopped nagging him about it, as though it was shameful for any son of his to be so stupid. Dave had a first and a Ph.D. and Oliver was letting him down.

Through the kitchen window Helen saw Emma stretched on the grass in her bikini, surrounded by books, her shoulder-length hair tucked up inside a wide-brimmed hat. She had exams too, but with Emma there had never been any problem with studying. The trouble with Emma lay elsewhere, as far as Dave was concerned. Two teenagers, always at loggerheads with their father, and there was still Tim to come. It made her wince, thinking of going through it all over again.

Automatically she picked Tim's bag from where he had thrown it on the floor, poured herself some lemonade from the fridge, and went out to join her daughter. The purple clematis on the pergola was just coming into bloom.

'Hi, there. How's the revision?'

'Rotten. I'm sure I'm swotting all the wrong questions.'

When Emma said that, it meant that she was reasonably confident. She had never failed an exam up to now.

'I've been thinking, Mum – if I don't get into university I might go abroad. Jake's cousin is out in Thailand helping to set up fish farms or something.'

'What sort of fish do they eat in Thailand?'

'God knows. That stuff you eat raw, probably.'

'Isn't that Japan?'

'I don't know, but it sounds like a good idea, doesn't it? Jake's into intermediate technology. He had an argument with the economics teacher about it.'

Helen thought: If I'd have told my parents I was going half-way round the world with my boyfriend, they'd have died. Her father nearly did die.

But Emma would just look down her nose and say airily, 'You can't tell me how to live my life', just as she had to Dave the other day. Emma didn't keep her life secret, hiding everything away as she had had to do, and Helen admired her for it. She had never had the guts to be like that. She had given in.

'I don't suppose you'll have any difficulty getting the right grades. But you must do what you think best.'

'Oh, by the way, someone rang for Dad. She's left a message on the answering machine. Iolanthe or something. A student of his, I think. Sounded very sexy. She wants Dad to ring her back.'

'Does she?' Helen, purposely vague, finished the lemonade and went in to mix herself a gin and tonic.

In the kitchen she pressed the button on the answering machine and a girl's voice, a little stilted because she was talking into a machine, but soft, confident and very young said: 'Hello, David, this is Ianthe. I've got a problem with that last set of data. Can you ring me? I'm at home till about eight. Thanks.'

David. Whatever made her call him that? Nobody ever called him anything but Dave. When Helen was at college she had called the lecturers 'Doctor', and they had called the female students 'Miss'.

She gulped on the gin and tonic. It was the second time Ianthe had rung that week. Dave, do you realise what you are getting yourself into? Helen knew girls like Ianthe; she understood them. So innocent and yet so calculating. She had been there herself, once.

The machine beeped, the tape in the machine whirred back into place. Deliberately she pressed the button that would erase the message. In a few months it would be their twentieth wedding anniversary. It was stupid, but she felt like bursting into tears.

2

'You can't go in trousers!' Dave objected, noticing all of a sudden what she was wearing, as he frantically tried on ties, one after the other. There were almost a dozen of them lying discarded on the bed.

'Why not? You are,' Helen retorted.

She sounded scathing, which wasn't like her, but the answering machine message still rankled. It had been childish to erase it, particularly as Ianthe was bound to mention it. Dave hadn't arrived home until after eight, too late to respond, but she might have rung again this morning, while Helen was in town.

'Very funny!'

He decided on the silk one his sister had given him last Christmas, which he had never worn. He hardly ever wore a tie for work. That would have to change, once he got the Chair. *If* he got it.

He retrieved the other ties from the bed and bundled them back into the drawer. 'I mean it. Haven't you got a skirt or a dress or something?'

'Velvet trousers are perfectly OK for dinner parties. It's a designer label. So is the shirt. I bought it at the dress agency in Oxford Road.'

'You mean it's second-hand?' he asked incredulously.

'One previous careful lady owner, I believe the expression is.'

'I thought you were going to buy something new.'

It was hand-painted silk, a one-off, knocked down to a ludicrously low price, but he had always looked on her weakness for old clothes as eccentric. She had a black cocktail dress with beading down the front which dated from 1935 and a couple of high-necked Edwardian blouses which she had lovingly restored with the help of modern washing powders and a book on hand-smocking.

'Dave, do you know how much this shirt alone would have cost new?'

'I think I'd rather you wore the thing with the beads on than that.'

He leaned over to fasten his shoe laces, stiff in a new suit, and Helen made a face behind his back. It wasn't just Ianthe: she resented being on show. It was Dave who was in the contest for the professorship not her; she was just an optional extra, an adjunct, taken along to make sure they didn't talk shop all evening. This wasn't America, where corporate wives were scrutinised as carefully as their husbands. So long as she didn't use four-letter words, or get roaring drunk and proposition the vice-chancellor, that ought to suffice.

'I couldn't see anything I liked in the off-the-peg stuff. It's all either for teenagers or for sixty-year-olds. I walked round Macintosh's until my feet ached.'

Macintosh's was the large department store in town, and it was years since she had been anywhere near its clothes department.

'Why don't you wear something a bit more sedate . . . ?'

He stopped, but Helen knew he had intended to add 'at your age'.

'Emma likes it.'

He shrugged. 'QED. Where is Emma tonight, anyway?'

'With Jake, I suppose.'

'What, staying over?'

Who would have imagined that Dave would turn into the very essence of a Victorian father as far as Emma was concerned? His little girl was grown up and he had not yet come to terms with the consequences.

'I don't know, but she's eighteen. She knows about contraception and safe sex. Now, whether you like it or not, she's on her own.'

It might have been easier if she'd been a bit more discreet, but that wasn't Emma's way. What Dave really couldn't swallow was finding a young man in his own bathroom one Sunday morning, wearing nothing but a towel, his damp hair combed back in a ponytail, and leaving a trail of wet footprints on the carpet.

'And because we don't let them stay here, they stay at Jake's! What kind of parents has he got, for Christ's sake?'

'Ones who bow to the inevitable, I should imagine. We mustn't antagonise Emma, Dave. She's going to university in October, and if you're not careful she won't come back.'

'She will when she wants money,' Dave said gloomily, thinking of the effect the next three years were going to have on his bank balance. 'But letting her boyfriend stay the night's not on, not with Tim in the next bedroom.'

At least Helen agreed with him about Tim. She wanted to fend off the awkward questions for just a little while longer. Childhood was pitifully short already, though she knew he slept too soundly to hear much through the wall. But the alternative was to be hypocritical, give Jake a sleeping-bag on the settee, and warn him to be back downstairs by the time Tim woke up.

The fleeting summer weather had ended abruptly and rain was beating against the bedroom window. Helen, trying to apply lipstick, shivered in her thin blouse.

'Don't drive her away, Dave,' she appealed seriously. 'That's all I ask.'

'Don't be silly. As if I would.'

But Helen knew how easy it was. There were times in her student days when she might never have gone home, even for the sake of a bed and a roof over her head, if it hadn't been for her mother. So as not to disappoint her.

As a little girl she never brought her friends to the house. By instinct she knew her father had really wanted a son. It was something never expressed in words, but certain. A boy might have enjoyed hearing about his wartime exploits, would have joined the Scouts, would have gone to cricket matches. But it never occurred to him to try and interest a girl in that.

So as soon as she was old enough she kept away, spending her Saturdays hanging round the local riding stables and her Sundays, after chapel, with her best friend Susie, who lived in a detached house with a study and fitted carpets and a Labrador.

Susie had a white organdie party dress with red velvet hearts sewn on it that Helen would have killed for. Her family owned a boat on the Grand Union canal and a holiday cottage in Derbyshire, at a time when other people still made do with a guest house at Skegness. Naturally, they had a car.

Susie's mother had been in the Wrens during the war and once she had had all her clothes blown off in an air-raid. To the young Helen, the thought of being found stark naked amid the rubble was the very height of romance and daring.

Mrs Dobson had the sort of grand manner that people like the Butchers were in awe of: something intangible to do with class. She wore nail varnish and bright red glossy lipstick; cashmere sweaters and tweed skirts with real pearls; smart little cocktail frocks for evenings. She was about the same age as Helen's mother, but Marion's usual garb consisted of a worn flannel skirt and a hand-knitted twinset. To go out she put on a brown hat that looked like a toffee, stuck on her head at an angle, and a threadbare camel-hair coat. When Helen thought of school speech day she blushed just thinking about how old her father looked and that awful monstrosity her mother would be wearing on her head.

In the Easter holidays, after they had both passed the eleven-plus, she and Susie went to Oxford to visit Susie's grandmother, all by themselves on the train. The Butchers were doubtful about sending their daughter to a stranger, but Susie's mother had been so adamant that they didn't like to refuse.

Susie's grandmother believed in exposing children to culture at an early age and she took them to see Queen Elizabeth's glove in the Ashmolean Museum (Helen never forgot that glove), the grand staircase of the Radcliffe Camera, Blenheim Palace with its painted ceilings. They went to the theatre to see a French farce and afterwards to a teashop to eat chocolate éclairs. There was an awful lot of giggling. The Butchers occasionally went to the cinema, but it was only to see films her father deemed suitable like *Around the World in Eighty Days* and *Reach for the Sky*. There was never anything frivolous. James Butcher had no idea of a child's need for frivolity.

Back home again, Helen spent her time painting stately homes and churches, copied from photographs in library books. When she declared she was going to be a painter, her father just said, 'Painting isn't a job, my girl.'

Only very slowly did it begin to dawn on Helen how ugly their house was, with its dark red-and-gold wallpaper, the home-made rug with a picture of faded roses, the beige and brown tiled fireplace, the cheap reproduction of a ship in full sail over the mantelpiece.

But she never dared to say so. Her parents would not have been insulted – just baffled. They never talked about feelings, about their own inner lives, and they had bred it into her.

At thirteen going on fourteen, Helen knitted herself a black sweater in secret and saved up all her money for a frou-frou petticoat, a creation of layered pink net that was all the rage. It stood up by itself and and she kept it at Susie's in case her mother found out; a frou-frou petticoat was not a garment that was easily hidden. With these clothes she wore purple eyeshadow and very pale, almost white, lipstick which she kept in the garden shed along with a wet flannel to wipe it off again before she came in. She was supposed to look like somebody called Juliette Greco, who was an existentialist, whatever that was. After a while the flannel started to smell.

She wasn't allowed out much, only on Tuesday evenings to the chapel youth club, but on Saturdays she spent the day with Susie. They went to town on the bus, visiting the coffee bars, playing Elvis Presley records on the jukebox, and smoking menthol cigarettes because that sort were supposed to be better for you – 'cool as a mountain stream' the advert said. There was no question of a health warning; in those days everybody smoked.

On Saturday nights she often stayed over. Susie's parents were usually out so they had the house to themselves, to play loud music on the radiogram and to ring up their friends, though Helen had no intention of telling her mother that. Marion didn't approve of children left alone in the house.

'Why don't you bring Susie over here sometimes?' her mother occasionally wanted to know. 'Her parents won't want you at their house every weekend.'

'Why shouldn't they?'

'Well you eat enough for two, for a start. I don't like to impose.'

It made Marion uncomfortable, knowing how much Susie's parents did for Helen. Susie's father was a solicitor and a JP and they moved in quite different circles from the Butchers. It never crossed her mind that some people didn't care what the grocery bills added up to.

'They can afford it,' Helen said. 'They've got cupboards full of booze – you should see it – gin, whisky, everything.'

'Don't say booze, love. It doesn't sound nice.'

Helen just shrugged. She loved them, of course. At least, she supposed she did. Her father sounded knowledgeable, giving his opinions as though he knew it all but, apart from his war books, the only reading matter in the house was the *News of the World* and *Woman's Weekly*, whereas Susie's father could speak French and Spanish and helped them with their science homework. The Dobsons carried on good-natured arguments, yelling at each other from room to room, but Helen noticed that if Marion disagreed with her husband, she never said so, she just gave an embarrassed sort of giggle and held her tongue.

When Helen was in the third year at school James Butcher retired from work and took to sitting endlessly in the armchair, in his sagging cardigan and carpet slippers, barking out orders as though he was still in the army.

'He's like his blooming Monty,' Helen said to her mother, out of earshot, when he started up. (She never used words more daring than 'blooming'.) 'Tell him to get his own tea. I would.'

But Marion was never anything but patient. 'He's all right really,' she said. 'Doesn't mean any harm.'

It was then that Helen started to feel so protective towards her mother. Whatever was wrong, she blamed it on her father.

Automatically Helen slid into the passenger seat, making a space for her feet among the maps and the discarded cassettes which lay higgledy-piggledy on the floor. When they were together Dave always drove. She looked at him in silhouette, stiff in his best clothes, far away from her. Mothers should tell their daughters how self-centred men were, but they didn't. They kept it secret, as though they were ashamed.

*　　*　　*

In the fourth form there was a school trip to London for those taking art at O level. Helen, who had never been to London, was up in the air for joy.

'We're going to the Tate Gallery and the National Gallery – that's one group. Some are going to the Victoria and Albert instead of the National. We shall have to catch the train at seven o'clock . . .'

But her father, looking up from the cash book where he patiently noted down each detail of the household expenses, said: 'You can't go to London. Where are we going to get the money?'

Helen stared. 'But I have to go. Everyone's going. It's part of the course.'

'Part of the course, my foot! We sent you to the grammar school so that you'd be able to earn your own living one day, not go on school trips to fancy art galleries.'

'Sent me! What do you mean, sent me? I passed the exam.'

'Yes, but we've got to pay for the uniform, the blazer, the sports stuff. I'm retired from the town hall. We can't afford school trips. I don't know what you want to be taking art for anyway. What's the use of it? You'd have done better with domestic science. Cooking always comes in handy.'

'Domestic science is nothing to do with cooking any more,' Helen said helplessly, on the verge of tears. She had never imagined they would forbid her to go. 'And art's my favourite subject . . . It's what I want to do.'

'People take photographs nowadays,' her father pointed out. 'Painting's no use to you in this day and age.'

He had no time for anything old-fashioned. The pretty Victorian pottery and substantial furniture his family had left him – the contents of the house in Shropshire – had all gone to auction houses and jumble sales. It was only the piano that Marion had managed to save.

'Painting isn't just what things look like,' she frowned, searching for the right words to express it. 'It's about feelings. And ideas. It's . . .'

James Butcher snapped the book shut. He had his own ideas of what his daughter ought to be. He had never had any choice in life and he didn't expect her to have any either.

'You're filling your head with rubbish, my lady. I've seen what they call art – lumps of stone with holes in and pictures of people with ears where their noses ought to be.'

Helen was ready to answer back but out of the corner of her eye she saw her mother, silently pleading for restraint, though powerless. Anyway, what was the point of arguing when he was being deliberately obtuse?

'I'm going, whatever you say,' she blustered. 'I've some money in the post office. I'll take it all out and you can't stop me.'

It cost her every last penny of her birthday and Christmas money but she went, and for ever after she remembered it as a magical day – the sort of perfect day you can only have at fifteen. She hadn't been to a museum or an art gallery since the Ashmolean and she rushed from room to room, enchanted, on fire.

After that she threw herself wholeheartedly into art, painting and drawing as much as she could. She could run up passable caricatures of the teachers which were published in the school magazine and she helped with scenery for the end-of-term play. In the exams she received the top grade and it was only natural that she should go on to study art in the sixth form.

Her father said nothing; art wasn't discussed again. Eventually nothing was discussed. Helen stayed in her room and came down only at meal times, like a lodger, though she knew quite well what went on below her in the sitting room: the quiz shows on the television with their high-pitched laughter and canned applause. Would they double their money or open the box? Her father didn't like talk when the television was on, so there was no conversation.

But on Wednesdays he went to Scouts, so Mrs Jacobson from across the road dropped in and she and Marion gossiped and laughed a bit, and shared a half-pound box of Black Magic. It was a very small rebellion.

She dreaded Emma ever feeling about her and Dave in the same way she had felt about her parents – Emma, who had been her consolation after so many months of hell.

'It's a quarter to,' she said, with a glance at the clock. 'We'd better get a move on. Am I driving home, or are you?'

They hadn't been out together for ages; perhaps this was just what they needed.

'You can, if you like, but I don't want to drink much either, not tonight.' He glanced apprehensively into the rear-view mirror. 'I feel all wrong in these cuff-links.'

'Don't worry,' she said, making an effort, trying to reassure him. After all, she didn't really know about Ianthe. It was only a feeling.

'You're the one who'll get it. You've worked your guts out for twenty-odd years for that department.'

'I wish I could be so sure.'

It was only about ten minutes' drive to the university from where they lived. They had a roomy Victorian semi, bought just before prices started to climb in the mid-seventies. The mortgage was nearly paid off, the two elder children were almost off their hands and Dave wanted to put another millstone round his neck. Head of department these days meant paperwork and public relations, balancing resources, looking for sponsorship. No wonder none of the other lecturers had applied for it. As well as the usual papers and articles, Dave was working on a book because it would supposedly lend prestige to the university. That was his excuse for always working late. And for the past three years he had been making annual trips to Malaysia and Singapore, touting for students, trying to persuade them to study in Britain instead of the States. Next year it would be China. The humble geography department had turned into the School of Geography and Earth Resources to keep its image up.

'Resources – we don't have any resources,' Dave would grumble, but he still wanted to be head of it all. The culmination of his career was to be Professor David Croft, although they had never really discussed what it would mean to either of them. He just assumed she would go along with it.

'Who are the other candidates? Tell me again, so I can memorise their names.'

'Richard George is the first one. He's second in command at one of the old polys. I've met him several times. Very bright. A couple of years younger than me. He's got a good research group going where he is. The other's a bloke called Conrad

Jones. He specialises in weather systems, climate change, that sort of thing.'

'High profile stuff,' she commented.

'Oh, yes. The media love it. And he'd be bringing a new area of expertise to the department. I met him at a conference in Australia a few years ago. He's been teaching in Hong Kong, but what with things the way they are out there, I suppose he's decided to come home.'

'Wives?'

'Richard George is bringing his, but I don't know anything about her. Jones is divorced. Married a Chinese girl out there, apparently.'

'A girl? Heavens, it sounds like Madame Butterfly!'

'All right, a woman,' Dave corrected himself. They stopped at the traffic lights and he glanced at her. 'I like the outfit, you know.'

Helen said nothing, but gave him an encouraging smile. The loyal wife act; on the whole she was pretty good at it. There was a lot of rivalry between academics at the best of times and she knew how nervous he was, like Tim before football on a Monday morning, when the others laughed at him for having two left feet. Usually Dave was calm and sure of himself, with a glint in his grey eyes. But that nonchalant smile of his had been absent recently and she could feel the aura of tension around him. It was his moment of truth. And he wasn't the dinner party type.

'I wonder what you ever did to Reg to make him come up with this idea in the first place,' she mused, trying to persuade him to lighten up a bit. 'I didn't know he was into sado-masochism.'

The evening had been the idea of Professor Bannister, the retiring head of department, known to staff and students alike as Reg. It would foster goodwill, he said, and allow the three candidates to meet other members of staff in an informal setting. The vice-chancellor would be there, and several of the lecturers. Probably some of the research students too, handing round the name badges and the cashew nuts beforehand.

And that meant Ianthe. Perhaps Helen would get the chance to see what she looked like at last, after these past few months of more and more messages on the answering machine. Neither she nor Dave had ever mentioned her name to each other, as though it was taboo.

'He means well, poor old Reg.' Dave said charitably, as they splashed through the puddles into the car park. 'We're not late are we? There are plenty of cars here already.'

'Dead on time.'

They parked the car and made a dash for it through the rain, Helen trying to negotiate the gravel in her decent shoes. The dinner was in one of the private rooms at the university staff club, an old stone house which had been standing nearly a century before the university campus had come up to surround it. The place was still as draughty and inconvenient as it had been in its heyday, with high ceilings and dark wood panelling, and all its charm seemed to have been taken away by the carpet tiles and harsh modern lighting.

They hardly had time to order drinks at the bar before Professor Bannister's wife descended on them under full sail.

'So there you are, you two! My dear, you're looking quite wonderful, isn't she Dave? I'm so glad I've found you before anyone else does, to reassure you both that it's to be absolutely informal tonight. I just hope you'll accept it in the friendly spirit it was intended. Do come and meet everyone else. Reg has just gone to find the vice-chancellor.'

So at least the velvet trousers passed muster with the professor's wife. Mrs Bannister was a stately woman with perfect, unforced manners and the sort of accent British actors had in post-war films. If Helen hadn't known her better, she would have believed that they had both schemed, she and her husband, how best to make them all squirm. The idea of this dinner for the three rival candidates was quite bizarre, but Mrs Bannister seemed totally unaware of it.

Obediently, they followed her into the next room where the company was gathering. Looking round Helen nodded to a few people that she recognised, but there was no one who could possibly be Ianthe.

Soon this could be me, Helen thought, studying Mrs Bannister. Grey hair in a bun, pink cheeks, no makeup. She was the old-fashioned sort of professor's wife who invited younger members of the department round for Sunday lunch, serving up crudités and avocado dips in the garden beforehand, welcoming their partners with a sympathetic ear.

Helen wasn't sure she was up to it, and her dining table certainly wasn't, with its felt pen marks and the places where Oliver's Stanley knife had slipped. They would need to replace the torn deck chairs too, and Dave would have to finish off that garden path he had been laying for the past two summers.

Doctor George's wife seemed much more the right type than she did, dressed in rather a loud cocktail frock, blue with purple flowers, and a voice to go with it. A marriage guidance counsellor, apparently. Perhaps she had to shout to make herself heard over the hapless divorcees, though no doubt she would be diplomatic and caring, if necessary. But her husband didn't seem to have much about him, with his codfish handshake. As far as personality was concerned, Helen judged that Dave could easily be the winner between the two of them.

'Now,' Mrs Bannister said, turning from the Georges to indicate one of the other lecturers, 'you know Dennis, of course . . .' (she certainly didn't want to invite Dennis the Menace for Sunday lunch; she knew from bitter experience that he was a groper), 'and this is Conrad Jones. I believe you've met before, Dave. Doctor Jones, this is Helen Croft, Dave's wife.'

Conrad Jones gave Dave a nod of recognition and looked straight past him towards Helen.

'I believe Helen and I already know each other,' he said, with a scrutinising look.

Helen stared, frowning, fumbling in her memory. For a moment nothing registered. Then she remembered a skinny sort of boy of twenty-one or two, ripped jeans before ever they were fashionable, brown hair covering his ears, slightly supercilious eyes, a determined chin. His hair was steel grey now, his face slightly bronzed. In his purple-and-white striped shirt and tailored grey suit he reminded her of a candidate for the American senate. But it was the same person.

'Nico?' she asked in surprise.

'They call me Conrad, these days. Always did, actually. It just didn't seem to fit the image at one stage.'

'You never told me that.'

'So you're old acquaintances?' Mrs bannister cooed, eyes wide. 'How very interesting. Didn't you know this, Dave?'

Dave looked from Conrad Jones to his wife and back again, brows knit in puzzlement. He had prepared himself for much tonight, but certainly not this.

'Didn't have an earthly . . . When was this exactly?'

'In France. In 1968,' Helen said. She turned to Mrs Bannister, trying to explain. 'I was over there for my study year as an *assistante* in a French school. But the school was on strike for most of the summer term, like everything else. You probably saw it in the newspapers. *Les événements,* they called it. The whole country almost ground to a standstill.'

'Yes, I do remember something about it,' Mrs Bannister said. 'And you were in all that? It must have been rather . . .' she fumbled for a suitable adjective '. . . intimidating.'

'Not when you're twenty,' Nico said. 'Rather exciting actually, wasn't it, Helen?'

Dave, left out of the conversation, was at a loss, but Mrs Bannister just said: 'And you've never met since? Well, we'd better leave you to talk about old times. Come on, Dave, here's Reg now.'

He was reluctant, but she bustled him expertly away as Professor Bannister came into the room, accompanied by the vice-chancellor and his wife. Behind them, carrying a tray of nibbles, came a pretty girl with a shock of light auburn hair, half on top of her head, half tumbling down in pre-Raphaelite waves. She was not particularly slim, but her legs, encased in shiny tights beneath a short black skirt, were extremely shapely. There was a fragile look about her, a bloom like a fresh peach.

Helen completely forgot about Nico. She had a terrible certainty that this was Ianthe and her white wine wobbled precariously. She was used to seeing geography students in old t-shirts and wellington boots.

'Rather a coincidence, this,' Conrad Jones was saying, nursing a martini. (Nico drinking a martini?) 'How long ago must it be . . . ?'

'Don't start counting years, Nico, for God's sake. I don't need reminding how old I am. And since when were you called Conrad?'

Trying to skirt round him so that she could keep Ianthe within her field of view, they seemed to do a strange little dance. This was all so ridiculous. She was cross with Dave for looking at them so stupidly, gaping like a fish out of water. And she was cross with Nico, just for being there, spoiling Dave's evening.

'I was christened Conrad in the chapel in Swansea where I was born. They called me Coni at school, so I just switched it round and called myself Nico. I suppose it was all those Italian films that were popular in those days – *La Dolce Vita, La Strada*. Remember them?'

'Vaguely. I never watch black-and-white films. My children think they're out of the ark.'

He smiled at her abruptness. 'Look, I didn't orchestrate this, you know. How was I to know you were married to David Croft?'

She was watching Dave who, having paid his respects to the vice-chancellor and to Professor Bannister, had detached himself and was speaking to the girl. It was Ianthe all right. They were standing side by side, heads together, deep in conversation, but frustratingly just out of earshot. Ianthe laughed, face upturned, and tossed back her hair with one hand in the way that girls do. Eagle-eyed, Helen looked for some little gesture, the body-language that would give them away.

'No, no, of course you didn't. I'm sorry. It's just all so . . .' 'Embarrassing' was what she wanted to say, but she managed to substitute 'unexpected' just in time.

'How many children have you got?'

'Three. Two boys and a girl. And you?'

'None, I'm afraid. No wife either, not any more.'

'Yes, Dave said you were divorced.'

'That's one reason I came back from Hong Kong. There were others. The political situation, of course. Boredom. I'd been there for fifteen years.'

She remembered that Nico's boredom threshold was just about as low as a three-year-old's.

'And what do you think of it, now you're back?'

'Not much, to tell you the truth. Everything's run down.

Tacky and tasteless. People living in cardboard boxes. Television programmes where people do banal things for money.'

'The revolution never came, Nico.'

Inside, she thought, 'At least he won't think much of the geography department – seventies' concrete and lecture halls that haven't been painted for upwards of ten years.'

'And what about you? What are you doing now?'

Helen, trying to put Ianthe to the back of her mind, was planning her strategy. She had been caught out many times before but she wasn't going to be caught out again and have to read the scorn in his eyes when she said: Well, I'm just a school secretary, actually.

'I paint,' she said, on the spur of the moment.

'Oh, yes, I remember. You used to have several on the go at once. We couldn't put our feet on the floor in that little room of yours, could we, for half-finished canvasses?'

Never finished, any of them. She couldn't carry them home, so they had ended up in some French dustbin. They weren't any good, anyway.

'Not quite the same stuff, these days,' she mumbled, wondering if she should claim to be a portraitist or something more abstract. Nico had never been very interested in art, anyway. He wouldn't know the difference.

'You've been married a long time, I take it?'

'Twenty years, give or take.'

'Funny, I met your husband in Sydney once. We shared a taxi to the airport. He paid the fare. I expect I owe him.'

Against her better judgement, she laughed. Other people would have started wittering about what a small world it was. One thing she did remember about Nico was that he never dealt in polite banalities.

'If you let me have a fiver I'll make sure he gets it,' she said dryly.

Dave looked up from his conversation with Ianthe and saw them smiling straight into each other's eyes.

After about an hour of circulating and forced pleasantries, they went in to dinner. The menu was the normal sort of food that was dished up on these occasions; smoked trout filets, noisettes of lamb, chocolate torte. Helen was placed next to the vice-chancellor, far away from both Dave and Nico, and she had a little time to collect herself. Nico Jones! She hadn't thought about him for years.

But perhaps it wasn't such a coincidence as it seemed at first. He and Dave were about the same age; both with a first-class degree; both still in academic life. On the day she met Dave a group of them were going to a bowling alley. There were two spare postgraduate students, one in physics, one in geography, and someone asked her which she'd prefer as a partner.

She remembered saying: 'Oh, I'll take geography. I've been out with a geography graduate before.'

Rather a quaint phrase, when you came to think about it – 'going out'. As far as she could recall, she and Nico had never had anything so formal as a date.

The vice-chancellor, she learned, was keen on gardening. Over the noisettes of lamb they chatted about double-digging; by the coffee they had embarked on slugs.

In the end, it was the sort of affair that just petered out. After coffee, everyone retired to the bar where the vice-chancellor dutifully did a last round of the candidates, having a word with each of them in turn. He didn't spend much time with the codfish, but whether that was a good sign or not Helen couldn't decide. Then he and Professor Bannister, with their respective wives, withdrew with a rather royal wave, leaving the others to their drinks and their false jollity.

None of the three hopefuls wanted to be the first to leave in case it was seen as surrender, so they stuck it out, buying drinks for those of the lecturers who were still around, as one by one the lights in the other rooms of the staff club were extinguished and the catering staff went home.

It was when Helen was slipping out of the ladies that she spied Ianthe, sitting on a stool at the bar. Her skirt had crept even further up her thighs and she was giggling. Dennis the Menace, his tie loosened, was flicking a peanut down the front of her blouse. Neither of them had been invited to the dinner itself, so they must have been sitting at the bar all evening and Dennis was definitely much the worse for wear. Helen remembered that he usually started on three or four pints of beer, then graduated to whisky. His wife had left him years ago and he was always the last to stagger home from these departmental jamborees.

'Some people never know when to call it a day,' she said pointedly to Dave, who was standing not far away, eyeing them with obvious annoyance, though he didn't approach. This evening he had to be aloof, no longer one of the boys.

'Are you implying that I've had too much to drink?' he flashed.

'Not you, those two. That's Ianthe, isn't it? I wonder if I ought to warn her about Dennis.'

'What do you mean, warn her?'

Did his voice rise slightly, panicking at the thought of her speaking to Ianthe, or was it her imagination?

'He's a lecher. Though I suppose these days she could sue for sexual harassment.'

'I wouldn't interfere if I was you. Look, do you want to go home? They'll be closing the bar any minute.'

He spun round on his heel and caught sight of Conrad Jones.

'Hell, here's Jones again,' he said in an undertone. He had been trying to avoid meeting him again all evening.

Then out loud to Nico: 'Hello again. Strange that you and Helen should already know each other. What were you doing in France in 1968, if you don't mind my asking?'

'Not at all.'

Nico sensed that he had better tread carefully and Helen could tell he was being excessively polite. 'I'd just graduated and I thought I'd have a year off, see a bit of Europe. France was a very interesting place to be that year. We had a few run-ins with the gendarmes. I'd been in Florence before that. And Munich.'

'And after that Hong Kong?' He spoke stiltedly, though he was curious.

'I was in the States for a while first.'

'And are you home for good now?' Helen asked.

'That depends.'

'Ah, yes,' Dave said. 'On the job, of course. Any other irons in the fire?'

He had been dying to ask that one.

'One or two. There's the French job. An EC pollution-monitoring station on the Mediterranean coast is looking for a head of research. That's up your street, isn't it?'

'It's the sort of thing I've been organising at our Earth Studies Centre in Devon for the past few years, yes.'

'Then there's the Oxford post. You must know about that. I'm a Cambridge man myself, so I'm not sure.'

Dave, who had never strayed from the same midlands red-brick, looked rather crushed. Oxbridge still held plenty of kudos and the vice-chancellor was a Cambridge man too.

'Peterhouse?'

'No, King's. Look, I'm aware that you consider this your territory. I'd be amazed if you didn't, but I'm still going to go for it,' – he glanced at Helen – 'old acquaintance with your wife notwithstanding. I hear she still paints, by the way.'

Helen saw that Dave was looking slightly puzzled. 'Oh, you mean those cat things,' he said vaguely.

She scowled. If he was going to blow her cover something had to be done to save the situation, and quickly. Dave had his back to the bar and couldn't see, but Dennis was moving in for the kill. His hand had strayed on to Ianthe's knee but he had obviously been feeding her drinks all evening and all she could do was snigger. Another peanut flew through the air.

'Dave,' she announced, 'I have positively got to go and rescue that poor girl,' and before either of them could say anything more, she was at Ianthe's side and had the dish of peanuts in her grasp.

'May I?' she asked brightly, putting one of them into her mouth. 'Such a waste, Dennis.'

With a grand effort she swallowed it. 'Don't take any notice of him,' she advised Ianthe with a knowing smile. 'He's been up to the same tricks for the last fifteen years to my knowledge. He makes a speciality of female research students. But then I suppose you've always got to be on the lookout for sleazy lecturers, haven't you, my dear?'

3

'Did you have to say those stupid things to Dennis?' Dave snapped as soon as they were in the car. 'Everyone in the bar could hear, and Ianthe thought you were demented.'

He had dragged her away as soon as he decently could, without even saying goodbye to Nico. As they had arranged, she climbed behind the wheel, kicking off her black shoes and feeling around in the dark for the old sneakers she wore for driving.

'Are you sure you're in a fit state for this?' he asked, wondering suddenly how much she had been drinking.

'Of course, I am. I only had one white wine. I was drinking mineral water after that.'

'Then I don't know what possessed you.'

'I was making a stand against creeps like Dennis.' She put the car into gear and they swerved out of the car park.

'And why ever didn't you tell me about Conrad Jones before? Making me look a fool! You might have warned me that my rival was one of your old boyfriends.'

'I didn't know who it was going to be, did I? When I knew him he was calling himself Nico. He was wandering round Europe doing odd jobs.'

'A sort of itinerant revolutionary by the sounds of it. Run-ins with gendarmes!'

'Don't be ridiculous! All students were left-wing then. Politics was big. Young people believed in things.'

Goodness knows why she was defending him. Nico was the only person she had ever met who called the Brownies a proto-fascist organisation.

'Are you saying they don't believe in things now?'

'Of course they do. They believe in saving the planet, but it's not something you can do single-handedly. After enthusiasm for that has waned most of them believe in keeping their heads down, so that they can get a job with a nice fat pay cheque, if they can get one at all.'

'Sounds like this Nico has had the best of both worlds. The revolution and the pay cheque.'

Helen knew the pay cheque Dave had in mind was *his* pay cheque. The showdown was very close now and he was scared, taking it out on her. The fact that she had once known Conrad Jones, however long ago, must have given him a knock he hadn't expected.

'And why the hell did you tell him you painted?'

'I do paint. What's all that mess in the utility room?'

'Yes, but it's not what you *do*.'

'On the contrary, Dave, it's the only thing that I *do*. Twenty pounds a time. Or at least nineteen ninety-nine.'

When she thought about it, it was rather like prostitution. She went on churning out her cats, whether she wanted to or not, at a fixed price, though she imagined that real prostitutes didn't pussyfoot around with prices like nineteen ninety-nine or forty-nine ninety-nine, or whatever they charged. It was the straight note, and no change given.

The windscreen wipers swished in front of them. Automatically she drove out of the campus and round the roundabout towards home as she had done a thousand times. She had made the required effort. What more did he want? Did he think she'd invited Nico here on purpose, just to make things difficult?

'How long did you know him for, anyway?'

'I don't know. A couple of months, I suppose. He worked in a bar.'

Behind them the city was lit with a dull orange glow and somewhere an ambulance siren wailed. Helen put her foot down on the accelerator as they joined the ring road.

She didn't add that they used to lie in bed all morning and then they would get up and spend the evening throwing stones at policemen.

'How was the bash?' Emma enquired, coming in from the sitting room where she had been working out in front of her fitness video in an electric blue leotard. It appeared that she hadn't stayed overnight at Jake's after all. It was one less subject for confrontation.

'It's over, that's the main thing,' Helen replied rather testily.

Dave, who hadn't said a word to her all morning, even when handing her a cup of tea, looked up from the Sunday newspaper. 'Your mother met an old flame, name of Conrad.'

Flame! The word smacked of hearts and flowers, undying love. It was certainly never like that with Nico. But Dave didn't really care. All he cared about was that Nico was after his job. He bit his lip, as he always did when he was angry.

'Mother's dark and secret past! Tell all, Mumsie!'

'There's nothing to tell. He wasn't an old flame. Just someone I knew in France, in the sixties.'

'Back in the dark ages, eh?' Oliver intervened, peeling perfectly good lettuce leaves from an iceberg to feed to his rabbit.

'The sixties! All pot and free love. "Bliss was it in that dawn to be alive, But to be young was very heaven,"' intoned Emma with relish. She was doing A level English.

'What's she on about?' asked Oliver, who almost never deigned to address his sister directly.

'It's Wordsworth, dummy. He said it about the French Revolution.'

'Nobody ever offered me any pot in the sixties,' Helen said, trying to steer them away from the subject of Nico. 'Pop stars smoked it, but most of the stuff you hear is just hype. When I first started college, you still had to wear gowns for lectures, and definitely no jeans.'

'You're kidding!'

'No I'm not.'

They could get high on a lot less than drugs in those days, not like the world-weary youngsters of these modern times. Emma would be going to university in a few months, if all went well. In the sixties your mother sent you off to university with a set of new underwear and a tin of home-made biscuits. Now it was a rape alarm and a supply of condoms.

'Didn't you ever smoke pot in the sixties, Dad?' Oliver wanted to know, peering round the side of the newspaper to see his father's face.

'Stop it, Oliver,' he mumbled. 'I don't remember.'

'That means he did,' Emma said triumphantly. 'And what about the free love bit? The flowers in the hair? The "make love not war"?'

'More war than love in Paris in 1968,' Helen said, then wished she hadn't. She really wanted to forget all about Nico.

'Is that where you knew this guy?'

'We went there,' she admitted, 'to see what was going on. There was a bunch of us. Mireille was one of them. You know Mireille – she was over here last year.'

'She brought some fancy wine, and you all had a barbecue and drank about four bottles of it. She fell down the steps in the garden. Pie-eyed.'

'She wasn't drunk. She fell over Tim's skateboard in the dark.'

'Oh, yeah?' Oliver said disbelievingly. 'And she knew this Conrad character?'

'Nico worked in a bar. That's what he called himself then. I didn't know he was called Conrad until last night.'

'And why was he at the vice-chancellor's do?'

'He's applying for the Chair.'

'What? Dad's Chair?'

That was the trouble. They had all taken it for granted. She had heard them talking to their friends; Dad was going to get promotion, Dad was going to be a professor. They liked the idea of it. The word 'professor' smacked of a bald head and a mid-European accent – someone kind and bumbling. Professors were cerebral; above anger, above hurt pride.

'It's not his Chair yet,' she said.

The phone rang and both Oliver and Emma rushed to answer it. Emma won, but it wasn't for her. She held out the receiver to her father.

'It's that girl again. Iolanthe. Isn't that some old opera?'

'She's called Ianthe,' Dave corrected. 'I'll take it in the study.'

'Ianthe?' Emma said incredulously, when he had gone. 'My God, what sort of a name's that?'

'Don't say "My God", Emma,' Helen said automatically, as she had done when her daughter was ten years old, and as her mother had done before her.

What did Ianthe want at half-past eleven on a Sunday morning? They had only been speaking to each other last night.

In the past she had never thought of students as a threat; twenty-year-olds thought anyone over forty had one foot in the grave, and Dave could never be described as trendy. He had a bush of curly greying hair, which he wore too long, and his clothes were baggy, every one an old friend. The students probably looked on him as an aging hippy.

But he was at a funny age for men. One of the teachers at school had been married for twenty-three years and one day her husband just got in the car, drove away and never came back. Without clothes, without even a credit card. It was the age when they realised that all those inflated dreams they had when they were young weren't going to come true. If Dave failed to get the professorship . . . Helen glanced at the photo of him on the dresser. He still looked quite boyish from some angles. She could sense it was going to be hell if he got it and hell if he didn't.

'Some people like literary names for their children,' she went on, picking up the conversation in a matter-of-fact tone.

'Did you and Dad trawl through literature looking for our names?' Emma asked with more than a hint of sarcasm. 'You must have started out with Jane Austen, gone on through D. H. Lawrence and ended up with Enid Blyton.'

'What's she on about now?' said Oliver again, with brotherly boorishness. He had gathered a salad for the rabbit fit to grace any dinner table.

'I wish you could have found someone a bit less wimpish for my name.'

'Isn't even poor old Jane Austen politically correct nowadays?' Helen asked, straining her ears to hear through two open doors what Dave was saying on the phone.

'Mother, really! All Emma ever did was sit around waiting for a man, her prince, her knight in shining armour. He's even called Mr Knightley! Nothing very subtle about that, was there?'

'In those days you didn't have much choice.'

'All they ever thought about was bonnets and husbands . . .'

'You can hardly expect somebody born in the eighteenth century to behave like a woman two hundred years later.'

Emma didn't understand what it was like being brought up in the fifties, never mind all that time ago: the way they had been promised everything they wanted. Like no other generation before them, they believed they had a right to whatever the world had to offer. They'd never had it so good. But there were still parents to contend with – parents to hold you back.

When universities were beginning to expand in the early sixties, any pupils with the prospect of a couple of A levels were being encouraged to apply, but the Butchers looked on it with a bewildered scepticism. Universities were for posh people.

'What's the point of it? You'd be better off getting a little office job for a while, until you get married. All that education's wasted on girls.'

It was 1964, but it could have been fifty years earlier. In her parents' eyes, girls left school early, got a job and dreamed about an engagement ring. Yet at school there had never been so much as a whisper that boys might be more valued than girls. Helen had never been confronted with any sort of prejudice.

'Married?' she repeated scornfully. When she imagined the future she never thought of marriage. Just a room of her own, an easel and paints. Sex maybe – she had been to teenage parties, with the bodies draped across each other, the furtive fondling – but not chummy domesticity.

'There's teaching training college,' Marion ventured. She had never even passed for the grammar school, never mind had the chance of a proper career, and she did want her daughter to do better, but university seemed like a distant mountain top, especially for a girl.

'Can you see me teaching? The classroom would look like a battlefield. But I wasn't thinking of university anyway. What I really want to do is go to art college.'

'Art college?' her father said with a sneer. 'What on earth's the use of art college? All those long-haired layabouts you see on television. What kind of people are you going to meet there?'

'I'm not going there to meet the right people. I'm going to learn to paint. Anyway artists aren't all anarchists.'

She fought the snubs with sarcasm but it did no good. All her arguments fell on deaf ears and there was no one to support her, not even the art teacher at school. He lived in his own little dream world, a painter *manqué*, trying desperately to sell his landscapes to bric-à-brac shops in Leamington and Stratford so that he could give up teaching altogether. He had no interest in any of his pupils' aspirations. Indeed at times he hardly seemed to notice any of them were there.

In his spare time he kept pigs and he had come to resemble one – pink with coarse thinning hair and a dismal grunt. When Helen tried to ask him to write to her parents, he just said vaguely: 'If you bring them in one day, I'll have a word, if you like.'

But she knew they would refuse to come; they found it intimidating being summoned to school. She couldn't even ask him to ring because they weren't on the phone. And the headmaster was too eager for as many of his sixth form as possible to get into university to take her side. This was a grammar school and art wasn't considered a proper academic subject. He expected his girls to be teachers, civil servants, possibly social workers – something respectable in straight skirts and sensible shoes. He put down her aspirations as being due to too many romantic novels featuring frail young artists wasted by consumption.

'You can't make a living out of art, Helen,' he attempted to point out, though Helen was sure it wasn't true. Could he really have failed to notice the thousand manifestations of art which were all around him? Who designed shop-window displays, book covers, soap box cartons? But arguing did no good. Knowing her parents' views, he refused point blank to sign the application form for art college.

Just to keep them all at bay while she planned her next move, Helen filled in a form for university entrance instead, though she hadn't the least intention of going. When they learned there was a grant, her parents didn't object to that so much. It seemed much more respectable than art college. For the first three choices she put down History of Art, then nearly tore the sheet up in frustration. Who was she trying to kid? She wanted to *do* art, to be part of a creative process, not study what was dead and gone. Disillusioned, she scribbled down French for the last three choices and handed it in.

In the other room Dave put down the phone and Helen poured herself another cup of coffee. The trouble was that she understood Ianthe all too well. The teacher, the older man. Hadn't she experienced it all herself, once upon a time?

She met Danny when she joined an art appreciation class which took place on Tuesday evenings in a room beneath the town hall. He taught art at another school but he was saving for a car, so he was augmenting his income by taking a night class. Helen, sick of Mr Granger's chocolate-box style and piggy eyes, found in Danny a fellow enthusiast. She eagerly drank in every word he uttered.

All the other students were housewives or old age pensioners so they were the youngest in the class: she almost eighteen, he twenty-three with dark wavy hair and hazel eyes – handsome, by anybody's standards, in spite of the old tweed sports jacket which was standard clothing for teachers at the time. Helen, who thirsted for beauty in everything, found it in him.

On the second evening, as the class dispersed, she hung back, hoping they could strike up a conversation.

'Need any help?' she offered, as he started to drag tables to the side of the room.

'Thanks. The caretaker grumbles if everything's not just so. Grab the other end of this, would you?'

'Sure.'

For a minute or two they heaved the tables and chairs in silence, but Helen's brain was on fire, as the possibilities presented themselves. Here was her chance; surely he could be persuaded to help her get to art college, if anybody could.

'How can you do this?' she asked, casual yet anxious to play her cards right. He might not want to be too familiar if he realised she was still a sixth-former. 'None of them seem to have got past school poster paints.'

'Some of it's pretty painful,' he agreed. 'But at least they're enthusiastic. Not like the brats in 2C.'

The noise of stacking chairs echoed in the empty room. It was more difficult than she had imagined breaking the ice, but she pressed on.

'Do you get the bus?' she enquired encouragingly, when the place was returned to spartan tidiness. 'I'm walking as far as Victoria Street.'

'I thought I'd go for a drink first. I'm hoarse from all this talking.'

They switched off the lights and together negotiated the labyrinth of corridors which lay in the bowels of the town hall, eventually surfacing beneath the colonnade where a pair of municipal stone lions guarded the front steps.

She made one final effort. 'Where are you going? The Swan?'

He was flattered at her insistence, glancing at her sideways, taking in her long legs and small breasts beneath a peasant blouse.

'Yes, want to come?'

'My bus doesn't go for another half-hour.'

'Come on then. You can tell me what you thought of the class. I don't want the whole thing petering out after three or four sessions. Helen, isn't it?' He smiled. 'Call me Danny.'

They fell into the habit of going for a drink after class, and to let him know that her interest was in him as well as in Art (it always had a capital A in her mind's eye) she turned up to watch him playing rugby one Saturday afternoon. Gradually, he took the hint.

'I'm getting my Morris Minor on Saturday,' he told her at the end of the first term. 'Why don't you come for a spin on Sunday to try it out? We could go up to Chatsworth, if you like. Have a look at some of the old masters.'

Helen felt a surge of satisfaction; her scheme was well under way. Very soon they got into the habit of spending Sundays driving all over the midlands, seeking out art galleries and stately homes.

But plans never go exactly as you hope. She had certainly never intended to fall in love with him, but as time went on she found she was more and more besotted.

There had always been a tinge of disappointment in her previous encounters with the male sex. She had expected men, but all she ever got were boys: boys at school, boys who were the sons of people her parents knew at chapel, boys at parties with beery breath, who wanted to put their hands down her dress. They certainly didn't want serious conversation and a glazed look would come into their eyes if she ventured to say anything half-way clever. It was a long time before it dawned on her how fragile the male ego was. It couldn't cope with brains.

Danny, older and, she was sure, wiser, was exactly what she had been longing for. To her, he was perfection.

It was the sixties, but the sixties had not yet started to swing, at least not in small towns in the midlands. Skirts were still knee-length, the Pill was for married women only and girls were cautious. It all happened very slowly. One week the hand on the knee, the next on the thigh above the stocking top, spinning it out, making it last, thrilling with the anticipation of what was still to come.

Young people know nothing about eroticism nowadays, Helen thought. 'In, out, and shake it all about', as Oliver said disparagingly, when the sex scenes came on television. Instant gratification was no substitute for those step-by-step pleasures, illicit but delicious. That, at least, she had to thank Danny for. Technically she remained a virgin. If it had lasted a little while longer she was sure they would soon have been proper lovers.

Of course, her parents knew nothing about Danny. She spun them a yarn about waitressing on Sundays, though they were rather surprised at her sudden conversion to Rugby Union. In fact she did work in a coffee bar for a few hours on a Saturday morning so it was not an out-and-out lie. She was expert at covering her tracks.

When the storm broke the rugby season had been over for about a month and Helen was in the middle of her A levels. Danny needed new curtains for his bedsit and she had offered to make them up for him, so she had stolen away from revision to go shopping. But there, in the middle of the market, as they were half-examining some rolls of material, arms entwined, they came face to face with Mrs Jacobson from across the road.

'She saw you kissing someone – a man, she said!' her father yelled.

It was after eleven; he had waited up for her.

'A grown man, not a boy. I want to know who it was, and I want to know now.'

Helen flinched. Her father never shouted. She sometimes wished he would, but now it was happening it stung her with resentment, and also with horror.

'His name is Danny Williams. He teaches art at Righton Hill. We . . .'

'He's a teacher?' he screeched. Marion appeared at her husband's side in her nightdress, hovering over him, trying to protect him from himself.

'You've been making yourself cheap with a *teacher*?'

'He isn't *my* teacher!'

'What does that matter? You're a schoolgirl. He's no right to be stringing you along like that.'

'I'm eighteen. I can do as I like.'

But that was not considered adult then. Eighteen-year-olds could not vote or legally do any of the things young people were allowed to do a decade later.

'Eighteen! What's that? I'm going to sit down and write a letter to the headmaster of Righton Hill and see what he has to say about it.'

'Go easy on her, Jim,' Marion urged him, trying to calm the waters. She was worried about him lately. He was often short of breath and his cheeks were shrunken until he seemed almost like a skeleton. 'And if they're fond of each other . . .' Marion, in spite of the life she had, still believed in romance.

'Fond of each other! You'll be telling me next that they're in love. Stupid girlish notions. An art teacher! I suppose he was going to help you get into art college. Well, this puts the lid on art college, my girl, I can tell you that.'

She coloured, angry that he should read her mind so easily. But why did he automatically think it was something wrong? He didn't know Danny. He didn't actually know her. He just assumed.

She locked herself in her bedroom – the classic act of a rebellious daughter – but nothing she could do or say made any difference. He wrote to Helen's headmaster and to the head of Righton Hill, complaining about Danny's unprofessional conduct and demanding what they were going to do about it.

Every day, like a man with nothing else on his mind, he lingered in the garden waiting for the postman, expecting his reply. Helen watched him with loathing from her window as he peered over the gate, craning his neck to see to the end of the road. Then suddenly he turned and stumbled, grey-faced, and fell down on the gravel path. Marion was at the shops and Helen had to run across to Mrs Jacobson's to use the phone.

She remembered kneeling beside him, trying to find some words to comfort him until the ambulance came, but she couldn't muster any. He made no sound, but his glassy, old-man's eyes rebuked her. This was her fault – the punishment for what she had done. She was too old to smack and this was the only way.

Through it all it never crossed her mind that Danny would desert her without a struggle, but he did. The phone in the house where he lived was constantly off the hook and when she went round to his bedsit he pretended to be out. All she got was a postcard depicting Rodin's sculpture of *The Kiss*, with four words scrawled on the back: 'I'm truly sorry, Danny'. It was a grand romantic gesture designed to appeal to her naivety. He must have known her inside out. After that, romance seemed to lose its bloom once and for all.

Nearly thirty years on she still smarted when she thought of what a fool she had been to believe in him. The anger was still there, and the trampled pride. Yet she could hardly remember anything about Danny himself. Had he had any real feelings for her or she for him? It didn't matter any more.

There was no question of art college now. She knew that as she sat stiffly beside her father's hospital bed when they thought he wouldn't pull through. She had received his unspoken message: give up art school or give up me. And with Danny gone, the fight had been knocked out of her. All she could think of was getting away from home – anywhere would do. A university about fifty miles away had given her a provisional offer to study French. She got an A for art but she scraped a B for French and accepted it.

'Be quiet, you two. Don't you ever talk about anything interesting?' Oliver said.

Dave returned to the table, slightly flushed, Helen thought. She knew every nuance of his face as he no doubt knew every one of hers, if he cared to take any notice.

'She wants to go down to the cottage next weekend, to check some data before she finally writes up her thesis and she needs my input. Do you mind?'

Input – that was certainly an apt name for it. The whole thing seemed like a heaven-sent opportunity for both of them.

'It's half-term. Why don't we all go?' she suggested, deliberately to provoke him, though she knew the children wouldn't want to. They were as tired of the cottage as she was.

'Oh, no, Mummy, I don't want to,' Tim piped up quickly, right on cue, with a slight whine in his voice. 'It's so boring at the cottage. And Ryan Crosland's having a swimming party.'

So Tim had got to the bored stage. She calculated it probably lasted at least eight years. Oliver hadn't got over it yet.

'Emma and Oliver can't go either,' Dave pointed out. 'They've got exams. And you've got the Summer Fayre, haven't you?'

'It's not compulsory. I work at school during the week. Isn't that enough?'

Though of course he wouldn't understand that. Apart from ten days at Christmas he hardly ever took a holiday. If they added up all he was owed going back twenty or more years, it would probably make a sabbatical.

Oliver said, 'We can stay here on our own. We don't need a nursemaid.'

'Perhaps not, but Tim does. Can't you skip it this time, Helen?'

To be honest she was glad to. She wouldn't have been worried if she had heard that the cottage and the Earth Studies Centre had both sunk beneath the waves. Though she liked the cottage. At least she had liked it, once.

The cottage didn't belong to the university. Dave's Aunt Bunny had left it to him in her will and he had taken Helen to see it just after they met, in that ancient car of his. He had let her paint flowers on the wings in psychedelic purple, but it didn't help the car go any better. That was before the motorway was built and it had taken them most of the day, stopping every few miles to let the radiator cool down.

He was in love with her then: newly, happily in love. They drove over Dartmoor, then through the narrow lanes, every so often catching a glimpse of the sea, until they came to a sheltered inlet on the river, a village street too steep for cars, the calm water sprinkled with boats.

The cottage faced straight on to the street, the door surrounded by the fronds of fern and dark pink valerian. They collected the key from the post office and let themselves in. It was dusk and the electricity had been disconnected, but they found some dry wood in the coal shed and a box of candles.

The rooms smelt of the sea, of dead flowers, of cloves. Aunt Bunny's belongings were still there: dark oak with runners embroidered in lazy-daisy stitch, rag rugs and cracked willow pattern. In the scullery there was an old stone sink and a wooden draining board.

They hadn't brought any food with them so they got fish and chips and sat in front of the fire, eating them out of the paper. They made love in the old bed with its home-made puffball quilt. Dave asked her to marry him in that bed; she wondered if he still remembered.

When they started living together they went down as often as they could and Helen threw all her creativity into it, painting the walls white and sanding and varnishing the floorboards. She scattered around Indian rugs and collected huge Victorian vases from antique shops to fill with dried flowers and trailing plants.

The cottage was the reason Dave had suggested the idea of the Earth Studies Centre in the first place. Those first affluent days when universities had been building and expanding were already only a distant memory, but the modern austerity had not quite set in. There had been a bequest to the department, enough to equip the centre, which was situated about a mile away beyond the headland, right down by the shore. Ecology was becoming the buzz word, and the geography department was keen to update its image by tacking 'Earth Resources' on to the end of its title. The centre became a monitoring station for marine life, and for pollution.

At first it was only Dave and a couple of colleagues who went there in the summer vacation, but gradually the students started to come too, at first sleeping in tents in the garden, but later on invading the whole cottage. The university paid for the outhouse to be converted into dormitories – downstairs for boys, upstairs for girls – but they all ate in the kitchen and it was Helen who fed them.

It had been manageable to start with, when the children were tiny and there were only one or two students. During the day Emma and Oliver played with the children next door which left Helen time for painting; not the stereotyped images of thatched cottages or yachts on the harbour, but off-beat subjects like a rusty bicycle thrown against the landing stage, or the rotting door of a derelict hut hanging off its hinges. At night there was always a willing babysitter so they went to the pub when it still had real wood panelling and leather chairs. Day trippers had not yet found the place.

But by the time Tim came along there had been a change. Everyone was supposed to muck in, but Helen's standards were quite different from those of the students, particularly when there were children in the house. She spent her time rescuing precious papers from sticky fingers, pulling hairs out of the sink and saving Aunt Bunny's furniture from the ravages of cigarette burns and beer spills.

Nowadays there was a television and a stainless steel sink with mixer taps. On the walls hung posters for Greenpeace and Amnesty International, stuck up with Blu-tack.

Every week she still took the camper van into town and stocked it high with supplies at the supermarket, but nobody ever said thank you. Nobody even noticed, except when she asked them for their share of the housekeeping money.

The postgraduate students were allowed to stay there in term time if they needed some data. They were given the key and told to come and go as they pleased, so every summer she had to scrape the grime off the cooker, scrub the floor, clean the toilet – chores nobody else bothered with. She tried to keep their own bedroom and the children's rooms out of bounds, but she couldn't supervise it when she wasn't there. She felt invaded, in her own house.

And over time the quiet atmosphere of the village had gone. The motorway was less than five miles away now and the pub had plastic fittings and Austrian blinds, with a juke box and fruit machines and a quiz night and karaoke during the season.

She imagined Dave with Ianthe. In *her* bed. There was no duvet; just blankets and a traditional quilt, with white sheets and the last of Aunt Bunny's pillowcases, hand-edged in crochetwork. She had wanted it to stay in keeping with the age of the cottage. If the curtains were open you could see the harbour, and beyond it the sky; changing from dark grey to clear blue with every shade between.

When she went down again – hateful thought – she would look for auburn hairs on the pillow: the trick of a spiteful old witch – the sort of woman she didn't want to be. She was becoming mean-minded, for after all she had no proof.

She could have confronted him, asked him straight out, but she didn't want to. Ignorance wasn't bliss, but it was a cop-out. There was too much on her mind already, what with the Chair and the children, not to mention her rotten job. And if she didn't know, then she didn't have to do anything about it.

They had never discussed what would happen to the Earth Studies Centre if Dave got the Chair. He would hardly have any time for his work down there, yet that's what he liked most; the hands-on, day-to-day business of research. And what would happen to the cottage – their cottage?

If you stayed here,' Dave said, 'you might be able to persuade Oliver to do some work.'

'Roll on Friday,' Oliver said cheerfully. 'Last day of school for ever and ever. I can't wait.'

'You'll be going back in September, don't you fret,' his father said, 'if it's only to resit the exams you fail.'

'There's no such thing as failing now,' Emma intervened. 'They don't want us poor dears to have chips on our shoulders for the rest of our lives.'

'That may be so, but in reality we all know which grades are passes and which are fails. And as far as I'm concerned, Oliver can go on sitting the exams twice a year until he gets decent grades, so he'd better get his finger out.'

'Don't you ever listen, Dad? I'm not going back. I'll get a job.'

'There aren't any jobs, can't you get it into your thick head?'

'I'll stack the bloody shelves at Tesco's, but I'm not going back to school.'

'Don't say "bloody", Oliver,' Helen said wearily. 'I don't want Tim picking up bad language.'

She had probably said it several thousand times. It sickened her to the pit of her stomach, these same old arguments. Round and round and round. Oliver was marvellous with his hands. He could fix the washing-machine or the car radio with no difficulty at all, but that wasn't good enough for Dave. And Emma was leaving home. What was it going to be like with no Emma, however sarcastic she could sometimes be? No more shopping trips, no more cosy, feminine conversations about things that men didn't understand. Just the thought of it made her feel wretched.

'I just wish he'd get real! The teachers all think I'm a waste of space. They can't imagine me as an accountant, so I don't know how you can. Next Friday I'm making a bonfire with my school uniform at the bottom of the garden and if you don't like it you can go and —'

'Shut up, Oliver!' Helen yelled suddenly. 'Shut up, shut up, shut up!'

They all stared. She was at a funny age herself. They probably thought it was her hormones.

4

That night Helen shut herself in the utility room with her paint and easel. Tim was in bed, Oliver was playing on his computer, Emma was revising, Dave was under the camper van. He was changing the oil, doing something with spark-plugs. It was supposed to be for the trip to the cottage, but Helen sensed it was because he wanted to get away from her; from everything. The interview was tomorrow. Saturday night had only been the prelude; Monday morning was the crunch.

The utility room was her favourite place in the house with its row of wellingtons, the smell of onions, pots of courgettes waiting to be planted out, the monotonous whir of the washing-machine. A hundred years ago it had been the washhouse and although the old stone flags had been covered with ceramic tiles and an extra window had been let in at the side, the whitewashed stone walls remained. Most of all she liked it because she could lock the door, with an old key, four inches long.

The phone rang. Ianthe again? Nobody else would bother to answer it if she didn't. Warily she put her brush down on a rag and padded barefoot into the kitchen to pick up the receiver, expecting to hear Ianthe's sweet young female voice. But it wasn't Ianthe, it was Nico.

'Helen?' he asked, in a low voice. Rather furtively, she thought. 'Look, there's something I never got round to asking you last night. Is Dave going after this French job?'

She wondered what he would have done if Dave had answered. Would he just gently have put the phone down?

'No. I'd never heard about it before last night. He's only interested in the Chair.'

'So there'll be no competition?'

'Not from Dave.'

'That's all I wanted to know. They're seeing people the week after next in Nice. Tomorrow, after the interview here, I'm going down to Cambridge to stay with my sister. Did I ever mention her to you? Sophie – she teaches classics.' He mentioned one of the better-known colleges. Helen might have guessed he wouldn't have just ordinary relations.

'Then I thought of driving down through France,' he continued, 'stopping off at some of our old haunts on the way.'

'Revisiting the scene of the crime? It sounds marvellous. I haven't been back to that part of France in all this time.'

'Why don't you come with me? Make a jaunt of it.'

'Don't be ridiculous, Nico! I'm married, remember?'

'Just as friends. Where's the harm?'

'Same old Nico! I know your jaunts. Six hundred miles, non-stop.'

'So the answer's no?'

'I'm afraid so.'

'So how did it go?' she asked Dave on Monday night. He looked exhausted, drained, whereas she would have expected him to be euphoric.

'Who knows?' His voice sounded distant, as though he didn't want to talk about it.

'When will they tell you?'

'In about a fortnight or so. It has to go before Senate.'

A fortnight of being on tenterhooks. She didn't think she could stand the tension.

'I've made steak-and-kidney pie. Ready in about ten minutes.'

She might just as well not have bothered.

'Have you? Do you know the Mini's clapped out? It won't go up any sort of a hill in fourth.'

Helen had been telling him that for weeks. Steak-and-kidney pie was his favourite dinner and she had been hoping it would cheer him up, but making an effort became tedious when there was no response.

That evening they sat in the same room, but neither of them

spoke. Each time he moved – shuffling papers, drumming his fingers as he concentrated on his book – it seemed to grate on her nerves. She didn't know what he was thinking but just lately she couldn't have cared less. Yet at one time they had almost been able to read each other's thoughts.

The children, sensing the atmosphere, kept away and at nine o'clock Helen sought the refuge of a hot tub with some of Emma's bubble bath. When Dave came up to bed she pretended to be asleep.

On Tuesday morning the telephone rang at a quarter to eight while Helen was cleaning her teeth. She opened the bathroom door, wiping her mouth on a towel and leaning surreptitiously over the bannisters as Dave lifted the receiver in the kitchen, eavesdropping, in case it was Ianthe. A cat and mouse game.

'Hello?' A pause. 'Oh, yes, I remember . . .'

He sounded detached and cool. He wouldn't have spoken like that to Ianthe. But nobody rang at this time of the morning unless it was urgent.

Afraid it might be Nico again, she crept half-way downstairs, straining her ears like a child listening to a forbidden conversation. For a long time Dave said nothing, listening to the person at the other end. He was pouring out coffee at the same time, spreading marmalade on toast.

Eventually he said, 'I'm terribly sorry, we didn't realise . . . Yes, of course I'll tell her . . . No, I appreciate that . . . Yes . . . yes, thanks for letting us know.'

Something suddenly clutched at Helen's heart. In a panic, she rushed down to the kitchen.

'Who on earth was that?'

Dave continued to munch on the toast. He had turned the radio off when the phone rang, and at the touch of a button it sprang back to life. A time check. Coming up for seven forty-eight; something about a lorry that had jack-knifed on the Old Kent Road.

'Duncan Morris. He was ringing about Carole.'

Carole? Who was Carole? Her mind played tricks. She couldn't remember.

'Oh, you mean Kicker?' she said, after a moment. Nobody ever called her Carole. 'Why, what about her?'

He looked up slowly. 'She died yesterday.'

Afterwards it struck her how tactless he had been. He could have said: 'Something's happened to Kicker. Bad news I'm afraid. Sit down, and I'll tell you', but he didn't. He just went on eating his toast as though it meant nothing. She hated people to beat about the bush, but surely he could have made an effort – just this once.

She frowned in bewilderment, hardly believing it. How could such a thing be true? They were the same age, she and Kicker. Her legs felt like jelly.

'Kicker's dead?' she repeated stupidly. 'But she can't be.' It sounded idiotic. As though he would lie. 'Whatever happened to her? Was she in an accident or something?'

'Breast cancer, apparently. She died yesterday evening. Duncan's ringing round everyone to tell them.'

Helen wrapped and unwrapped the belt of her dressing-gown tightly round her hand. In her ignorance, she thought people recovered from breast cancer these days.

'But I don't understand. How long had she been ill?'

'He didn't say.'

She had written the usual bouncy letter for Helen's birthday, in that ample handwriting of hers, all loops and flourishes. The same old sarcastic comments about the state of the country, the collapse of the school system and nobody giving sweet F.A.

Kicker, why didn't you let me know?

Yet what could she have said? 'Dear Helen, this is probably the last time I shall ever write to you . . .'

She had a dreadful urge to scream but she didn't. Women her age didn't scream. The children would be down for their breakfast in a minute. Numbly she would have to go on getting out the Weetabix and cutting bread for toast, just as she always did. Kicker was dead and she had to get used to the idea.

'I wish you'd have let me speak to him. When's the funeral? I'll have to go.'

'He didn't say. I don't suppose he's arranged anything yet.'

'Why didn't you call me down? I don't know how long she's been ill – anything . . .' Her voice was high, accusing him.

Frantically she searched for the phone book, found the handwritten number and dialled it, fingers trembling slightly. It was engaged. She slapped the receiver down in disgust. How stupid of Dave not to have called her. There was so much she desperately wanted to know.

'He said he was going through her address book, phoning everyone in it.'

Croft. That means he had only done A and B. Now he was phoning somebody beginning with D, like a game. It was horrible.

'It usually takes about a week these days.' David offered inadequately. 'That means the funeral ought to be about the middle of next week. But you're surely not thinking of going?'

'Of course I'm going. She was my best friend.'

He was incredulous. 'You haven't seen her for years!'

'What's that got to do with it? If you're going to the cottage I can't go in the van. I'll have to go on the train. The Mini won't make it, not to Carlisle . . .'

'So you're definitely not coming to the cottage?'

'I can't now, can I?'

They had both wanted an excuse, but not this one – never this one. Her chest felt tight, as though she was winded. Full of self-reproach, she thought that if she could make the effort to go up to Carlisle now that Kicker was dead, why hadn't she made more effort to go when she was alive?

At twelve thirty she came home from school to try phoning Duncan again but this time there was no answer at all. She thought of making some scrambled eggs for lunch, but the automatic gas lighter on the cooker wasn't working. Jerkily she opened a matchbox and matches spilled out all over the worktop and into the beaten egg. Tears of frustration sprang to her eyes. How could she even think of eating when Kicker was dead?

To try and calm her nerves, she walked down to the newsagents and looked along the row of cards, tactfully labelled 'Bereavement'. They said things like 'beyond the veil' and 'called by the Master', not 'struck down with a fatal disease in the prime of life' – in agony, in sorrow. There were pictures of crosses, flowers and churches: no hospitals, no scalpels, no drips.

Helen rejected them in disgust. There was no way she could buy anything like that – so smug and full of certainty. Kicker would have laughed her head off. She had never suffered fools gladly. Helen could see her now in her black PVC mac, that curly hair, that smile. Kicker always smiled, whatever shit the world threw at her.

Eventually she selected a card depicting the Seine at Asnières by Renoir. It reminded her of Paris when Kicker had rowed them both on the lake in the Bois de Vincennes. In the morning they had been to the Jeu de Paume to see the impressionist paintings.

Though they never realised it at the time, it had probably been one of the happiest days of their lives.

The first time Helen saw Kicker she was bathing a dog. When the A level results came through it had been too late to start applying for a hall of residence and the only choice left was to look for digs. Universities still considered themselves to be *in loco parentis* and flats were almost unheard of, particularly for first-years.

Kicker was destined to be her room-mate in a large thirties' terrace house presided over by a spinster landlady of a certain age called Miss Dumbleton who came to be known as Dumbo. They had never met before. It was just the luck of the draw – someone in the accommodation office matching up two names from a list. They might have hated each other.

That first term Marion took her daughter over in the car. The Butchers had treated themselves when one of their insurance policies had matured, and in any case a car was a necessity now that James couldn't get about as well as he used to. Marion had passed her test first time, much to her own amazement.

When Dumbo opened the front door and invited them into the spacious kitchen, Helen was confronted with the sight of Kicker, already at home after only half an hour in the place, busy bathing a little white cairn terrier, suds up to her elbows.

She took one look at Helen's mother and said accusingly: 'I bet you're a bloody Conservative.'

Helen was horrified, but strangely her mother didn't turn a hair. People took remarks like that from Kicker.

Kicker was definitely not a Conservative. Her father was a trade-union official in the days when the trades unions thought themselves the privileged children of the Labour party. Kicker had been arrested in Trafalgar Square on a CND march. She professed to having read Marx's *Communist Manifesto*, and her chosen subjects at university were French and politics, with philosophy thrown in for good measure.

'I'm going to be President of France,' she would simper, when anyone commented on what a crazy course it was.

Despite all that she blued the whole of the £50 grant her father's union had given her on expensive underwear.

That underwear floated into Helen's mind. Black bras and full-length slips ornamented with lace and a formidable pantie-corselette with suspenders dangling from it. Kicker was no Twiggy – she weighed fourteen stone and was almost five feet eleven inches tall – and tights (that great invention of the late sixties) had yet to see the light of day. They didn't make fashionable top clothes in large sizes, but everything underneath was slinky.

It was Kicker who first taught her to fight.

'You should have gone to art college and said balls to the lot of them,' she said bluntly. 'It's your life.'

But Helen was resigned to French now. She tried to put art college out of her mind. And meanwhile there were other things to fight for. Together they joined the student Socialist Society, going on protest marches against apartheid and sit-ins in solidarity with the American civil rights movement. With Bob Dylan they sang 'The times they are a-changing', and they believed it.

When there was a local by-election they went up and down the rows of terraced houses near the university distributing leaflets, knocking on doors, persuading people out to vote. Much to Kicker's amusement, Helen had never met any real working-class people before. James Butcher, even though he was not well off, had a white-collar job and the local council estate, if not out of bounds, had definitely been looked down upon.

'God, you've led a sheltered life,' Kicker would say, but playfully, never accusingly.

When the Labour candidate was announced the winner from the town hall balcony, they danced home at midnight singing *The Red Flag*. It was heady stuff.

With Kicker there was never any problem making friends. She barged up to people like a battleship, introducing herself, telling them her life story, and they responded in kind.

Her family life was nothing like Helen's. They made a long weekend of it quite often and hitchhiked back to her home town. Kicker's mother worked at the Co-op and her father was a welder; the floor was strewn with toys left by her young brother and sister; meals were *ad hoc* affairs which took place whenever anyone was hungry. Sliced white bread, shop jam, roast dinners and fry-ups were the order of the day, not the nourishing stews and homemade fare served up at regular hours by Marion Butcher.

Kicker's father brought them huge mugs of tea in bed every morning, pushing his jovial moon-face round the door, dressed only in his vest and trousers. Helen realised with a shock that she had never seen her father in his vest.

Three hundred pounds in student grant went a long way then and the first Easter they went to Paris for a fortnight, staying at a youth hostel on the outskirts of the city, gobbling up art galleries in the morning and shops in the afternoon. When they ran out of money they sold copies of the *International Herald Tribune* in the Champs Elysées to earn a few francs. Kicker knew about things like that and had no scruples about adopting a capitalist lifestyle when she needed to. The year before she had worked as an au pair for the owner of one of the biggest vineyards in the Beaujolais. Their bathroom, she insisted, had no towels, just a great big machine that blew hot air all over you. Helen never knew whether to believe her or not, as she imagined Kicker's ample body being blow-dried, without benefit of towel.

Helen loved France, but her enthusiasm for her subject had never been high. She scraped through the exams by a whisker, whereas Kicker always landed marks that destined her for a two-one. Helen copped out by reading all the set texts in English; Kicker had already read everything under the sun from Ian Fleming to *War and Peace* and she handed in brilliant essays on Sartre and Proust as a matter of course. Helen dragged along behind in her wake.

Neither of them bothered much with boyfriends. Kicker was more of a drinking than a dancing partner, though she always talked airily about the men, real or imaginary, in her past, and in Paris she dated a black Senegalese student who was six foot seven.

Only Helen understood her insecurity: her disappointment that men found her too formidable to be attractive; her week's starvation diet that ended up in binges of chip butties and Mars Bars on a Saturday night.

In bed, when she thought Dave was asleep, Helen buried her head in the pillow and wept. What hurt most was that Kicker had been ill and she hadn't even known. They could have written or phoned; said they loved each other; said goodbye.

For years they had led separate lives, she with the children, Kicker as head of modern languages at a large comprehensive, but sometimes the phone would ring out of the blue and there they would be, talking about food or films or books or how awful the government was, giggling and intimate as was only possible with another woman.

Who said that any of them would be alive this time next year? And what if they were? Was she going to get into the Mini every day, arrive at quarter to nine, spend her days washing grazed knees, typing letters to the local authority about the state of the boiler and to the parents about jumble sales and swimming lessons and trips to museums? Would Dave be going to that geography department and to the Earth Studies Centre until he got a gold watch? (Did they still dole out gold watches? she wondered.) Until they both rotted?

Dave heard her crying and reached out to her in the darkness.

'Hey, are you all right?'

Of course, I'm not all right, she wanted to yell. *Are people who are crying all right?*

'I'm just thinking about Kicker.'

'You haven't seen her since I don't know when. She called in that time, d'you remember? Tim was only a toddler —'

'Yes, but I always knew she was there. I expected her to be there. When we were old.'

He tried to catch hold of her, to comfort her, but she thought of Ianthe and turned the other way, pulling her knees up to make herself into a cocoon. Trying to keep the world out.

At school, in the staff room, they chatted about the Summer Fayre: the arrangements for the teas; presents for the brantub; face-painting; fancy dress. It was a pep talk. The deputy head was reciting her spiel about team spirit. Helen realised that she had been coming to the Summer Fayre since Emma was in the nursery class. That made fourteen years.

'It would save a lot of time and effort if we just asked all the parents to contribute a fiver or a tenner at the beginning of each term,' she said, putting into words what she had thought for ages. 'Then we could avoid all this fuss and trouble.'

A ripple went round the room and at once she felt the disapproving stares and perceived them closing ranks against her. Of course she had no business to an opinion. She wasn't a teacher, just the secretary.

'Helen, surely you don't believe that?' one of them said.

'Well, yes, I do, as a matter of fact.'

A reproachful silence descended, but Helen didn't care. The worst even Mrs Rose could do was to give her the sack and she wouldn't be that lucky.

At lunchtime, once again, she went home to try ringing Kicker's husband while nobody was there. The head wouldn't appreciate her ringing Carlisle on the school phone. This time he was in and he described in a calm voice – a voice cultivated especially to deal with painful things – what had happened.

Apparently two years ago Kicker had found a lump in her breast, which had been removed. She hadn't bothered telling anyone; the whole traumatic experience had been over so quickly. She had just tried to get on with her life.

But ever since last Christmas she had been feeling ill. The doctor had suggested depression and advised her to rest. Then one day in March Duncan had found her collapsed on the kitchen floor. By then it was too late to do anything about it.

'But surely the doctor was at fault for not realising . . .' she objected, inadequately. 'If they had known earlier . . .'

'Nothing can bring her back,' was all he could say.

She wanted to ask more, much more, but they hardly knew each other. They had only met once. Kicker hadn't married him until she was well into her thirties and Helen hadn't been able to go to the wedding because she had been expecting Tim.

She ached to share with him those memories of Kicker that she treasured, but although he sounded patient and resigned, he probably just wished she would get off the line.

After she had put the phone down she lingered. *Tried to get on with her life.* Duncan's explanation would have been believable to someone who didn't know her, but Helen did. Kicker was all bravado on the outside, but fragile on the inside, acting her way through life. She hadn't told anyone because she was scared rigid.

Helen couldn't face school, not until she pulled herself together. And the thought of the Summer Fayre made her wild. The way they all acted, it was as though it was the most important thing in the world.

She sat down and tried to eat a sandwich but the phone ringing again made her jump. It was her mother.

'Don't come over on Friday afternoon, dear,' she said. 'Frank's taking me on a coach trip to an abbey or something and I don't know when we'll be back. There's a pub lunch, and afternoon tea on the way back.'

So even her mother didn't need her any more. She had cried last night in bed, but Dave had been there. Now that she was alone she gave herself up to long choking sobs, her head on the kitchen table.

Much later, when she had dried her eyes, she dialled directory enquiries and asked for the Cambridge college where Nico's sister worked. It was a long shot, but there was no other way. No, a voice at the other end said, there was no classics lecturer called Sophie Jones. There was a Sophie Jones-Morton; would that be her? Helen laughed. It almost certainly was. This was a lot easier than she thought it would be. Unfortunately, however, Dr Jones-Morton was out of her office.

'Can you give me her home number?'

The woman hesitated. 'Well we're not supposed to.'

'Please. It's quite important. I'm a friend of her brother's.'

At last she acquiesced. Helen wrote down the number and dialled again.

'Nico, is that you?'

'Helen? How did you find the number?'

'It wasn't difficult. Listen Nico, is your offer still open?'

'What? You've decided to come with me?'

'I want to get away. To clear my head. Would you mind?'

'Of course I wouldn't mind. I wouldn't have asked you.'

'When are you going?'

'I'm booked on the evening sailing, Dover–Calais, Friday. I shall need to leave Cambridge in reasonable time to get through the jams. It's bank holiday weekend, so the M25's going to be choked. Can you be here by mid-afternoon?'

'Yes. I'll be catching the train. I'll ring you from the station.'

'I'll expect to hear from you then.'

She put down the phone and went to find the paintings she had left neatly in a box ready for the Summer Fayre, each one with its own price tag. Up on the landing she pulled down the loft ladder and heaved the box up, covering it carefully with some plastic sheeting. This year they could whistle for their cats. Then she locked the front door and drove back to school with gritted teeth.

It wasn't very difficult to come up with an excuse. Sometimes, in an idle moment, the notion had drifted through her mind – how would she get away if she really had to? She had planned it in imagination a dozen times, but with spring bank holiday and half-term coming up it couldn't have been simpler.

'I had a visit from Malcolm Booth today,' she said casually, over supper. 'One of his teachers has dropped out of the French exchange visit – broken his ankle or something – and he's looking for a replacement urgently. I said I'd go. I hope you don't mind.'

'When is it?' Dave asked. It wasn't such an outrageous suggestion; she had been on French exchange visits in the past when they had been short of a teacher.

'They leave about Friday teatime.'

'What, this Friday?'

Helen smiled sweetly. 'Yes. I shall be away for a fortnight. The first week's half-term, and they can get a temp to cover for me at school during the second week.'

'Isn't it awfully short notice?'

'A little, but it shouldn't affect you. After all, you're going down to the cottage on Friday.'

Let him go, let him incriminate himself. Two could play at that game.

'Yes, but what about the children?'

'Emma and Oliver are all right on their own. You could take Tim along with you.'

'With me?'

'Or Mother will have him,' she mentioned, as a deliberate afterthought.

She looked for fleeting signs of relief in his face when she said it, but couldn't quite grasp them.

'But what are we going to eat?' Oliver wailed.

'You ought to be able to throw something into a pan at your age. I set out to be a modern mother, bringing up my sons to fend for themselves.'

'You've failed,' Oliver replied, putting on a tragic air. 'I'm like that kid on the advert. His mother tells him how to boil an egg down the phone.'

'Rubbish. You got together a perfect stir-fry the other night when Ben stayed over. Otherwise, buy a packet. Stick it in the microwave. I can't be responsible for everything.'

'What about Kicker?' Dave asked.

'As I said before, the Mini probably wouldn't make it to Carlisle. And I don't really know Duncan very well. I'll send flowers.'

In reality she didn't think she could face Kicker's mother after all these years. She had been such a jolly little woman. What could they say to each other that would possibly make any sense?

Funny, when they were at university Kicker's parents couldn't have been any older than Helen was now and they had seemed ancient.

'Where are they going this year?' Dave asked. They both remembered other years when they had waved off either Emma or Oliver, after enduring two weeks with a French teenager in the house, both times the type who hogged the bathroom and ran up huge international phone bills.

'Usual place,' Helen replied evasively. 'I don't know exactly where I'll be staying yet. I'll ring and let you know when I get there.'

'I hope the coach doesn't break down,' Oliver said. 'When I went we were late at Dover and didn't cross until half-past four in the morning. Then the brakes failed or something. The teachers all had nervous breakdowns.'

'They should have decided on the Chair by the time you get back,' Dave said.

'I expect I'll ring to find out.'

Helen, feeling sorry for Emma and Oliver, but not for Dave, went shopping to fill up the freezer with oven chips and pizzas, plus a stock of yogurt, fruit and orange juice just in case they decided to eat something reasonably nutritious. Perhaps it would be as well to hide the key to the drinks cabinet and put Dave's beer in the shed under some old packing material. The best ornaments could go away too, but the thought of exams would probably prevent them from having a party.

She stopped her trolley, looking up and down the aisles. As friends, he had said, and probably he had meant it, but that was when he hadn't thought she would accept. And facts were facts. They had been lovers and he would probably expect them to be lovers again.

'This is the 1990s, for God's sake,' he would say. 'Did we go through the sexual revolution almost single-handedly for you to start being a prude at your age?'

Your age! She thought of Ianthe – that firm skin, lips with a slight pout. Her own body didn't seem any different from what it had been, not from the inside. She did aerobics every week and she had never been one of those women who needed to be on a perpetual diet, but the fact remained that she had had several children. Like an old bed you had slept on for twenty years, it was only when you tried a new one that you realised how slack and squashy it had become.

She found them at last, in the aisle marked toiletries, tucked discreetly between the vitamin C and the blackcurrant cough lozenges. Condoms. Helen stood there, plucking up the courage. She felt like the only woman in the world who had never used one – every other method under the sun, but never that. They had never been very popular in her day (heavens, it sounded like a different century!).

She had used a diaphragm at first, then the Pill. Later when the coil had disagreed with her, Dave had agreed to a vasectomy. You were supposed to use a condom for a certain time after the operation, but it had coincided with her last month of pregnancy with Tim and after that they hadn't touched each other for months, by mutual but unspoken consent. Tim had kept them up all night anyway. Circumstances hadn't been ideal.

Helen's eyes wandered over the range on offer. Superfine, extra long, gold-coloured, ribbed for heightened pleasure; the mind boggled, or else she was very naive. There was the female condom too, whatever that was like – she had visions of a transparent bin-liner. On the premise that the female of the species was deadlier than the male, she decided that it might be more than she had bargained for. She didn't want to show Nico her utter foolishness. She grabbed a couple of packets at random, hiding them under the dishwasher powder and fled to the checkout.

When she had put the groceries in the car she went to one of the boutiques on the square that sold up market underwear and splashed out on a pair of satin pyjamas. Just in case.

'Pop your signature on here, dear,' the very young assistant told her kindly, presenting the bank debit slip.

It was just as well she was doing this now. Shop assistants were already starting to sound patronising. Soon the wrinkles would be starting to show and it wouldn't be long before everyone was treating her like a little old lady. If she wanted adultery, this was definitely going to be her last chance.

5

'What time are you leaving?' she asked Dave on Friday morning, as she drew back the curtains. It was only a quarter to seven but she had started to pack, the satin pyjamas hidden right at the bottom of her suitcase.

'About four,' he said, still only half awake. 'What about you?'

'The bus leaves at five but I'm having the afternoon off. Going for a briefing with Malcolm. Emma's meeting Tim from school, giving him his tea and taking him to Mother's in the morning.'

'Right.' He turned over, head under the covers to avoid the light. 'Have I got any shirts?' He meant clean shirts.

'In the airing cupboard.' She omitted to mention that she hadn't got round to ironing them.

There was a card each for Emma and Oliver on the breakfast table: good luck cards for their exams, since she wouldn't be there in person when they began in earnest. She had no qualms about leaving them during this part of the process. It was the results she was dreading, Emma's even more than Oliver's.

She had the feeling that Oliver would eventually make a success of life, whatever his present animosity towards the education system, but for Emma these results would dictate the whole of her future. And no matter how often she came back for the holidays she would never really live at home again. It would be the end of an era in both their lives.

Her elder son was touched by the card in his unemotional, teenage way.

'Hey, you're only going for a fortnight,' he reminded her. 'Not for ever.'

She put her arm around him. Emma scarcely ever hugged her any more, but thankfully Oliver still responded to maternal embraces, even though she had to look up to him now. Whatever Dave said, she felt a sense of pride in her tall son.

'Don't let him sleep in on the exam days, Emma,' she said. She knew Dave wouldn't bother to look at their exam timetables which were pinned up on the kitchen noticeboard.

'The trouble with men,' said Emma, pouring milk on to cereal, 'is that they need mothers all their lives.'

'And if you do decide to burn your school uniform this afternoon, Oliver,' Helen continued, 'try not to burn the house down with it.'

On the way to school, Helen wondered idly if she was really cut out for this. Certainly, her first shot at sex hadn't been all that hot. That was why Nico had come as such a relief, because with him emotion didn't enter into it. It had been all animal sensation, without the least pretence of anything like love.

Perhaps it had been the times, perhaps her age, but suddenly virginity didn't seem so prized as it had been. She and Kicker recounted near misses to each other as they lay in bed, wondering who would be the first. Kicker fancied the socialist candidate in her home town, even though he had a wife and baby, but at least he was experienced. A lot of their fellow students didn't seem much more clued up than they were.

Helen had known Paul Valentine since they were children. The Butchers and the Valentines both went to the same chapel and the children called each other's parents Auntie and Uncle. Helen never really liked Paul much. He was tall and rather gangling with fair hair which he pasted down with Brylcreem – quite attractive in an old-fashioned way, but not very lively, though he was always grinning. He reminded her of someone on a toothpaste advert.

When they were teenagers Paul was the sort of person Helen used to bring if she needed a partner and couldn't think of anyone else. That's what he had always been to her – a last resort.

Her parents certainly approved. Paul was ultra-polite and started work in a building society after O levels. It was normal then; leaving school at fifteen or sixteen to become a fully paid-up member of the adult world. Nowadays dependence stretched to twenty-one and often well beyond. For his eighteenth birthday Paul's parents splashed out and bought him a little red MG. It was his only indulgence; Paul, on the whole, was a very steady lad. He always wore a suit and tie and after work he was studying for his professional exams.

Helen tried to stay away from home during university vacations. Susie and her family had emigrated to Canada and she seemed to have lost touch with her other friends from school. Above all she didn't want to see her father. She argued with him now when he made remarks about her clothes or her ideas, something she had never done before. She provoked him on purpose by wearing her shortest skirts and playing loud music. But she always put in an appearance for her mother's sake, and whenever she did there was Paul asking her to the pictures or to go boating on the river.

At least at the pictures you didn't have to talk and it got her out of the house. Afterwards they would go back to his place and he would snuggle up to her on the settee, while his parents watched television in the other room. When he put his hand inside her blouse she didn't bother to stop him. After all he always paid for the best seats at the cinema and the car was very nice. She supposed he deserved something in return. (Girls thought that then; Emma would have been outraged.)

During her second summer vacation she blued the remains of her grant on a two-week trip to Spain with Kicker, the first week in Granada, the second on the coast. After that there was nothing for it but to get a job and she found herself waitressing in a high-class café, serving cream horns and buttered scones to the wealthy Conservative voters of the town where she lived.

As it happened, Paul's building society was just across the road and after work on Thursdays they fell into the habit of going for steak and chips and then on to the pictures. Later it was back to the settee at 15, The Mount, the address on an exclusive new estate where the Valentines lived. She put up with him because there wasn't much else going on.

After Spain she felt depressed. Her course included going to France for a year to teach English and she was dreading it. She knew she would be hopeless at teaching and they had dumped her in a place down in the south-west, a small town miles from anywhere. In the sixties nobody in England had heard of the Dordogne.

Her body might have been on the settee with Paul, but her mind was certainly absent. Before she knew it his hands were inside her knickers and his trouser zip was undone.

'Why don't we do it?' he asked, nuzzling at her ear.

Helen came back to the settee with a jolt. 'Do what?'

He kissed her on the nose. 'You know – it!'

'What, here? What about your parents?'

'They've gone to bed. The telly went off ages ago. Come on Helen, what do you say?'

'I've never had sex, not properly,' she said, trying to disengage his hands. 'Have you?'

'N . . . ooo,' he admitted. 'I thought you might have . . . what with you being a student and everything . . .'

'Universities aren't all orgies, you know.'

'Fountains of wisdom, where students go to drink, that's what I heard,' Paul said jovially.

Helen made a face. It was a very old joke. All the same, she would quite like to get it over with so that there wouldn't be any more mystery. With Paul it would be safe, and she could keep the knowledge for next time. Besides, standards were starting to slip. At one time a girl had refused sex unless she was engaged, or unless she was in love, or unless she was going steady. Nowadays, she just did it for the hell of it.

'You'll have to get something.'

'Get something? What?'

'For God's sake, I don't want to end up pregnant.'

'You mean a Durex? Couldn't you go on the Pill or something?'

'It's not as easy as all that, Paul. This isn't like London where you can go to some anonymous clinic. I'd have to go and see Dr Carlton. He used to be involved in the Scouts with my father. He'd never agree to it unless I was engaged. Anyway it's much more complicated for women. All you have to do is go to the barber's and buy a packet of them.'

She surveyed him calmly. 'Your hair could do with a cut.'

'You mean you'd do it, if I got some?'

'Why not?' The prospect struck her as quite funny and she needed something to cheer her up.

He went for a haircut but he never got up the courage to ask for the Durex. Helen just laughed.

'Faint heart never won fair lady,' she remarked, without the least bit of emotion, but the idea stuck in her mind and she decided to go and see Dr Carlton after all, spinning him a story about getting engaged. James Butcher went to the hospital for his heart check-ups, so chances were the doctor didn't meet her parents all that often. Her father hardly left the house these days, anyway.

He was an old-fashioned doctor who was still cautious about prescribing the contraceptive pill and he sent her to the nurse to be fitted out with a diaphragm, which turned out to be a little dome of rubber on a flexible metal frame. It came complete with a pink plastic box and some talcum powder stuff which apparently prevented the rubber from perishing.

'You're very narrow,' the nurse remarked as she showed Helen how to fit it, 'but once you're married you'll remedy that.'

She gave a little guffaw and Helen fled in embarrassment, the little plastic box in her handbag. All it needed now was the time and place. Paul's parents were going out on Thursday night, so they decided to skip the pictures and come home early.

Even then it was not so simple. Paul didn't want to risk the bedroom in case his mother got a whiff of Helen's perfume or found stains on the sheets and guessed what they had been up to. That left the settee, since Paul hadn't the imagination to suggest the hearth rug.

They locked both front and back doors and shut the cat in the kitchen. Then Helen went to insert the diaphragm and came back with her tights and knickers in her hand, her miniskirt revealing the whiteness of her thighs. Paul took a deep breath and fell on her.

Helen was sure it was one of the most miserable experiences of her entire life. It was like a battle without desire, without love and seemingly without end. Paul came before they had even started, so they waited a few minutes and tried again. It must have been nearly half an hour before he even managed to penetrate her and by then she felt sore and physically drained. In the end she decided the best policy would be to lie back and just let him get it over with. It was one more illusion shattered for ever.

At work the next day she kept away from the café window in case she could be seen from the building society opposite. In her lunchbreak she stayed in the rest-room and at closing time she flew to the bus stop like the wind. That evening she went out so that she wouldn't be at home if he phoned, but next morning there was a letter on the mat addressed to her.

'My darling, I haven't been able to stop thinking about you all day. Or I should say thinking about us. Last night was so wunderfull . . .'

She shook her head in disbelief. It was farcical. The man couldn't even spell and he thought he could write a love letter. It had all gone far too far. She had never imagined this. All she had wanted was a bit of sexual experience, no questions asked, and he had to go and fall in love with her.

All week she avoided him and when he rang to confirm their usual Thursday date she told him she was feeling a bit off-colour and could they skip it this week? Besides, she had to start getting her things together for France. He sounded disappointed, but she couldn't be held responsible for that.

But a few days later he was waiting for her as she came off duty. It hadn't been the best of days; she had been in trouble with the manageress for spilling a plate of toasted teacake and getting butter on a customer's fur coat. All she wanted was to go home and have a lovely warm bath, to wash off that cloying smell of whipped cream that seemed to cling after a day in the hot kitchens. At the end of the week she would pick up her last pay packet with profound relief.

'Come for a steak,' Paul pleaded, and since she was hungry and it would only be fishcakes at home, she reluctantly agreed. They sat in a corner of the restaurant, on opposite sides of the plastic table, while a record of gypsy violin music grated over the loudspeaker just above them. For pudding there was chocolate ice cream with a rather soggy fan-shaped wafer stuck in the top of it. Helen's eyes were starting to close.

'Will you come back home? Mum and Dad are out again.'

She had her excuse all ready. 'I can't do anything tonight, Paul. Time of the the month, you know.'

He flushed a little, but his grin hardly slipped. If he ever got the sack from the building society, there was a great career waiting for him in commercials.

'Then I'll show you this now.'

From his pocket he brought a small box and Helen's blood ran cold.

'What is it?'

His face lit up with pride as he opened it. The solitaire diamond caught the light. It must have cost him a very great deal.

'Helen, let's get engaged.'

'What!'

'I know it's sudden, but it's what I really want. Please, darling, won't you think about it?'

'But I don't want to get married! I've got two more years to go at university. I'm going to France next week, for heaven's sake!'

Surely only people in romantic novels went in for this sort of behaviour. She ought to be wearing a crinoline, or one of those flapper dresses with fringes round the hem. He was holding her hand, but if it hadn't been for the Spanish waiter hovering in the background he would probably have gone down on one knee.

'I know we'd have to wait,' he was saying, 'but I don't mind that. It'll give me a chance to save up a bit. For a deposit.'

'What?' she shrieked again.

'On a house,' he said, unnecessarily.

'This is ridiculous.'

He didn't seem to hear her. 'I was awfully touched, you know, when you went to the doctor for that . . . when you went to the doctor's. I hadn't the guts, but you did. And you wouldn't have done it if you hadn't liked me quite a lot.' He gazed into her eyes. 'I love you.'

Kicker would have laughed aloud and told him to stuff it. But Helen had been brought up to be polite and she had never quite broken the habit. She felt sorry for him really. After all, she had gone along with him, just for the meals and the nights out, when she hadn't the least interest in him. Feminism had knocked that sort of attitude right on the head, thank goodness.

'Paul, please, the waiter's looking,' she said in embarrassment, trying to extricate herself from his grasp. 'We can't get engaged. It never even crossed my mind. And I told you, I'm going to France on Tuesday.'

'Well if it never even crossed your mind, you can think about it now.' He thrust the ring into her hand. 'You're coming home at Christmas, aren't you? We'll talk about it then. Honestly, Helen, I mean it. Keep the ring for now, and see if the idea grows on you.'

On Friday and Saturday she was working and Paul had promised to drive his parents up to Blackpool to see the illuminations. They wouldn't be home until Sunday afternoon. Monday, she said firmly, had to be devoted entirely to packing. That left only Sunday evening, and fortuitously both sets of parents were at home. A repeat bout of wrestling on the settee was definitely out of the question, but Paul turned up anyway, at about seven, and sat in the kitchen, legs dangling from a stool, watching her cope with some last-minute washing.

'Can I come and see you off?' he asked.

'There's no point. I'm setting off pretty early from here. I've got to get to Victoria by eleven.'

'I could take you to the station.'

'I've already ordered a taxi,' she argued, then saw the pointlessness of it all. He wouldn't see her until Christmas. It would do no harm to be gracious.

'Have you tried the ring on?' he asked curiously.

She denied it, but she had. It was too big, the solitaire flopping rather drunkenly to one side.

'I really think you ought to take it back,' she said, wringing out underwear into the sink. 'You hardly know me, have you ever thought of that?'

'Of course I do. I've known you since you were six years old.'

Sitting together in Sunday school was hardly a good preparation for marriage, but he seemed oblivious to that. And she hadn't the heart to lay it on the line and tell him that the whole idea was nonsense.

At the station, he seemed not to notice her aloofness, as he attempted to deposit a lingering kiss upon her lips. That must have been how he got to be the manager of a string of estate agents – he wouldn't take no for an answer.

'Have a good trip. Don't fall for any Frenchmen!'

As Emma would have said, it was enough to make you throw up. With relief she watched him disappearing as the train gathered speed. What on earth was she going to do? Write him a 'dear John' letter or wait until Christmas when they would have time to discuss it all more sensibly? She wondered vaguely if he was expecting her to start saving up. A bottom drawer, as they called it then; a dinner service, a cheese board, flannelette sheets.

She took out a cigarette in a gesture of defiance, remembering Paul did not approve of women smoking.

Uneasily, Helen realised that she had been doing it all her life – not facing up to reality, hoping that if she did nothing things would change. She was doing the same now, running away from Dave and from Ianthe, burying her head in the sand like a coward.

That was the worst winter she had ever spent, that winter in France after Paul and before Nico. The lodgings she found consisted of a dark little room with a gas ring in one corner and a shared bathroom. There was no carpet, just threadbare lino. The landlady was a widow who owned a dress shop, and who looked as though she had stepped straight out of a French surrealist film. She was about thirty-five with bright red lips and waist-length raven hair which by day she wore in a sedate bun. By night she wafted about in a long green dressing-gown with the hair in a loose plait down her back.

To Helen she spoke in French but to the black cat, whose coat matched her coiffure, she spoke in whispered Spanish. Late at night Helen could hear muffled voices at the front door and then again at about six o'clock in the morning. Madame had a lover. She wore a wedding ring but what had happened to her husband Helen never found out.

There were only twelve hours of teaching a week but those

twelve hours were hell. Helen hadn't the remotest idea how to teach or what to teach. None of the pupils took the slightest notice of her, even if she yelled at the top of her voice. The rest of the time she could do as she liked, but there wasn't much amusement in a town of ten thousand inhabitants: a few cafés, one cinema, not another British person for forty miles.

The English teachers took pity on her. They invited her for meals, earnestly giving her details of the study years they had spent in England. They too had been exiled to unheard-of places; Northampton, Thirsk, Andover. They offered her bacon and egg fried in butter and China tea with too much milk in it.

But at least there was time to paint. She hired a bicycle and rode out into the countryside to sketch Romanesque churches and the surrounding terrain with its rocky outcrops shaded by trees in their autumn colours. The town itself was situated on a coalfield and many of its inhabitants were employed at the chemical works, but it was surrounded by wilderness; not quite the Dordogne, not quite the south. The locals called it 'midi moins le quart'.

People were friendly, but they were not friends. Paul's sentimental letters, badly spelled, were all she had to come between herself and loneliness. She had never gone home to an empty room in her life before and she never would again. That was something she was never to forget.

Eventually, she made friends with Mireille, a student who worked at the school. Mireille helped look after the boarders outside lesson times, supervising meals and sleeping in the dormitory, trying to earn some sort of a living while studying for her degree.

The nearest university was a three-hour train ride away with two changes. It was like living in Sheffield and going to university in Cambridge twice a week, but Mireille didn't think it strange. The lectures often contained a couple of hundred people and there were no grants. If your parents had no money, you just did your best. It was a dismal system. Helen recognised that her own life was pretty good in comparison. British students didn't know they were born.

She ought to have gone home at Christmas but she chickened out of it. The ring was safe in her handbag, unworn, and Paul seemed very far away. After Christmas dinner at Mireille's she took her bike out over the frosty deserted roads to paint the bare trees on the horizon above the coal mine with a bottle of calvados at her side to keep her warm.

'Is that note ready, Helen? The children must take it home this afternoon. It should have gone out ages ago.'

Helen handed Mrs Rose a sheet of paper for her to read over. 'It only appeared on my desk this morning,' she said.

The head peered over her glasses. 'Oh, I wasn't blaming you. Far from it. I just didn't seem to have the time . . .'

'I could have written it myself, if you'd mentioned it.'

It made her feel like the rawest office junior when she wasn't allowed to draft the letters. It didn't need much gumption. Or they could have sent out the letter they sent last year or the year before that.

'Skilfully has four "l"s, hasn't it? What a nuisance! It can't go out like this, Helen. A school, you know . . .'

Helen snatched the paper from her hand, scrutinising it. 'Three "l"s, Mrs Rose,' she said steadfastly.

'Oh, surely not . . .'

Calmly Helen took down Chambers Concise from the shelf and handed it to her. Mrs Rose's eyes hardened at the challenge. She riffled the pages rather nervously.

'Good gracious, how strange! I always thought . . . I suppose we all have our blind spots, don't we?' she stuttered.

Helen didn't look at her. She was gathering up her handbag, taking her jacket from the hanger.

'I'm afraid I'm going to have to leave you to photocopy them yourself. I've got to rush. I'm going to France, you know. Have a good half-term won't you? And enjoy the Summer Fayre. I've decided not to put my cats in this year after all.'

Mrs Rose looked puzzled and the letter seemed to wave about in her hand like a white flag. But Helen was not in the mood for a truce. Impetuously she stuffed the royal wedding mug into her bag, together with a hand mirror and a makeup case from the desk drawer. Now was the time to make her protest.

'I'm going to France and I'm not coming back. But I've finished all the typing.'

'But I don't understand . . .'

Helen looked out of the window. A black-and-yellow car was turning into the school drive.

'That's my taxi now, right on the dot. If you ring the newspaper today you should get an advert in by Monday. Goodbye.'

Three hundred and fifty copies of the letter to go out and she had hidden the last two packets of duplicating paper right at the back of the stock cupboard, under a consignment of coloured card. Altogether, it was turning out to be a very satisfactory day.

6

At twelve o'clock she was at the station. It was years since she had been on a train and the thought of it gave her a sense of wistful romance, reminding her of student journeys through Europe long ago. But this train wasn't the romantic type. It was a modern, no-nonsense, two-carriage sprinter train with an intercom and seats in blue spotted velour. There was even a phone. Helen hadn't realised trains had phones these days. She fished in her bag for some change and rang Nico to tell him what time she would be at the station.

Afterwards, when there was nothing more to do, she stared out of the window and thought of Kicker. Then, as her eyes filled with tears again, she tried not to think of her.

They crossed the flat lands of East Anglia between Peterborough and Ely with its dykes and church spires standing out against the sky. The wind tossed the sparse trees beside the track: hawthorns and elderberries just coming into bloom. The countryside was all straight lines, in green and cream against a leaden sky. As she stepped out on to the platform in Cambridge the breeze blew her hair into her face. Beyond the red automatic doors of the station foyer she could see Nico waiting for her in the short-stay car park, hands in pockets, smartly turned out in a grey denim shirt and trousers.

'Hi!' he said. 'I wondered if you'd be able to get away in the end, what with Dave and the children and everything.'

'I said I'd come, didn't I?'

He opened the boot of a car that Oliver would have given his eye teeth for – a large white monster with a dashboard like an aeroplane – and deposited her suitcase in it next to his own.

'A rung up from the old 2CV, isn't it?'

'It isn't mine. I've hired it for a month, until I get myself sorted out. Sophie wasn't keen. It hardly fits in her drive.'

'At one time, Nico, you used to despise status symbols.'

'I move with the times,' he said with a grin. 'In the sixties I was a left-wing, penniless student. It was the thing to be.'

'And now you work out at the gym and wear designer labels?'

'We've been lucky, our generation. There were, the baby boom, born after the war. When we were young it was fashionable to be young. We got the free milk and the orange juice and the education. Now we're the consumers, the ones with the money. I made a bit on the stock market in Hong Kong. Out there, it's as normal as putting a bet on a horse.'

He indicated the station buffet. 'Hey, do you want a coffee or something, before we start?'

Helen shook her head. 'We'd better get on, I suppose. We can get something at Dover, when we know how much time we've got.'

'Always organised, our Helen.'

She felt him scrutinise her beige linen trouser suit, green blouse, low-heeled shoes, mid-brown hair not yet starting to turn grey.

'You haven't changed much, you know, though the clothes are smarter. I remember you in miniskirts and long hair with lots of black eye-liner.' She slipped into the passenger seat and he obligingly adjusted the air-conditioning. After the Mini it was sheer luxury. 'What did you say to Dave about all this?'

'Nico, I don't want to talk about Dave, all right?'

'I thought you might have come to talk me into withdrawing my application.'

'Heavens, did you?'

He gave a lopsided smile, almost a smirk. 'Stranger things have happened, Helen. Especially if he hasn't anything else lined up.'

'If that was the case, I could have told Prof. Bannister several unsavoury details about you, but I didn't. To be perfectly honest, Nico, at this moment I don't give tuppence who gets the Chair.'

'So that's it!'

She ignored whatever he might mean by that. 'I thought this was a trip to France,' she said coolly. 'Why don't we get going?'

They swung out into the traffic and she leaned back against the soft leather. Nico overtook a bus and slipped through the lights just as they turned red.

'Careful,' she warned. 'They have hidden cameras at junctions nowadays.' Anything, so long as they could get away from talking about Dave.

'Do you know what I hate about England now, after so many years away? It's this nanny society. Eat by, best before, belt up, safe sex, do as you're told, keep in line, even being watched at the traffic lights.'

'At one time you thought everyone ought to have a car. It was their right. Their slice of the cake. Well, your wish came true. One day there'll be complete gridlock from Lands End to John o' Groats.'

'You don't expect me to get a bike do you?' he asked, cutting in front of a little old lady in a Volvo.

'No. Not your style at all. Though if you'd moved with the times, I'd have thought you'd be into conservation. Global warming and all that stuff. Didn't I hear that you special-ised in it?'

'Global weather patterns, actually. It's not quite the same thing. Let me tell you something, Helen. Nobody really knows if there's any such thing as man-made global warming yet, but journalists don't mention that. They just think it's a good story. And good luck to them, I say.'

'Of course it wouldn't matter to you. You have no children.'

'At the beginning of the century people thought London would drown in horse shit, but of course it didn't happen. Something turned up. People always like to make a drama out of things.'

'Complacency won't help.'

'Actually it's complacency that gets my goat. Not about global warming, just the country in general. You're all so bloody complacent. The government does as it likes and all you can do is sit back and let it happen. No backbone any more. No stomach. And you don't realise Asia is out there ready to take over the world.'

'You like a fight, don't you, Nico?'

'You might say that.'

And his biggest fight now was with Dave. In the old days it had been the system. And he was still a maverick. On the edge of the system, yes, but not yet quite part of it.

It was Florence where they met. Not only did Helen stay away at Christmas, but she stayed away at Easter too and went to Italy to visit her pen-friend.

She had been writing to Adriana since they were both fourteen, ever since Helen had seen a picture of Botticelli's *Birth of Venus* and Adriana had heard the Beatles – exchanging dreams, Helen in poor Italian, Adriana in very creditable English.

They spent a fortnight going round the galleries together: the Uffizi for the grave Renaissance faces of Botticelli, San Marco for the glorious angels of Fra Angelico, the Accademia for the *David*, who looked every second as though he would come alive and step down from his pedestal. Helen felt light-headed at the magnificence of it. This made up a bit for her solitary winter in that cold little room.

Adriana's parents owned a bar in Piazza Santo Spirito on the other side of the river from the main tourist trail. Here the only foreigners who wandered into the square were those who were looking for Browning's house in the nearby Via Maggio. In the afternoons, when Adriana had to help behind the bar, Helen sat outside at one of the pavement tables, surrounded by murmuring Italian voices and staring at Brunelleschi's plain facade of the church of the Holy Spirit.

It was warm already and occasionally she wandered, bare-armed, down the narrow streets, attempting to sketch the shops of the leather-workers and blacksmiths which didn't seem to have changed much since the Middle Ages. It was a timeless place; only the occasional screech of brakes reminded her that it was the twentieth century.

The only nuisance was Gianni, Adriana's brother, who seemed to have taken a fancy to her, attracted by her English miniskirts which were shorter than any yet seen in Italy. He had a knack of appearing suddenly and sidling up to her, rolling his dark brown eyes.

When he had some time off, he said, they would go dancing. English music – very good. She understood that much, though most of the time she couldn't make out his Florentine accent.

'Take no notice of him. He is *fidanzato* . . . engaged,' Adriana informed her calmly, though where his fiancée was Helen never managed to discover. She got the impression that an arrangement had been made and Gianni was bound to honour it, but what he did in the meantime was his own affair.

Meanwhile Adriana discreetly tried to divert Helen's interests elsewhere.

'That's Nico,' she said one evening, indicating a boy of about her own age who was among the crowd watching football on television in the bar. 'He's English too. He lives in a *pensione* in Piazza Pitti.'

'What's he doing in Florence?'

'Something at the British Institute, I think. He has a nice . . . what do you call it? Bottom?' she added with a giggle. 'Hey, Nico,' she shouted in Italian, 'here's a compatriot of yours.'

'English?' he asked, sauntering over to join her when half-time came. 'So am I. At least, I was born in Wales, but it's the same thing as far as they're concerned over here. Live in Southampton. Just come down from Cambridge.'

He was very slim and lithe, already sunburned so early in the year, with shabby clothes, his hair long over his ears and neck, and plenty of shrewdness in his eyes. Adriana's opinion of his bottom was certainly not misplaced.

Helen never asked him what his real name was. She just took it for granted it was Nico and she certainly never saw any cheque book or passport or driving licence that told her any different. In those days Nico didn't believe in documents.

'Working at the British Institute, are you?' she asked, making conversation.

'I have been, but I'm sick of it. All I do is put letters into envelopes. I'm thinking of moving on.'

'What, home?'

'No, not yet. I've a few months yet before I have to find a proper job. I thought I might try France.'

'I'm in France myself,' she replied. '*Assistante* in a school.'

'I thought the French constitution outlawed torture.'

'It's not so bad really.'

'Oh, no?'

'Only one term to go,' she said. Florence was heaven; she didn't want to think about going back.

'How long are you here for?'

'Only a fortnight.'

'Seen much?'

'The *David*, the Uffizi, the churches.'

'The usual stuff, eh? All dead and gone. It's not the real Florence. That's round here, where the craftsmen work, or out on the northern side, in the new suburbs near the football stadium. Florentines, believe it or not, care as much about football as they do about art.'

They slipped into conversation, both eager to speak English again, after so long grappling with a foreign language.

'Haven't you been up to Piazzale Michelangelo?' he asked and she shook her head.

'It's the best view of the city from there. I'll take you, if you like.'

And before she had time to give an answer he was shouting to one of the others watching the football. Helen caught the words '*signorina inglese*' and saw a nod and a thumbs-up sign.

'Come on,' he said, catching hold of her wrist. 'We'll borrow Paolo's scooter. He doesn't mind.'

'What, now?' His careless spontaneity was rather alluring.

'No time like the present.'

Just outside on the pavement they found the motor scooter and Nico was already revving up the engine as she climbed on to the pillion and adjusted her skirt appropriately. Crash hats, she supposed, were only for the faint-hearted.

'Hold tight!' he yelled, and she had to, because he set off at breakneck speed, dipping and swaying along the ancient streets, threading his way between parked cars and in and out of the stream of traffic. Her hair billowed out behind as they streaked along beside the river and up the hill towards the crowded square.

'Wrong side of the road's a bit hair-raising, but you have to drive like they do, or you'd be flattened,' he said when they came to a standstill, seeing she was out of breath. 'What did I tell you about the view?'

She turned and saw just what he meant. From here Florence lay before them, lit up brightly, like jewels on black velvet.

'Great isn't it? Do you want an ice cream or a beer or something now we're here?'

They drank beer, then smoked American cigarettes.

'What made you come to Italy?' Helen asked curiously.

It was a time when many students were heading for Amsterdam to smoke hash or hitting the hippy trail to India, but Nico wasn't into peace and love.

'They've got the biggest communist party in western Europe. I thought it was worth a look.'

Surely not someone else who wanted to put the world to rights? But she wasn't surprised. Student activism was a normal part of life all over the continent.

'You a Marxist or something?'

'I guess so. It's a framework for redirecting history, a process for moving forward, isn't it?'

Helen sucked on the cigarette, below her the towers of an ancient city, behind her the roar of cars and motorbikes. She wasn't convinced that history needed redirecting.

'Forward to what?'

He shrugged his shoulders and intoned every contemporary student's creed. 'Freedom, workers' rights, death of capitalism.'

'Yeah,' Helen said. She believed in it herself.

After that they met in the bar quite often, but Gianni took exception to this Englishman muscling in on what he considered his own territory and he was suspicious of the way they spoke in low voices in English, then laughed uproariously at what he didn't understand.

Gianni, however, had one more card up his sleeve. 'I take a few days off,' he said to Helen in his broken English a couple of days before she was due to leave. 'I never seen south of France. I give you a ride back.'

'A lift, do you mean? How could you? It's hundreds of miles!'

It was an outrageous suggestion, though it would certainly save her the train fare.

With a careless gesture he indicated that it was no problem. 'I have an uncle at Finale Ligure. We stay there first night. When you must be back?'

'Tuesday morning.'

He made a swift calculation. 'We leave Friday *mezzogiorno*. OK?'

But his mother and father didn't think it was OK. They had old-fashioned views about girls going on long trips with men they hardly knew, even when that man was their own son. English girls had a bad reputation with Italian parents, and apparently they knew Gianni all too well.

Helen would have gladly given up the idea, but Gianni had got the bit between his teeth and he didn't want to change his mind. There was a lot of shouting and door-slamming while the project was discussed in the little flat above the bar.

It was stalemate, until Nico offered to go with them. The job at the British Institute had run its course and he was ready for pastures new.

'Why don't we deliver Helen back at school together?' he said to Gianni. 'Then we can spend a few days on the Riviera – see the casino at Monte Carlo, that type of thing.'

Gianni was not enthusiastic, but it was the only acceptable compromise. To the approval of Adriana's parents it was decided that the three of them should go together, as mutual chaperones. For Helen's last day in Florence all faces were wreathed in smiles.

Helen was used to the bad time-keeping of the French but the Italians were even worse. She wasn't sure how, but Friday midday slipped by, turning into Saturday morning and then into Saturday afternoon, but there always seemed to be something to prevent them leaving. It was after five o'clock when they eventually started, Gianni embracing his family as if he would never see them again. He took along with him a smart leather suitcase; all of Nico's luggage fitted into an old canvas ex-army rucksack.

They all climbed into Gianni's little Fiat, the record player blaring out the latest pop songs from England which were all the rage in Europe. Helen could tell that the boys were deeply suspicious of each other's motives. In fact they were icy cool and didn't address each other very often, channelling their remarks through her, in either English or Italian. She wondered idly when they would come to blows and if they did what her reaction ought to be.

It was late when they reached Finale Ligure. Gianni's uncle's hotel was on the sea front and from her bedroom Helen could hear the brush of the waves on the shore. After dinner they strolled, three abreast, along the promenade under the palm trees in the mild evening air, with Helen in the middle.

Nico had insisted, with a glint in his eye, that he and Gianni should share a room, so that they could wake each other early in the morning, which meant that Gianni, who had been eyeing Helen hungrily ever since they left Florence, wouldn't have a chance if he was contemplating slipping along to her bedroom in the middle of the night.

'Up by five if we're to get a good start,' Nico said severely and Gianni flinched, but in the event it was nearly six before any of them were out of bed, Nico and Gianni blaming each other for sleeping late in loud Florentine dialect which Helen didn't attempt to understand. Then after bolting down some coffee from the bar across the street, they got back in the car and started out full pelt for the French border.

Gianni held his foot to the floor, with the car windows open, the record player turned up loud, the Mediterranean always on the left, sparkling in the sun. Imperia, Bordighera, Ventimiglia, Menton. The chilliness of yesterday had gone. Today the two of them were scoring points off each other. Helen's Italian was basic, but she knew enough to realise that.

Every so often Gianni took her hand and kissed it. Nico responded by whispering to her in English. To annoy Gianni, the other two started to sing stupid songs like *One Man went to Mow* and *Ten Green Bottles*. Then more pop songs. Gianni retaliated by going at breakneck speed. Once past Nice the roads were narrower, yet to be replaced by motorway, but by lunchtime they were nearly in Aix en Provence and they came to a shuddering halt in a tiny hamlet.

'We go to find shop,' Gianni announced, and without another word or an invitation to join them they were gone. Helen took the opportunity to scramble out of the car to relieve herself behind a rock, and to rinse her hands in a stream at the side of the road.

Eventually they returned with lunch: some bread, beer, a tin of sardines and some apples. It was rather like a picnic out of Enid Blyton. And when they had finished, much to Helen's exasperation, they both lay down on the grass verge and went to sleep.

For two hours she waited, but then she could stand it no longer. She got in the car and hooted the horn.

'You may have forgotten this,' she said tartly, 'but I'm supposed to be back at school the day after tomorrow, and we've still got an awful long way to go.'

But the hectic morning had been too much for all of them. After another hundred miles, even with Nico taking over at the wheel, they had all had enough and they started to look round for somewhere to stay the night.

'How much money have you got?' Nico asked, and he and Gianni emptied their pockets.

It was certainly not enough for luxury accommodation and they both refused to let Helen pay her share. Their egos would never allow that. So they booked into a shabby little hotel right on the town square where they could only afford one room. It contained a single bed which they allocated to Helen and a double bed which they took for themselves.

But the wine was very cheap and later, as dinner wore on, they both became drunker and drunker.

'I'm going to bed,' Helen told them at about ten thirty. She had had quite a lot to drink herself. 'I suggest you two take a turn round the square to sober yourselves up.'

'Why? We aren't drunk, are we Gianni, baby?'

'What is drunk?' Gianni asked.

'I'll teach you,' Nico said kindly, putting an arm around him. 'It's intoxicated, tipsy, plastered, three sheets to the wind, sozzled . . .'

'Shut up, Nico. Just go for a walk.'

In the bedroom she waited a while but they didn't come, so she turned out the light and went to sleep.

Next morning she found them sprawled together on the other bed like exhausted puppies and when she returned from the primitive shower room down the corridor they were still fast asleep. In any case they were both still far too drunk to drive a car.

She zipped up her bag and stood over them.

'Well, *ragazzi*, I'll be on my way.'

Nico opened one eye. 'Where are you going?'

'To the station. Neither of you is in a fit state to move and I have to be home by tonight.'

Gianni tried to lift his head from the pillow and failed. Helen bent to kiss them both in turn.

'Bye,' she said. 'Thanks for an eventful journey.'

She did not expect to see either of them ever again.

7

Helen picked through the pile of CDs she found in a plastic case in the glove compartment, marvelling at the selection. Perhaps he had changed, but Bach's B minor mass and music by William Byrd didn't strike her as being to Nico's taste.

'I picked them at random out of Sophie's cupboard, then found most of them were church music,' he explained, in answer to her look. 'I never really got past the Rolling Stones myself. How about you?'

She had a vision of them tearing flat out through the south of France singing *This Could be the Last Time* at the tops of their voices with Gianni glaring at them glassy-eyed. But the world had moved on.

Just about the lightest in Sophie's collection was a recording of Debussy. 'Will this do?' she asked, holding it up for his approval, but he made no comment.

Helen didn't ever remember them discussing music, though she supposed they had discussed politics – those idealistic politics of the time, when young people believed the world was going to get better and better through a mixture of love and socialism and militant protest. They had no inkling of damage to the planet; all that was far into the future. It was going to be the dawning of the age of Aquarius, a mystic new beginning. It was letting it all hang out, it was doing your own thing. Well, they had done that all right.

A couple of weeks after she was back at school, at the very end of April, a small grey 2CV drew up outside the house in the middle of the afternoon and she heard feet on the stone steps leading up to the front door. Madame was at the shop and she went to answer it herself.

'Hello,' Nico said coolly. 'This is a one-horse town, if ever I saw one.'

'Nico! How did you find out where I lived?' she exclaimed, astonished that he had managed to track her down.

'Gianni had it written on a piece of paper in his wallet. Didn't I mention that I had a first in geography? I knew it would come in handy one day.'

'You both behaved like idiots.'

'Male competitiveness, I'm afraid.'

'Is that your car? Where are you going?'

'Wherever the whim happens to take me.'

'And I'm your whim, am I?'

'You might say that,' he acknowledged with a grin.

Passers-by were beginning to stare; everyone in the little town knew the English 'Miss' by this time and she quickly grabbed him by the sleeve.

'I think you'd better come in.'

Over a cup of coffee, he brought her up to date. He and Gianni had returned to the Riviera, where they had spent a couple of days together before the drinking money ran out and Gianni had to go home. Nico found a job as a tour guide in Monte Carlo for a few days. The Americans were good tippers and he had made a bit of money at the casino. Hence the car. It was rather a jalopy, but it could do sixty-five with a following wind.

'I thought you didn't believe in capitalism,' she mentioned pointedly.

'If it's the only way the workers can get a slice of the cake, it's OK – for the meantime.'

'Until the revolution, eh?'

Helen didn't like to mention that getting a first from Cambridge hardly suited him for membership of the proletariat.

'And how goes it here?' he asked, changing the subject.

'Bloody awful. But there's not long to go. Roll on the end of June!'

'They don't put this place in the travel brochures, do they? Out of all the towns in all of France, how did you come to pick on this one?'

That line seemed to remind her of something but she couldn't quite remember what.

'I didn't. It picked me. I expect it's a case of mutual disappointment.'

It was nice to speak English, nice to grumble. They sat together on the bed which doubled as a sofa and she offered him more coffee and some biscuits. She was not at all surprised when he kissed her. She had been expecting that he would.

'Can I doss down here tonight?' he asked. 'I've got my sleeping-bag. Or will your landlady object?'

His arms were tight around her and they kissed again, this time more lustfully as his hand crept up towards her breasts. Helen had a feeling that the sleeping-bag would probably be superfluous. She knew almost nothing about him and she felt rather suspicious about the car, but he was English and she had fancied him from the start. As far as she was concerned he could stay for as long as he liked.

'She has her lover here several nights a week. She can't really say anything to me.'

That was the green light, if either of them needed one. Before she knew it they were writhing about together on the bed and she was enjoying herself hugely. She wanted to get the image of the fiasco with Paul right out of her head for good.

'Are you a virgin?'

(Men always asked you that in those days, Helen remembered, and wondered if they still did. They seemed rather nervous of being the first, except of course if they were intending to marry you.)

'Does it matter?'

'Not if it doesn't to you. Shall I take that as a no?'

Fortunately she had brought her diaphragm from England, just on the off-chance, and she excused herself and went to fit it.

'Actually I'm sort of engaged to a chap in England,' she admitted, while he still had time to change his mind.

'Christ, I didn't know people got engaged any more! Adriana didn't mention it.'

'I never told her. I'm not going to marry him. I just haven't got round to breaking it off yet. I'm afraid it all sounds rather ridiculous.'

Why was she apologising? It was nothing to do with him.

'Well if you don't care about him, I certainly don't. Anyway, marriage is dead, isn't it?'

He was skilfully peeling off her knickers and running his hands up between her thighs. 'You know, I've been thinking about your legs ever since Florence.'

She laughed. 'I'll say this, you get full marks for persistence.'

Sex with Nico was very easy. There were no emotional strings. He didn't expect anything of her and she didn't expect anything of him. It was a way of getting rid of all her other frustrations. A way of not thinking – about her loneliness, about the rest of her life when she had to leave this place. Besides, Nico was the first excitement she'd had since she'd been here.

They spent the rest of the afternoon and most of the evening in bed. It was like getting a box of chocolates; once it was open, they couldn't resist sampling more and more until they were both utterly sated. Then after a makeshift meal of bread, *saucisson* and cheap red wine they fell asleep in Helen's single bed.

Next day she left him there while she went to school, but she only had two lessons that morning, so she was back by ten thirty, carrying warm croissants and some apricot jam.

'Do you always get up at the crack of dawn?' he enquired, surfacing bleary-eyed. She breathed in the smell of his naked body, fresh from the bed.

'The railway line's only fifty yards away. A train goes past at seven twenty, another at eight ten, another at quarter to nine. It's like an alarm clock.'

'I've slept in worse places. That hotel near Narbonne for one.'

They both laughed, while she prepared some coffee and he pulled on a pair of jeans.

'If I stick around here, what will Madame say?'

'Are you referring to me, or to the landlady?'

'The landlady, stupid. Will she object?'

'How long did you have in mind?'

'Dunno. I spent all my money on the car but I can always get a job somewhere or other.'

'Got a work permit?'

He shrugged. 'Nobody's ever asked me for one.'

'Well don't blame me if you get arrested.'

His French turned out to be almost as good as his Italian and within two days he had found a job as a barman at the Café Rex in the main square, afternoons and evenings. Monsieur Taupin didn't pay a lot, but he gave Nico all the leftovers he could eat which saved on the housekeeping money. When Helen went there after school he was always deep in conversation with one of the customers, more often than not about politics.

(De Gaulle? All right in the war but what did he know about the workers? The Americans? Warmongers and worse! Look at the evidence – Vietnam, the civil rights problem. Martin Luther King had been assassinated only a few weeks previously.)

Was he just showing off? Whether he was or not, he had made the acquaintance of more people in a few days than she had in nearly nine months.

And she liked having him around. He scattered his clothes on the floor but at least the place looked lived in. She had been wretched before, with no more than a handful of friends and school only just bearable. Now she spent most of her evenings in the café and when Nico finished at midnight there was the prospect of a boisterous night in bed. It was something to look forward to; something to make her feel human again. Who cared if she was tired in the morning?

She didn't take much notice of what was going on in the world. Now that the nights were lighter the English radio stations were becoming fuzzy, like hearing messages from outer space. When she wasn't at the Rex, she had her assignment to work on – fifteen thousand words on an aspect of the region she was staying in. She had chosen Romanesque art, stealing whole chunks from obscure books in the local library and stringing them together, carefully missing out the more grandiose descriptions. It was May already and it still had to be tapped out on her old Olivetti portable.

When Nico mentioned to her that the students in Paris were rioting she didn't think anything of it. So what was new? The French had been rioting for the best part of the last two hundred years; 1789, 1830, 1848, 1871. The time had come round again, that was all, and she didn't blame them. If she had had to put up with conditions like theirs she might have been rioting herself.

'Don't tell me I've shacked up with a fascist?' he asked in reply to her noncommittal look.

She was painting, trying to catch the early summer light which glanced off the shutters and the window-boxes on the other side of the street. Next year, back at university with finals looming, there would be no more time for this.

'I've never read *Das Kapital*,' she conceded, 'though I suppose I do consider myself a socialist. And people like Jean-Paul Sartre are part of my course. But French politics isn't really anything to do with us.'

'You're bloody naive, d'you know that?' he said, surprisingly vehement, making her look up sharply into his face. 'Everything's to do with us.'

But she had heard it all before from Kicker, who really was working class, not a doctor's son with a Cambridge degree. At that moment she was more interested in painting than in politics.

'Give it a rest, Nico. Can't you see I'm trying to concentrate?'

She perceived he was bored by the Debussy. When it was finished she turned on the radio instead, flicking through the stations until she came across some heavy rock. It was the sort of stuff she always told Oliver would rot his brain cells.

'That better?'

He grinned. They were on the M25 by now and the traffic was nose to tail, but moving. There was no escape from this mad adventure, even if she'd wanted to change her mind. Anyway each time a doubt crept in the thought of Dave and Ianthe, together at the cottage, hardened her heart.

Yet she was perplexed. What was Nico doing, inviting her on this trip and not some woman fifteen or twenty years her junior? He had kept himself in shape and in a way he was more attractive now than he had been at twenty-two. He was certainly smarter, with the expensive clothes and fast car that made up the accoutrements of a successful male. And the bum was still pretty firm. He could have had a girl Ianthe's age.

Silently she cursed them – him and Dave. Unless they had beer bellies and bad breath it was still easy for men in their late forties to be considered sexy, while she was teetering on the brink of that age when all the beauty creams in the world weren't going to hide the slowing down of nature. Women who tried to fend off time were just considered tarts.

'Nico,' she said tentatively, 'may I ask you something?'

'Go ahead.'

'What did you ever see in me?'

'What? Back then?'

She nodded, wondering if he would dare to tell the truth.

'Well, for one you had fabulous legs.'

Involuntarily he looked down at them, but she was wearing trousers again, as she had been on Saturday night, so whether they had stood the test of time neither of them was in any position to say.

'And second you were never sentimental.'

What he meant, she assumed, was that she had never expected him to be in love with her. That would have made him drop her like a hot potato.

'Seems like you still aren't, if I read this Dave thing right.'

'I thought I said we weren't going to talk about Dave.'

'OK, I get the message. You often used to tell me to shut up and I suppose I quite enjoyed it. I hate timid women with no brains.'

That was not quite the scenario as Helen remembered it. Men didn't like it if you contradicted them and Nico was one of the worst offenders.

'I always thought men weren't keen on women with brains. They certainly weren't in those days. They'd run a mile if they thought you'd read anything more taxing than Mills and Boon.'

'Yes, but then they married the ones with no brains and found out what idiots they'd made of themselves. You see it over and over again. I did it myself, in fact. Within a year the whole thing's a bore.'

'Is that all you stuck it out for?'

'Nearly nine actually, God knows why. We spent the whole time screaming at each other. Never again, I can tell you. It's best the way it was with you and me. Go for it while you can, then walk away when you start to disagree and don't look back.'

On the surface it sounded as though he had learned a valuable lesson about himself, yet here he was, re-enacting the scenes of youth, playing the same old tune. If that wasn't sentimentality, she didn't know what was.

'So that's your ideal relationship, is it? A month or so, and call it quits?'

'Why not? That way nothing gets broken.'

'I didn't think, somehow, that you believed in broken hearts.'

'Too right,' he agreed. 'I didn't mean hearts. I probably meant plates. She was a fiery little thing, was Rosie.'

'Rosie?'

'I never could pronounce her Chinese name. She smashed most of the china on my head. Even the expensive stuff my mother brought out from England.'

Broken crockery – was that all he could remember out of nine years of marriage?

Still, she wasn't really surprised. She had always been aware that he hadn't taken their own relationship any more seriously than she had. It had been easy come and easy go, thrown together and thrown apart again. That was the way they had both wanted it.

Perhaps, on reflection, they had never really had very much in common, even at first, except their Englishness in a foreign land, their shared background of post-war Britain. It wasn't xenophobia, but it was probably self-satisfaction. Perhaps they hadn't really discussed anything in depth at all. There had never been much talking. To tell the truth, she had been more interested in his body than his opinions.

The M2 was less crowded and he drove in the outside lane, exceeding the speed limit whenever he got the chance. His driving certainly hadn't changed for the better. The visibility was deteriorating now and black spray began to fly up from the wheels of the lorries in front as the rain grew heavier. In British fashion, they fell back upon remarks about the weather, then sank into silence, except for the repetitive din of bass drums from the radio.

And if they hadn't talked much then, how long was their small talk going to last this time round?

At the ferry terminal the holiday queues stretched for miles and their sailing had been delayed.

'Why don't we have dinner somewhere while we wait for this lot to clear?' Nico suggested, pulling out a restaurant guide. 'Let's see if anything in here fits the bill.'

Helen's eyes opened wide. In the old days he used to think food freaks were the ultimate bourgeois, but of course that had been life on a shoestring. Food had been fuel, nothing more. They ate bread with *charcuterie* or slabs of dark chocolate, tinned ravioli, ready-cooked chicken pieces. If they were still hungry they stuffed themselves with éclairs from the *patisserie* just across the street. Mostly they just lived on cigarettes and black coffee.

Nobody had worried about fat or sugar; nobody had heard of cholesterol. Not like Emma who scoured labels for animal fat and artificial additives; who brought out her pictures of emaciated, featherless chickens when Helen forgot to buy free-range eggs at the supermarket.

'How about a takeaway Chinese?' she suggested, with a mischievous glance.

'Are you kidding? All those soggy noodles and sickly sweet sauces . . .'

'Joke, Nico,' she interpolated patiently.

She had forgotten that he didn't have much of a sense of humour. Oh, they had laughed all right, but it had been high spirits, never teasing. One thing he had certainly always taken seriously and that was himself.

'You can't get decent Chinese cooking in this country unless you pay a fortune. That's something Rosie could do all right, I'm glad to say.'

Strangely, Helen had never met a man who admitted his wife was a bad cook, even if he hated her. Perhaps it had some deep psychological meaning. She leaned over his shoulder to catch a glimpse of the guide and the expensive perfume of his aftershave wafted towards her. He was as well groomed as a model with trousers carefully pressed, shoes polished, his jacket hanging up on the hook behind him to avoid the creases. Even the guide was pristine; no dogears or torn pages. This Nico might have been a completely different man, that other life sloughed off like an excess skin.

'The White House sounds rather nice. It's ages since I

tasted Sunday supplement food. We usually survive on chicken nuggets and regular fries when we're out, for Tim's benefit.'

'What on earth are they?' he mumbled, poring over the page, brows bent in concentration and Helen wondered if they had been living on the same planet all these years.

'It's obvious you've never had children, or hasn't the fast food industry penetrated Hong Kong?'

The White House, when they eventually found it down a narrow lane a couple of miles out of town, was pretentious and overpriced. The elaborate edifice of guinea fowl breast and blobs of red cabbage surrounded by swirls of sauce wouldn't have fed a flea. Helen would have preferred the takeaway sweet and sour with lashings of monosodium glutamate, but Nico offered no criticism, so she said nothing, reminding herself to stock up with crisps and biscuits on the boat. Even the chocolate dessert left her stomach with a gaping hole in it.

To her surprise he refused coffee ('surely nobody drinks it anymore?'), but Helen needed the kick-start of a good strong coffee if the ferry was going to be hours late. But perhaps if he worried about his diet he was not such a maverick as she had first thought.

'We'll go Dutch, you know,' she said quickly, when the waiter brought the bill, then wished she hadn't when she saw what it came to. She didn't know how she was going to explain away a meal at such a fancy restaurant when the credit card bill arrived.

'You haven't told me about your paintings,' Nico said, as they strolled back towards the car. 'Had many exhibitions?'

It was as though he was remembering his manners. The only comment she ever remembered him making about art was something snide about Andy Warhol and why didn't she paint a tin of tomato soup.

She stuttered, thinking of the number of times her cats had appeared on a trestle table in the school hall.

'Oh . . . er . . . several actually. Only one in London though.'

'West End?'

'Not quite.'

Her cousin, who lived in Notting Hill, had once asked her to do a painting of the villa their family always went to on the

Costa Brava, and Helen had obligingly knocked one up from a colour photo, but that was the nearest the West End any of her paintings had ever been.

'What do you do, mostly?'

'3-D stuff these days, not paint much any more. I use Perspex a lot, old bicycle chains, waste materials – you know the kind of thing. It's sort of ecological.'

It was amazing what you could come up with using a little imagination, but since he knew less than nothing about art she didn't expect to come unstuck. But as she said it her mind boggled at the thought of sculptures made out of bin bags and old foil plates.

'Very avant garde. Do you ever sell them?'

'I got a four-figure sum for something I did last year.' (Well, wasn't £19.99 a four-figure sum?)

He seemed impressed, whereas years ago he would have told her that modern art was a load of bull – a con-trick by the so-called intelligentsia against people who had more money than sense; now he seemed to have taken the market economy to his heart. It was a hell of a change.

They were nearly back at the ferry terminal; it was her last chance to change her mind. Was she really going to step aboard the boat with this man whom, frankly, she hardly knew, let alone stand another week or so in his company? It was going to be a voyage of discovery indeed.

But after her triumph of the morning she was still up in the air. France meant sun and good food, and besides she was tired of being sensible. If she was going to make a fool of herself, then so be it.

The eight o'clock ferry didn't sail until almost 10.30. It was a rough crossing for the end of May and the boat was full of school children on half-term trips, looking tired and sick, the teachers with permanently furrowed brows worrying them into packs like sheepdogs.

Helen and Nico sought refuge in the bar where she sipped on a tomato juice and he ordered a malt whisky. They had only drunk mineral water in the restaurant, but apparently he hadn't decided to eschew every kind of stimulant.

'Bloody kids!' he growled. 'I've always hated the ferry.'

'Have you? I love it. It makes you realise that you live on an island and I always think it's a great start to the holidays.'

'You always were a romantic, Helen. It must be your artistic temperament.'

'I certainly can't be very hard-headed coming away with you,' she agreed cheerfully. 'By the way, any idea where we're going to sleep tonight?'

'I booked a place a few miles the other side of Calais. Single rooms.'

He eyed her and tossed back the rest of his malt. 'I thought you'd prefer that – for now.'

So he was giving her a let-out clause.

'Yes,' she said. 'I would. For now. You know, Nico, I've been thinking. I wonder if this whole thing is really a good idea?'

'What? You and me?'

'This trip, yes.'

'Why shouldn't it be?'

He ordered another malt and made short work of it. The ship heaved and rolled. By now, they were almost alone in the bar and even the barman looked a bit queasy, but Helen had always had a strong stomach and Nico hardly seemed to notice. The drink was having a mellowing effect.

'Do you remember how we raced from Florence?' he asked with a nostalgic laugh. 'Remember Paris? Remember how we marched and yelled ourselves hoarse?'

Students didn't march any more, did they? Where were the students of today, protesting against the corrupt regimes, the wars and insurrections all around the world?

'I remember the bare boards and the hole-in-the-floor toilets.'

He hardly heard her. 'That's the best time. When you're young. A few laughs, no responsibilities, plenty of sex. That's the real thing, don't you think so?'

Their glasses lurched across the table.

'Perhaps you're right,' Helen said, contemplating his face under the muted lights which showed up the fine lines around his mouth. 'But I hope there's still something left to look forward to, even at our age.'

'That's what we're going to find out, isn't it?'

*   *   *

The first thing she did when she reached her hotel room was to kick off her shoes and close the shutters. To keep herself in.

The bed was an old-fashioned country one with starched sheets, a fat bolster and a carved mahogany bedstead. The dressing-table had a triple mirror; the sort her parents had in their bedroom when she was little. She remembered sitting in front of it for hours, tilting each mirror so that her reflection was repeated a thousand times, going on for ever.

In the corner, sitting incongruously beside a modern pearl-pink wash-basin, was an old prie-dieu. It no longer stood in front of a crucifix or a picture of the Virgin Mary, but a travel poster of the beach at Le Touquet. Helen knelt down on it in relief, hands clasped, though not in prayer.

A room of her own. A private place. She hadn't had one for twenty years; all this was worth it just for that. It wasn't a lover she wanted really, just a room to herself – some space. She wanted to throw her underwear on the floor and take up both sides of the bed. A little selfishness was what she needed, a little greed.

Softly, she rose from her knees and went to lock the door, just to make sure she wouldn't be disturbed.

8

The morning sun shone warmly on the wet tarmac, making steam rise from the puddles in front of the hotel. In the sky the clouds were as fluffy as those in a children's picture book. During the night the wind had dropped and it was real holiday weather.

'We won't stop in Paris on the way down,' Nico said, handing her a road map from his suitcase, then proceeding to stow their luggage in the boot. 'We'll save that for later. We'll go Reims, Dijon today, then head south tomorrow.'

'Aren't we stopping anywhere on the way?' she asked, slightly bemused.

He had slept off the effects of the malt and had been knocking at her door at seven thirty, already freshly shaved, though a little flushed. She wondered if he had been out jogging before breakfast. Helen had always rather despised people who did that.

'No. Let's go flat out, the way we used to. Do you remember Gianni? The way he revved up that little Fiat of his? But I could drive it faster.'

She could hardly believe it. He seemed to want everything to be exactly the same, as though she was an actress in his fantasy. In his imagination she probably still had long straight hair and smudged black eye makeup. Perhaps he had convinced himself that the fantastic legs were still there too, and everything else that went with them. What she might think about it didn't interest him at all.

Nevertheless she had had the courage to uncover her legs this morning, though the navy-and-white cotton dress she was wearing still came well below the knee.

They climbed aboard and the sleek car purred into life.

'On the way back we'll go along the coast,' he continued. 'Then north, to see if the Rex is still there, with Paris last of all.'

In a way she didn't blame him. Life had been carefree then, everything in black and white, as it was when you were young. Experience usually taught you otherwise, though it didn't seem to have taught him.

'All Madame's lovely black hair will be white by now,' she commented wryly. 'I shouldn't think we'd recognise anyone in the place. Mireille's parents are both dead. Did you ever meet them?'

'You keep in touch with Mireille, do you? I'd forgotten all about her.'

'We've always written. She comes over to England every couple of years. Brings us wine and stocks up at Marks and Spencer's.'

'Does she? I thought she'd be a dreadful old *hausfrau* by now. What was her boyfriend's name? Xavier, wasn't it? He was really under her thumb, poor bloke. I hope he kept her barefoot and pregnant for the next ten years.'

She had forgotten that Nico and Mireille had never quite seen eye to eye.

'Actually they're divorced. She lives in Provence now, out in the country somewhere. From the photos it looks like one of those places you see in glossy magazines. I don't think she's ever mentioned what happened to him.'

'Well out of it, I expect.'

Helen set her lips and looked out of the window. If only he knew. It was she who was the *hausfrau*, not Mireille. She who had never had a career, who didn't really paint, who bought her designer blouses second-hand, who had never once cheated on her husband – not until now. By this time even the thought of that was wearing rather thin.

They met Xavier one Sunday when the four of them drove out for lunch in some little village, perched precariously on the side of a hill. The countryside was stunning at that season, with its running rivers and new green vegetation springing up along the gorge. Food was cheap and they stuffed themselves with soup, crudités, asparagus, pâté, venison, various vegetables, salad, ice cream and coffee, all for next to nothing. The place was probably in the Michelin guide these days with the main course alone costing a small fortune.

Mireille and Xavier were getting married in the middle of June, even though they were both still students, and the girls spent the time discussing bridesmaids' dresses. On the way home Nico remarked: 'There's a general strike tomorrow. In support of the students and against the violence used by the police.'

'Yes,' Xavier acknowledged. 'I heard.'

Nobody else seemed interested and the conversation turned another way, but next morning they heard a noise coming from the main street long before school was due to start. It was a demonstration with people chanting slogans. The unrest seemed to be spreading throughout the country.

Later in the week Nico came rushing home from the main square where he had gone to collect the bread.

'Have you heard the news? The banks are going on strike on Monday. And trains, factories, post offices – the lot. All over the country.'

Helen looked in her purse. 'I've only got about ten francs.'

'Go and draw some more out then, before the strike starts. God knows how long it's going to last.'

Nico had no bank account – he was strictly a cash-only man – but he filled the car up with petrol as a precaution. There was talk of food shortages if the strikes went on for any length of time. On Monday, when Helen arrived at school, she found a banner hanging out of the window proclaiming a sit-in by some of the sixth-form students. Somebody told her there was a meeting of teachers that afternoon to vote on a strike and asked if she was coming.

Helen hesitated. She was English. None of this was anything to do with her. But she said she might.

'You ought to vote,' Nico urged her. 'You know what conditions students have to put up with in this God-awful system. They don't know they're born in England with their grants and their middle-class values.'

There was a glint in his eyes every time he talked about the strikes. He was middle-class himself but converts were always the most fanatical of the lot.

When it came to it, however, her vote made no difference; there was overwhelming backing for indefinite strike action by the teaching staff. Helen was delighted. It meant that she wouldn't have to face those endless chaotic classes with children who were daily slipping beyond her control. With any luck it would last for a month or more.

She found Mireille and Xavier with Nico at the Rex.

'I've just been to the post office,' she told them. 'They must be seeing all this on the news in England, so I tried to ring my mother to tell her I'm OK, but they won't let you make a call unless it's a matter of life and death.'

'You should have told them it was,' Nico said.

'Well, it wasn't, was it? But it might have been for other people.'

He saw the irritation in her eyes but he ignored it.

'Let's go,' he said. 'All of us. Let's go to Paris to see for ourselves. We've no proof that what the newspapers and television are feeding us is right. We don't know what's really going on. What do you say?'

Mireille and Xavier glanced at each other. The school was on strike and the boarders sent home. The university would be closed.

'I could do with a bit of excitement,' Xavier said, but Mireille wasn't so sure.

'How would we get there?'

'In my car,' Nico said. 'Tonight. We might as well go straight away if we're going at all.'

'What about your job?' Helen asked.

'Easy come, easy go,' he said carelessly. 'Old Taupin won't care.'

'I'm game for it,' Xavier agreed. 'Anything to get out of this place for a change.'

'What about petrol?' Mireille objected. 'It's getting harder and harder to come by. The garages aren't getting any supplies. We don't want to be stranded.'

'We can always hitch back if necessary. But it won't be a problem.'

Eventually even Mireille started coming round to the idea. She mumbled something about her parents, but it was only lip service. She was getting married in less than a month. Her parents wouldn't have any jurisdiction over her then, even though she wasn't quite twenty-one.

'We'll go at eleven, then,' Nico said. 'I'll get off early. If we drive straight through, we'll be in Paris by morning.'

It was between 250 and 300 miles, but Nico didn't stop. By the time it was midnight they had reached the *route nationale* and he drove as fast as the little car would go, while Mireille and Xavier dozed in each other's arms on the cramped back seat, but Helen forced herself to stay alert, so that she could keep Nico from dropping off to sleep. They sang the *Marseillaise* together, tapping out the rhythm on the dashboard, as they rolled on through the darkness.

As they were approaching Paris Nico turned off the road to look for something to eat in a neighbouring village.

'The baker's just opening up,' he said. 'You go and get a couple of baguettes. I'll scout round and see if I can find some petrol.'

The others tumbled out to stretch their legs and smoke a cigarette while Nico took the car in search of a garage.

'Did you find any?' Xavier asked, when he reappeared a few minutes later.

'Yes. Filled her right up.'

'We'll pay our share.'

Nico was noncommittal. 'No hurry.'

In those days, before the oil crisis of the early seventies, when petrol was cheap, nobody had lockable petrol tanks. It had taken Helen all this time to realise that he had probably not bought any petrol at all. He had siphoned it from someone else's tank. Stolen it.

Nibbling bread and chocolate from the baker's, they were soon on the road again, arriving in Paris early and parking the car in a street near the Boulevard St Michel, almost within sight of the Sorbonne.

'We'll go to one of the cafés – keep our ears open to find out what's going on.'

They by-passed the usual tourist bars on the main boulevard, with their red canopies and bright window-boxes, and ordered black coffee in a tiny side-street café which catered to a mainly student clientele. Xavier and Nico interrogated the waiter, while Helen and Mireille took their drinks outside and sat on the pavement.

'I'm not sure what we're doing here,' Mireille said, lighting another cigarette. 'We haven't anywhere to stay and nothing to pay for it with anyway. I should have been having a fitting for my dress today.'

'Yesterday you were all for it.'

'That was before I started to think about it properly.'

'It's only for a day or so, to satisfy Nico's curiosity. Anyway it'll be interesting to see things first hand, instead of on the eight o'clock news.'

'This isn't a game, you know,' Mireille snapped. 'It's all right for you two. It doesn't really affect you. But just imagine it – my father says there could be a *coup d'état* at any moment. And I want Xavier in one piece for the wedding. He's far too interested in this whole affair.'

'Don't you think you're a bit young to be getting married?' Helen ventured. 'Neither of you has got a proper job. What are you going to live on?'

Mireille gave a shrug. 'At least we'll be on our own, and near the university. My aunt's going to let us have a room, rent free. If Xavier passes this year, he can get some sort of a teaching job in September.'

'There aren't going to be any exams, not by the looks of it.'

'It'll straighten out,' she said with a grimace. 'It's got to. I can't put the wedding off now. I'm pregnant.'

'Does your mother know?'

'Not yet. But these things happen. She'll get over it. What about you and Nico?'

'What about me and Nico?'

'Do you like him?'

She used the word *aimer* which could mean either love or like, so Helen didn't know how to answer. It was one of the shortcomings of the French language.

'He passes the time,' she said with a grin.

By talking to some law students Nico somehow managed to scrounge some accommodation for them all on the fourth floor of an apartment building not far away. After they had trudged up the dark stone staircase, they found that the place consisted of one bare little room where the only furnishings were a torn net curtain and a brass chandelier.

'It's a bit basic, but we can bed down in our sleeping-bags,' Nico said, looking out of the tiny window to a courtyard far below which contained dustbins and old scrap metal. 'It'll do for a couple of nights.'

'I hope they're not expecting much rent,' Mireille said with a shudder, looking at the dusty bare boards. 'What a dump!'

'Who said anything about rent? The landlord won't know we're here if we don't tell him.'

Xavier nodded his approval, but Mireille had her own ideas about it. She and Nico always seemed to rub each other up the wrong way.

'Isn't that rather dishonest?' she demanded.

'As some famous philosopher once said, "Property is theft",' Nico answered glibly, and Helen wondered if he would still have said that if someone had wanted to borrow his precious little car.

'At least the weather's fine or we'd freeze to death,' commented Mireille. 'I take it there is at least a toilet?'

But Xavier and Nico weren't interested in her feminine regard for home comforts. Apparently some of the students who inhabited the same floor were having a meeting about tonight's tactics on the streets and they were eager to join in.

The rioting had died down somewhat during the last week or so, but now it seemed that a couple of the student leaders had been banned from the country and the trouble was all due to start up again in protest.

The girls said that if Nico and Xavier were going to a meeting they were going shopping.

'Shopping? At a time like this?'

'This is Paris. What do you expect?' Helen said, rather amused at Nico's earnestness, when he didn't give a toss about most of the things that other people took seriously. 'Anyway, I thought we'd come to watch, not take part in a riot.'

'The students aren't the ones to provoke violence,' Xavier pointed out solemnly.

'That's what your new pals say, but the television pictures say different.'

'It's rigged. To show the students in a bad light. Surely you can see that?'

There was no point arguing with them and certainly no point going to their meeting. Helen knew from her brief experience of politics that men didn't take kindly to women interfering in what they considered to be a masculine domain. It rankled with her a little, but Mireille didn't care.

'Leave them to it,' she advised. 'You and I are going to spend the afternoon in Au Printemps. They can get on with whatever little schemes they like.'

Later on, when they arrived back at the apartment the boys had disappeared so they wandered down the corridor, knocking on doors at random. The room at the end was a kitchen with an ancient gas stove and unpainted cupboards round the walls. It stank of stale cigarettes and alcohol. At the table sat three young males drinking beer and Helen noticed that they were reading Chairman Mao's *Little Red Book*.

'You are the girl of Nico, yes?' asked one of them in English.

'I speak French,' she told them. 'I'm Helen and this is Mireille. Do you know where they've gone?'

They indicated their ignorance with a twist of the mouth. Helen didn't really know what to make of them; outwardly they were well turned out with jackets and even ties, and one of them wore those heavy horn-rimmed spectacles that were popular at the time. Like Nico they were members of the *bourgeoisie* playing at working-class ruffians.

'All I want to know,' Mireille said, waving her hand imperiously at the jottings of Mao that western students had suddenly taken to their hearts, 'is what you hope to gain from all this. What is it all for?'

Collectively they looked astonished. 'We want to overthrow the government,' one of them said. 'It's as simple as that.'

Xavier and Nico returned carrying two brown-paper bags full of food. They didn't ask if the girls would cook – they just assumed – and that made Mireille angrier than ever.

'Why should we do your dirty work for you?' she flared.

'And if you think I'm cooking for those mates of yours as well, you can think twice. Who are they, anyway? They're not from round here.'

She had caught their provincial accents which Helen's ear was not yet acute enough to pick up, despite all these months in France.

'They're from Nancy,' Xavier explained. 'Wanting to find out what's going on, like us. Come on, *chérie*! We'll do it all together, if you like. We've got eggs and salad, that's all. An omelette won't take long to throw together.'

He glanced at Nico apologetically, as if to say, 'Never mind her. She's pregnant, that's all it is.'

Helen saw the look and interpreted it. The expression 'male chauvinist pig' still hadn't been invented but it was what she felt. She hadn't come to do the cooking either. Neither had she come to bring down the government. She had come in solidarity with all those students who were getting a raw deal. But at the same time she realised that this wasn't going to be the same as a gentle English by-election.

In the end, after some squabbling, they shared the chores equally, eating their omelettes in silence, drinking what beer the students from Nancy had left behind.

'We'll go at nightfall,' Nico said at last. 'We know the place where they're all gathering. Are you girls coming, or what?'

Helen glanced towards her friend. A demonstration was no place for a pregnant woman, and whatever their claims she knew that it wasn't meant to be peaceful. It would be blatant provocation of the riot police, just as they had seen so many nights on television.

But Mireille said, 'It's OK, we're coming. At least when you get your heads kicked in, there'll be someone to patch you up.'

Xavier was full of enthusiasm but Helen thought that if he had had any feeling for her at all he ought never to have let her come along. Being a girl shouldn't make a difference, but being pregnant did.

When the time came for them to start out, Mireille picked up her camera.

'What do you want that for?' Helen asked.

'I thought I might be able to make a bit of cash out of all this.

Magazines pay big money for photographs. You never know, if I can get just the right shot . . .'

'Do you know anything about it?'

Mireille slung the camera round her neck. 'Enough. My uncle's a photographer. This is one of his old cameras.'

'Well, just take care. If I'd known you were pregnant before we started . . .'

'Are you girls coming?' Nico shouted impatiently from the bottom of the stairs.

Mireille squeezed her arm. 'It's all right,' she said. 'I'll be fine.'

They marched, shoulder to shoulder at first, in long rows along the boulevard, the street lamps lighting their way. From the cafés there came shouts of encouragement, or of hatred, it was hard to tell which. Helen had her hand clasped tight in Nico's, trying to keep Mireille and Xavier in her sights, straining her eyes to keep her bearings. She could feel the stones he had collected for missiles hard inside his pocket. They chanted slogans against the government and various obscenities she didn't really understand. It was cold, even in the crush of bodies.

Then suddenly the column broke, scattering between some trees towards a line of what looked like robots, their shields up, helmets down. Nico dashed forward, taking aim with the stones from his pocket, and she followed him grimly as the front of the crowd bore down upon the police. Those with no missiles had just their own bodies as bulwarks against the enemy, but they charged on just the same, attempting desperately to break through the cordon, before being driven back by the merciless batons and shields confronting them.

Some, in the front ranks, were beaten to the ground and dragged away. She saw Nico tackle one of the policemen who had lost his shield, aiming a kick into the man's groin. Briefly they grappled and Nico fell to the ground, but Helen, only a yard away, opened her mouth and screamed at the top of her voice. It was enough. For a split second the policeman looked up and Nico dodged him deftly, like a snake, before jumping to his feet and making a dash for it, catching hold of her and dragging her towards the shelter of a nearby doorway.

'Are you all right?' she fussed, smoothing away some mud from his cheek, but he pushed her away impatiently. She realised suddenly that he was enjoying himself.

'Never better! The thugs! Look over there; people are starting to pull up the paving stones for barricades.'

He pushed something the size of a quarter of a brick into her hand.

'Here, you shouldn't have come without any ammunition. You know what you're fighting for. Shout *merde* to the lot of them!'

Twice more there was a determined surge forward on the student side and twice more they were furiously beaten back, each time with casualties dragged away. Helen was swept along with all the rest, yelling the same slogans, following in Nico's wake, terrified of losing sight of him. In the distance they could hear the wail of police vans, come to take their prisoners, and on the road, in the light of the street lamps, there lay lost shoes and policemen's helmets. A car in a side street had been set on fire.

But eventually the rioters started to disperse, the groups shrinking as more and more of them dropped out of the fray. It was time to call a halt. Nico was one of the last to give up, shouting defiance to the last.

'Come on,' Helen called to him. 'Come away. It's all over.'

And he burst out laughing, not hysterically, but seemingly from pure joy.

At the corner of their street they found Mireille and Xavier, clinging together and none the worse except that Xavier had torn his jacket.

As they headed for home there was no conversation. They were all breathless now, and almost exhausted. In their little room they collapsed into their sleeping-bags, all four of them together on the floor like a row of sardines.

For the next two days they stayed there, sleeping almost until noon, going out for bread and cigarettes, talking about tactics. One of the boys from Nancy had a guitar and they sang songs – protest songs in English by Pete Seager and Joan Baez. A sort of international solidarity. It was going to their heads – the danger, the sense of power.

In the evenings it was on to the street again. One of them was arrested – one of the Nancy boys, as Nico called them sarcastically. They never heard what happened, but nobody seemed to care. He was a martyr and his work was done. In the early hours they slumped into bed again without even the strength to undress.

Mireille's morning sickness always made her wake up first, and she rushed down the corridor to throw up in the toilet, followed by Xavier who fed her tea and stale bread to try and calm her stomach. As soon as they were safely gone, Nico would unzip his sleeping-bag and fall on top of Helen. He made love savagely, an outlet for the aggression of the street which was still inside him, and she responded in kind.

She had heard that warriors were mad for sex after the battle was over, and for a day or two she was carried along with the same euphoria; the blind excitement of the mob.

They stopped for lunch down a farm track beside a sluggish stream with straight rows of vines beyond it like a green-striped tablecloth. From the car boot Nico produced the elaborate picnic which the hotel had packed up for them. There was a mixed salad in a plastic box, vinaigrette ready to be drizzled on to it, ham, bread and peaches with a bottle of mineral water.

'Sorry about the disposable forks and plates,' he apologised. 'It rather spoils the effect.'

This from a man who never turned a hair in that greasy kitchen and who slept on bare boards without a murmur.

'It's a shame we haven't got any champagne. This is the right part of the world for it. All the villages round here have *caves*. Why don't we stop and sample some?'

'I hate all that tourist nonsense,' he said, rather brusquely. 'Besides I didn't think you approved of drinking and driving.'

No doubt he had interpreted her offer to drive when they came off the ferry last night as a criticism of his indulgence in the malt. But she didn't understand why he was in so much of a hurry.

'When did you say the interview was?' she asked again.

'On Tuesday. They're seeing people all week. I suppose it'll be a whole day affair. All those earnest questions. It bores you stiff.'

Life without the boring bits! Helen thought. Wouldn't that be splendid?

'I wouldn't have thought you'd be qualified for this job. It's not really your field at all, is it?'

'I expect I'll manage to convince them,' he said carelessly. 'I always thought it would be nice to live in the South of France.'

'At least you'll have good references from Hong Kong.'

'I should do,' he replied, taking a piece of ham and arranging it carefully on a piece of bread. 'I wrote them myself, tailored to suit every occasion.'

'What?'

He laughed at her surprise. 'Why not? I know more about me than anyone else.'

'But surely, if the work you were doing was so important, there'd be no need . . .'

'No, but unfortunately you don't know the whole story. As far as they were concerned, I'd been a naughty boy, so academic considerations all went out of the window.'

'You mean you got the sack?'

'That's about the top and bottom of it.'

He obviously supposed she would be agog to know more, though he was wrong. She had absolutely no desire to know what he had done. Naughty boy! There was nothing more pathetic than a man with talent who wasted it in puerile games. It was like a Shakespearian actor who made bad films just for the money.

'So that's what made you come home?'

'Yes, but I don't want to talk about it. You won't talk about Dave and I won't talk about that. Let's just say they lost one of the best researchers they ever had. Anyway I'd had enough of Hong Kong, so I wasn't sorry.'

They ate in silence for a while. It was warm now, at midday, and the doors and sunroof were open. Helen flicked crumbs of bread out on to the grass.

'You know, I always wondered if you'd go into politics. Every time there was an election I expected your name to come up. The country needs a few radical ideas after all this time. Capitalism's run wild since the sixties.'

'Has it?'

'Of course it has. Resources being gobbled up, currency speculation, what I call the Mickey Mouse-ification of world culture.'

She said it to provoke him into being the man she remembered him to be. Someone with values – or so she had thought.

He snorted. 'Intellectual crap! They make me sick, all those student leaders who turned into respectable Labour MPs and politics lecturers. They're only looking after number one, the same as anybody else.'

That talk about socialism and Marxism – had it been just so much eyewash, just so much mouthing of dogma, to make him appear trendy, when politics and youth went hand in hand? Though at the time, although she hadn't shared them all wholeheartedly, she had accepted his views at face value. It had never occurred to her that it could possibly be just a front. All at once it made her feel ashamed of what they had done in Paris.

'Why did you do it then, if you didn't believe in it?'

'What – that Paris stuff? For the thrill of it, I guess. Anyway it all came to nothing. The people who protested then are running the world now and nothing much has changed. Nobody believes in anything any more, do they?'

'Perhaps they ought to,' Helen said thoughtfully. 'You know you'd make a wonderful politician, Nico. You'd be adept at telling all those lies.'

He laughed and poured mineral water into two plastic cups, raising one of them to his lips. 'Cheers. Oh yes, I'm good at telling lies all right. Look at this stuff. Actually, I can't stand it, but the doctor says I've got to give up booze, for the good of my health.'

'What's the matter with your health?' she asked, surprised. To outward appearances he seemed amazingly fit.

'Had a heart attack last year. Only a slight one, but it was enough. The do-gooders descended, handing out advice. I'm still popping the pills.'

'You could have gone a bit easier on the drink last night.'

'I don't like doing as I'm told, didn't you know that?'

Without warning, he leaned over and kissed her on the mouth

but she sat there stiffly, unresponsive. His lips felt dry. There was no thrill there now, and they both knew it. The thought of going to bed with him again was loathsome. And she had thought that would be the easy bit.

He tried again, half-heartedly, then turned away. She wondered if he was as disappointed with his own response as he was with hers.

'You and me. We were good, weren't we?' he murmured with a forced smile, making light of it.

He expected her to laugh too, to agree with him, but all she did was pick up the remains of the picnic; the peach stones, shreds of lettuce. It was a woman's job and she was used to it.

The heart attack explained much. He wanted to recapture those old thrills before it was too late. Somehow. He was just a pathetic man approaching fifty who had suddenly realised that he wouldn't live for ever. Comforting was a woman's job too; yet she didn't feel pity for him, just contempt for all his crassness.

After the failure of that kiss a curtain of embarrassment descended between them which she hadn't felt before. When they had first met at the vice-chancellor's dinner they spoke to each other as they had always done – the way that grown-ups lapse into infancy when they meet their old schoolmates, with no barrier of time between them. They nudge and call each other names the way they did at ten years old. It's not until some time later that they discover they are different people, trailing life's baggage behind them.

So that they wouldn't need to talk, she fiddled with the radio again, trying to find a French station.

'Still understand it all?' he asked. 'It's wonderful what comes back to you, isn't it?'

But, Nico, not everything will come back, she thought, however much you hope for it.

'They say that you can't speak a language until you dream in it. I could dream in Italian but never in Cantonese.'

'Do you ever have nightmares, Nico?' she asked softly.

He frowned. 'Why should I?'

But she saw a fleeting panic in his eyes. People who have nightmares are scared, and he was petrified. But, like those other two mad car dashes they had made together, he was unstoppable, driving himself on to he knew not what.

Into the crash barriers of life, Helen thought philosophically, and then all their problems would be solved. But fate, she knew, was too subtle for that.

After a welcome shower, she came downstairs to dinner, but Nico hadn't yet put in an appearance so she wandered out on to the balcony which looked over a formal garden of box hedges and standard rose trees surrounded by gravel.

It felt strange to be alone, without Dave, without the children, and she leaned rather awkwardly against the parapet. She wasn't used to hanging round strange hotels and for the first time in years she felt like a cigarette, just to give her hands something to do.

'*Bonsoir, madame,*' she heard at her elbow and she half turned to respond to the greeting, though diffidently. She had forgotten that men hate to see a woman by herself; they can't imagine that she might prefer her own company to theirs.

He was a pale round man who looked rather like Mussolini on a bad day.

'English?' he exclaimed in delight, recognising her accent. 'You are all alone?'

'I am with a . . . gentleman.' (What a word!)

He looked crestfallen.

'Oh, I am so sorry. I beg your pardon.'

He said it with a lecherous grin, then turned away. Helen shuddered at the unpleasantness of the predatory male. There were books, weren't there, which gave instructions to lonely people looking for their ideal partner? She had seen people fumbling through them surreptitiously in bookshops: what to say at parties; how to strike up conversations in supermarkets. All those meaningless chat-up lines, leading nowhere. If she and Dave separated would she really have to go through that again? Back at square one?

And here she was screwing her life up even more.

'Who was that?' Nico asked, as her would-be admirer beat a retreat.

'I haven't the slightest idea,' she replied, straining to be upbeat. 'I'm starving. What are we going to eat?'

It seemed that he had been studying the menu in his room and had already ordered.

'I've asked for the *specialité de la maison*,' he explained. 'Their chef's a top man. I'm sure you'll approve.'

She looked around the dining room with its heavy red plush curtains and damask tablecloths, freesias and roses carefully arranged in bowls of coloured glass. It was another expensive country hotel, way above what she could afford, but if the company had palled, she was damned if she wasn't going to enjoy the food and the surroundings while she had the chance.

The waiter brought a bottle of red wine and Nico quickly downed a full glass of it after the ritual of holding it up to the light and swirling it round his mouth. At one time he wouldn't have known a Cabernet Sauvignon from pickling vinegar. At core, Helen thought, he was nothing more than a series of personas, making himself up as he went along, seeming to have no ultimate reality.

'You're a fool, Nico, do you know that?'

'What's that supposed to mean?'

'You're killing yourself. You work out and you won't drink coffee and you think that's enough, when in reality it's the booze you've got to kick.'

She should have said all that, but she didn't. He had never taken kindly to sermons. It was his life, not hers. Definitely not hers.

Instead she accepted the ample glass of wine he offered her. It was too thick, too cloying, like blackcurrant juice with a kick. Red wine always went straight to her head these days. But he had been right about the food. The meat was tender and succulent in a creamy sauce with plenty of alcohol thrown in, and this time there were no concessions to the waistline.

As the meal progressed a second bottle of wine appeared, then a third. She had wondered what was going to happen next and getting drunk seemed as good an option as any. Nico seemed to feel the same.

There was a family party not far away from them in the

restaurant; uncles, grannies, cousins, all talking at once, so that Helen had to listen hard to hear what he was saying.

'Tomorrow we'll be in Nice. Or Cannes. Whichever you like. Back to the scene of the crime, isn't that what you said? They never found me, you know. Never found me!'

There was a hint of triumph in his voice which she didn't understand, and he continued, somewhat incoherently: 'At least I suppose this time the car's paid for, even if it still isn't mine.'

She had heard that all right, or she thought she had.

'What are you talking about?'

'That old *deux chevaux*. Don't you remember it?'

'Of course I remember it!'

'I stole it. Didn't I ever tell you?'

'You know perfectly well that you didn't.'

He wouldn't have told her tonight if he hadn't been drunk, that was certain. But by now he was utterly, determinedly drunk.

'I picked it up in Cannes and had some new plates made for it. There were so many of those cars then. Tin cans on wheels. I knew they'd never find it.'

'I suspected you stole the petrol but I never thought you stole the car.'

'Clever of me, wasn't it?'

If she had been sober herself she might have protested more vehemently, but she couldn't muster the energy. After a starter of stuffed mushrooms and the main course they had eaten salad and Roquefort and were now embarking upon a dessert; some sort of a tart with crisp almond pastry. Helen felt her head beginning to go fuzzy. The restaurant was hot, the family party behind them beginning to grow even shriller. There were toasts and someone started playing a guitar.

'Bastard.'

He took it as a compliment and smiled wanly. 'I just wanted to try it, to see if I could get away with it. I think you should try everything in this world, don't you?'

'Even if you end up in jail?'

'Who cares? It wouldn't have worried me. In those days nothing worried me.'

That was it – the appeal of the sixties. Perhaps for a year in that decade, perhaps only for a few months, perhaps only for a day, but at some pinpoint in time it was as though there was nothing left to worry about. The *angst* of the Aldermaston marches was over; you could leave school and walk straight into a job if you wanted to; skirts were short; sex was OK. Feminism was still in the future, waiting to upset the applecart once and for all. Nobody knew they were ruining the planet. It had been perpetual adolescence: all the fun, without the responsibility. They hadn't needed the pot; they had been high on idealism. Or innocence.

Then again perhaps it didn't really happen. Perhaps it was a figment of the collective imagination of those who were young then.

'A brandy to finish off, I think,' Nico said, ordering two Armagnacs with the coffee.

'I don't really think I ought —'

'Rubbish. It's the best thing for rounding off a meal like that.'

He looked so respectable now in his crisp white shirt, his dark trousers, his well-tailored jacket, but he had come near to being in jail, once. She supposed they all had.

On the third night they were separated. Nico was getting more and more daring, always insisting on being at the forefront of the action, dragging Xavier along with him. More and more Helen was lingering behind with Mireille while she took her photographs, trying to shield her.

'What's she doing it for?' Nico asked contemptuously. 'Taking photos is asking for trouble – from both sides.'

In the darkness and confusion Helen lost him and back in their squalid little room she waited tensely, while the others slept. Tonight she had seen a boy staggering away with a red gash across his face, the flesh opened up from chin to temple. It didn't matter who had done it; she was getting sick of the whole business – the violence, and the futility of it.

Was Nico in jail or in hospital, and if he was how would she ever find out? Paradoxically it made her furious, seeing him breeze in unscathed next morning, while she hadn't been able to eat or sleep for worrying.

'Where on earth have you been? I thought you'd been hurt – or arrested.'

She was near to tears but all he did was shrug his shoulders.

'Lying low in a cellar until morning. Thought it was safest on the whole. Where are the others?'

'Buying bread, and having coffee if they can afford it. Nico, it's time we were going home. I'm fed up with all this, night after night. And Mireille and Xavier haven't any money left.'

'I can let them have some. It's no problem.'

'They don't want to be beholden to you. Besides, where have you got money from all of a sudden?'

He looked at her, innocent as a baby.

'I saved it. I got a few tips at the Rex, and old Taupin wasn't a bad sort, considering. Anyway, how are they going to get back?'

He noticed for the first time that their sleeping-bags were all rolled up ready to go and realised that she meant it.

'If you won't come, hitchhike I suppose.'

'But we're doing it all for the likes of them! Or don't they realise that?'

'It seemed like that to start with, but everything's got out of hand. Besides, they're supposed to be getting married soon. And their parents will be worried sick.'

'Parents! Who cares about their parents?'

'They do, Nico, strange as it may seem. Their parents will be supporting them, don't forget, when everything's back to normal and the universities open up again. And I agree with them. This is no way to solve a problem. People are getting hurt every night. What do you think it can achieve in the long run?'

'I thought you were all for it?'

'I was,' she admitted, 'but I'm tired of it now. I'm tired of this awful room, tired of men I don't even know telling me what to do. You can't have a proper wash and I hate even going into that kitchen.'

'You can't just leave – walk out.'

She looked at him earnestly. The first excitement had gone and without it there was little left.

'Yes I can. I can go any time I want to. This isn't my war.'

It sounded hypocritical and perhaps it was. Because she was English she could walk away from it whenever she had a mind to.

'Anyway I've been robbed. My engagement ring's gone and it must have been worth a packet.'

She had always kept Paul's ring at the bottom of her handbag, and how those Nancy students had got hold of it she didn't know, but she was convinced they had rifled through her belongings while she wasn't looking.

But they would only deny it if she confronted them, and she wasn't in any position to go to the police. Of course Nico wouldn't help, she knew that; they were of the universal brotherhood.

'I just don't know how I'm going to explain it away.'

'What, to your so-called fiancé?' he sneered. 'If he saw you performing in the sack with me, I'm pretty sure he'd have second thoughts about the whole thing.'

'That doesn't alter the fact that the ring's gone,' Helen said coldly. 'And I'm going too. You stay if you want to. We'll manage.'

'Bloody hell, what's the matter with you? You've got to fight for what you want in this world – fight, do you hear me?'

'Are you coming or not?' she asked.

'No.'

'What about later on?'

He had left some of his belongings behind in her room, but nothing of any value. He said he didn't know, but if he didn't come now she didn't believe he ever would.

She could hear Mireille and Xavier in the corridor and picked up her bag. Everything was settled.

'I'll see you around then. Bye Nico.'

It had all ended as quickly as that.

Kicker was a fighter too, but Kicker was gone and Nico was all there was. That was the reason she had come. She had longed to be saturated again with some of his old fighting spirit, only to find it wasn't there. Now alcohol was the only thing left that would make them drunk.

A man in the family group caught her eye and he lifted his glass to her across the room. She lifted hers in response and drank. The Armagnac was fiery, in contrast to the wine. The singing grew louder and they both joined in, though they didn't know the words.

Somehow, a little later, they managed to find the way upstairs. Nico fumbled with the lock to his room and lurched in with Helen right behind him. It was only by good fortune that they landed on the bed rather than the floor.

She wasn't really conscious of much that happened next. She knew he used a condom because she found it later – not one of hers so he must have come prepared. After she realised the inevitability of it all she just let it wash over her. She knew him well enough and the technique hadn't changed. He hadn't added any refinements. Probably nobody had ever told him there could be refinements. When she was twenty it hadn't mattered; she had been as hungry as he was. Now, as he panted away on top of her, she did nothing to either encourage him or fend him off. If she felt anything at all, it was rather sick and those clothes she still had on were sticking to her in the heat. This was the second reason she had come – for her revenge – but she was far too drunk to relish it properly.

Afterwards they lay quite separately on the bed.

'We're pissed, aren't we?' Nico said, stupidly.

'High as kites.'

He groped around for her hand. 'Accommodation's better than we used to have, anyway. Remember that dump in Paris? Cockroaches.'

'We didn't have to pay for it.'

'Good thing too. Down to the last centime, weren't we? It was only your ring that saved the day.'

Helen snatched away her hand and managed to crawl out of bed, smoothing down her dress and staggering to the window. She opened it, taking a gulp of cool night air. So he had stolen the ring too. She had been on the verge of guessing that at dinner, only her brain had been befuddled. Sold it probably. And it had taken more than twenty years for the penny to drop.

Then suddenly she felt an involuntary churning in her stomach as her body got the better of her. She only just made it to the toilet, and for ten minutes she knelt there limply, head down, retching up every bit of her dinner.

'Nico!' she called out weakly, but there was no reply. She wasn't surprised. A ministering angel he had never been.

When, in a little while, she had pulled herself together and returned to the bedroom to look for the rest of her clothes, she saw that he was fast asleep.

Back in the bathroom she splashed cold water on her face, her mind slowly beginning to clear. That ring had cost Paul sixty pounds, quite a sum in those days. He had been pretty upset about it too – probably more upset about that than about her admission that the engagement had been a sham all along. Looking back, she didn't blame him.

Carefully she padded back to the bedroom and felt in the pocket of Nico's jacket which was lying on the floor where he had dropped it. He was sleeping soundly, snoring a little. The curtains were open and there was enough light to see his outline; his pale legs and bare buttocks, the rumpled white shirt. He looked ridiculous now but he would look even more ridiculous in the morning.

She took out his wallet and his car keys. Then she retrieved her shoes and tights. Her knickers must have been hidden some-where in the bed and she would have to leave the chambermaid to find them. She didn't want to risk waking him up. In her own room she found another pair, took off her dress which was creased and soaked in sweat and put on some clean jeans and a shirt.

There were several thousand francs in the wallet and quite a lot more in traveller's cheques. That ring would have cost much more than sixty pounds these days; perhaps ten times that. And then there was the interest. He had various credit cards, cheque books, American Express – all the trimmings that he used to scoff at. She left the American Express card on the bedside table. At least he would be able to pay for the room. The rest she was taking with her. He owed her.

The hotel was quiet, even though it was only about half-past one. The family party had broken up and the dining-room tables were freshly set for breakfast. Helen opened the front door and crunched across the gravel drive to the car park. It sounded like thunder, in the silence. A dog barked in the distance, but apart from that nothing stirred.

Fortunately the car alarm only emitted one high-pitched bleep. She unlocked the car door, poked the key into the ignition and accelerated wildly down the drive and out into the road. Not long afterwards she had found her bearings and was heading south. The sickness had cured her lethargy and she felt clear-headed, almost euphoric. She remembered the words of a French record she had bought long ago.

'*Emmenez-moi au bout de la terre*': 'take me to the ends of the earth . . .' She was singing it at the top of her voice.

9

'Helen are you all right? You sounded very strange on the phone.'

A small dark woman, elegantly dressed, hurried along the platform to meet her. Helen lugged her suitcase down from the train.

'Yes, I'm fine now. How are things, Mireille? I didn't have time to ask you before.'

They kissed, then held each other at arm's length for a moment, looking for the changes.

'I didn't have time to tell you. I don't often get phone calls before six o'clock in the morning. Come on, I'll take you for a coffee before we go home. You look all in.'

'I think my adrenalin's stopped. I felt all right until now.'

Helen sipped on the coffee tentatively, wondering if her stomach would revolt again. She hoped the sickness had just been a combination of too much food and drink, plus Nico's not inconsiderable weight pressing down on top of her. Or the whole episode could have been purely psychological.

They sat in a dark corner, a contrast to the bright sunlight of the morning, and she spoke as softly as she could, so that nobody at the neighbouring tables could catch what she was saying. It was only about eight thirty but already the café opposite the station was bustling with regulars.

'So I left the car in a car park with the keys in the ignition,' she finished off. 'Before that I took all his money and traveller's cheques and threw the wallet and the credit cards over the side of a bridge.'

'Where was it? Do you know?'

'Not really. It was still dark. There was a river somewhere below, that's all I can tell you.'

She remembered getting out of the car, feeling the grass wet with dew under her feet. She had stretched out her arm and flung the wallet over the parapet, screwing up her eyes to see the tiny shape gliding through the air in the moonlight until there was a hollow splash. Then she had driven on, waiting for the sunrise. At dawn she had abandoned the car and taken the train, but she must have driven a hundred miles.

'He's bound to contact the police.'

'To trace the car maybe, but he won't mention me. It would be too humiliating for him, wouldn't it? I'd like to think he'll regard it as a good joke when the first resentment wears off, but I don't know. He never had much of a sense of humour.'

Mireille gave her a look that said that the English set far too much store by a sense of humour.

'Will he get to the interview in time, do you think?'

'Oh, yes, he's got days yet. It isn't until Tuesday.'

Amazingly, it was still only Sunday morning.

'Well, I can't say I blame you. I always thought he was a prat.'

'Yes, I remember – at least I do now. What we did in Paris seems to have been bathed in a romantic glow for all these years. Now it's all come back to me, I feel rather ashamed. It's funny how you don't always remember things the way they really were.'

'Or perhaps you block them out,' Mireille suggested.

Helen was asleep all day. It was getting dark when she woke and came downstairs to the kitchen, where Mireille was standing at the big pine table preparing salad. The house was miles from anywhere, at the bottom of a lane. An old farmhouse, Helen guessed, as they drove up to it, but she had been too tired to ask.

Mireille looked with admiration at the pyjamas.

'Was that for Nico's benefit? I wonder you bothered. There never used to be anything subtle about Nico.'

'Nico isn't quite as you remember him. He's the sort of man who's kept up with the times. Smart cars, jogging, designer suits.'

Mireille smiled, skilfully mixing oil and vinegar. 'Then I'm surprised he didn't pick on a girl half his age. Most of them do.'

'I wondered that myself,' Helen confessed.

'But of course there's one thing wrong about getting mixed up with a woman who's only about twenty. It's all right in bed, at least to start with, but deep down you've got nothing in common. The background, the culture, it's all totally different. What's the point of telling some poor girl about his exploits in May'68 when she wasn't even born yet?'

Helen chuckled. With any luck that would be Dave's stumbling-block with Ianthe.

'Do you want to get dressed before we eat?' Mireille asked. 'Though you look quite decent as you are.'

'Looking decent wasn't entirely the plan. I had visions of a mind-blowing seduction scene. In the event, the only way either of us could bring ourselves to do it was by getting stoned out of our minds.'

The thought of it in the cold light of day made her cringe, particularly after all those lectures she had delivered to Emma. And doing a runner in the middle of the night smacked of a Gothic heroine.

After the chuckle came a sigh.

'It seems as if I haven't grown up yet, even at my age.'

'What's grown up?' Mireille said, busying herself about setting the table, putting out silver cutlery and linen napkins. 'I used to think it was being like my mother was; when your oven's always spotless and your cupboards are all tidy and you can serve up a six-course dinner without being scared something's going to spoil. In other words, when you've got life sorted out. I still haven't achieved that and I don't expect I ever will now.'

Helen didn't believe it. To an outsider Mireille always seemed utterly together.

'You don't seem that way to me. Whereas I still haven't decided what I really want from life – who I am, even – and it's getting a bit late for that.'

With a gesture, Mireille indicated where she should sit. The kitchen smelt enticingly of lemon and tarragon.

'That's probably entirely normal. It always hits you when your children start to leave home. You don't quite know how to approach the rest of your life. And sometimes you have to come to terms with all sorts of unfinished business first.'

Helen wasn't sure that she had any unfinished business, so she let it pass. The meal was ready and Mireille opened a bottle of wine.

'Don't give up on Dave at this late stage, Helen. I've always envied you. Stability. Three lovely children. It's what I always wanted.'

Everyone wanted what they didn't have. It was human nature. What Helen noticed most about this house was the total, the blessed silence. But she was realistic enough to know she would be sick of it in a week.

'You could have had them.'

'With Xavier? I only married him to get away from home and to have sex.'

'Didn't everybody in those days?'

'Besides I wanted the wedding. You get all the attention on your wedding day. It's the only day in your life when you're the centre of everything. Nobody cares about the groom. It's the bride who's all-important.'

'I know. But it's a lot to put up with, just for a day.'

'But then girls don't seem to get married any more, do they? They have high-flying careers, just like men.'

Mireille had looked beautiful on her wedding day, that was certain, in a long lacy gown and a white hood over her glossy dark ringlets. It had been Helen's only taste of a French wedding and it had been quite a lavish affair for a family of medium income, with a civil ceremony at the town hall, a church service, drinks at one place, a reception and dance somewhere else, those cries of 'Long live the bride!' as the wedding procession passed by. That night the guests had chased all round the countryside trying to track the married couple down, bursting into their bedroom to toast the 'bedding', as French peasants had done for centuries.

A couple of years later had come news of the divorce. Helen never really knew the details.

'I was pregnant – do you remember? We wanted a big family, Xavier and I, or we thought we did. But when Nathalie was born we couldn't cope. Neither of us had a job, neither of us had finished our education. The baby never stopped yelling. In the end Xavier's mother came in and took over.'

'What, completely?'

'For nearly a year, it must have been. And of course it split up the marriage before it even got started.'

'What happened to Xavier? I don't think you ever told me.'

'He teaches chemistry in a high school near Rouen. We write on birthdays and I send his kids Christmas presents.'

'Is Nathalie still in the States?'

Yes. She married a New Yorker a few months ago to get a green card. They live in separate apartments in Greenwich Village.'

That, perhaps, was what Mireille had had to come to terms with. She looked across at Helen candidly and bit her lip. 'Women never learn, do they?'

They sat down to pâté, salad and cold lemon-scented chicken, followed by cheese, and accompanied by Mahler on the CD player. It was utterly peaceful.

'Of course I don't want to leave Dave,' Helen said. 'Not deep down. It would be like saying that the last twenty years of my life have been a failure. But Dave just expects life to go on for us in the same old way. Me at school, him at the department, all of us at the cottage, and I can't stand it.'

'Haven't you told him that?'

'We don't seem to communicate much any more.'

She didn't mention Ianthe, but she didn't need to.

'Another woman?' Mireille queried.

'One of his postgraduate students,' Helen admitted briefly. She made a quick calculation. 'He's probably still at the cottage alone with her at this very moment.'

'So he's admitted it?'

'No, but I can tell. I've seen the way they look at each other. And he's at the department every evening. He says he's writing, but I'm not stupid. And I doubt if we've had sex more than half a dozen times since Christmas.'

Mireille laughed wryly. 'So you think he's really been screwing this student on the floor of his office? Well you can't blame him now, after what you've been doing.'

'You mean we're quits? Yes, but the difference is that in my case it was a one-off that I don't particularly want to repeat. I realised last night that when you've got a problem with a man the last thing you ought to do is go out and look for another one. But with Dave and Ianthe there's more to it.'

'You mean because he's in love with her? So it doesn't matter when it's just physical, but when emotion's involved that's different?'

Helen considered. It was difficult to rationalise her mixed-up feelings.

'I suppose I mean that. But I don't regret doing it with Nico, even if I was stupid to think he'd be the same as he used to be. Dave makes me bloody angry and at least I've got my own back a little bit.'

'Well I think it's a shame. I've always thought you were very well set up. A lovely house in a very nice part of town. A wine shop and a book shop just round the corner. Very civilised.'

After her moment of confession, Mireille had completely regained her equilibrium.

'Is that what you like? How many miles is it to a shop from here?'

'There are a few shops in the village. And I go to Paris twice a month. This is a sort of ancestral home for me. My grandparents owned it, and my sister only lives ten miles away.'

'How do you manage your business right out here?'

'Phone, fax, satellite dish. I'm not a city person, you know that. I come from peasant stock and I like my garden.'

The kitchen door stood ajar. They were in the south and the evening air was still warm.

'I can smell the herbs from here,' Helen said, breathing in the scent of them.

'Yes, there was a shower while you were asleep and it brings out all the perfumes. I'll show you in the morning. You can give me some English expertise.'

'I'm no gardener, not really. Dave does most of it. All I do is prune the roses and plant a couple of hanging baskets for the patio.'

Mireille poured coffee and they went to sit on the sofa, opposite an old stone fireplace. In the empty grate was an earthenware vase containing an artistic display of bulrushes and teasels.

'Men do stray,' Mireille said, realistically. 'But usually they come back. And whatever people say there's more to marriage than that. Sex is nice but it's not the be-all and end-all. You're a team, you and Dave. Don't throw that away. He's damned intelligent, you know. And I mean really intelligent. Dave can talk very knowledgeably on most things without sounding like a know-all.'

'Can he?'

'You know he can. And I should imagine he's very sexy.'

Dream on, as Oliver would say. That side of their lives seemed to have slipped away completely.

'I know I have no right to complain,' Helen said. 'I'm not well off, but I can afford to live reasonably well. My children are healthy. When you look at the television news there they are, the women of Africa, women in war zones all over the world, my age but looking twenty years older. Compared with them, I'm in clover. Our parents' generation never expected life to be all roses either. But we did and that's why it hurts more. When you realise.'

Mireille smiled and wisely said nothing more. Her crisis had been over for many years now.

'Well you can stay here for a few days if you want to. I'm not expecting visitors. But I have to go to Paris the day after tomorrow to see some publishers. You just have a rest and a think.' She gave a sudden laugh. 'I wonder what's happened to Nico.'

Helen had a vision of his bare buttocks in the middle of a crumpled bed and couldn't help giggling herself.

'I expect he'll survive. He usually does.'

'You know, I can't understand why Dave isn't going after this job as well. It sounds as if he's got much better qualifications than Nico has.'

'I didn't know anything about it until Nico mentioned it. Dave's only interested in his Chair. It's what he's been working up to for twenty years.'

'And what if he doesn't get it?'

'The end of the world as we know it.'

She dared not even think about that.

'He ought to have something in hand, like Nico. That's why Nico always bounces back. He's always got one more card up his sleeve.'

'Apply for this European Union job, you mean? Dave doesn't speak French. Or not well enough.'

'Would it matter? He'd be working with people from all over Europe, not just France. It wouldn't be a barrier.'

'Perhaps not, but it's too late now. He's put all his eggs in one basket. Mireille, do you mind if I ring the children before it gets too late? I said I'd be in touch and they'll be wondering what's happened to me.'

Lying in bed alone, not tired enough to sleep, all of Helen's pain came back to her. She had been up in the air yesterday and now she was down again. There was time to think – about Kicker's death, about her marriage – all she had been struggling against. During the past three days she had managed to push it all to the back of her mind, but now it came flooding back, numbing her with resentment and misery. It would probably be Kicker's funeral tomorrow or the next day, and she wouldn't be there. Some best friend she'd turned out to be.

Next morning they ate breakfast outside, the summer air warming the old stones of the courtyard where a riot of red and pink geraniums were trailing from terracotta pots.

'We can only do this about twice a year at home,' Helen said, wriggling her bare toes in the sunshine. 'And then you get the traffic noise. How far are you from the village?'

'About a mile.'

Mireille heard something inside and went to look through the open window.

'The only noise round here comes from the fax machine. Would you excuse me for a moment? I think this is what I've been expecting.'

She went indoors and returned a minute or two later with some sheets of paper in her hand, breathing in sharply through her teeth in an expression of disgust.

'*Mon Dieu*, this is absolutely wrong! What does the man think he's doing? Illustrations like this could ruin the book.'

She wafted the offending pages in front of Helen's eyes. They were line drawings of children, rather pudgy children with angelic faces, like pictures from a book written during the nineteen-fifties.

'What are they for?' she asked. 'You know, I've never really understood what you do for a living.'

'Oh, I do project management and book packaging. Children's illustrated fiction, mostly. Somebody recommended this man to me as an illustrator. Unfortunately I didn't ask to see what he'd done before. I certainly didn't imagine his stuff would be so abysmal. Look at these children – they seem to be living in the dark ages. Heavens, the girls are wearing *skirts!* When did you last see a girl between eight and fourteen who wore a skirt willingly? I need something quirky and irreverent, not these little goody-goodies.'

'Are these what you were supposed to be taking to Paris tomorrow?'

'Yes, but I shall have to cancel until I get something better than this.'

'Do you want me to try?' Helen offered. 'I might be able to do a couple of outlines, if you tell me what you want.'

'Can you draw? I didn't know.'

'I wanted to go to art school, but it never happened. I could probably have a reasonable stab at it. If there's something I do know about, it's children and what they like.'

Mireille paused for a moment. 'Oh, yes, I remember now, you used to paint. You did a picture of my sister sitting on the balcony at home. My mother kept that for ages on her bedroom wall.'

'Did she? I'm glad. Your mother was very kind to me. I never really said thank you.'

But Mireille was more interested in her friend's new-found talent than reminiscences.

'Will you really try and sketch something out if I explain what's needed?' she asked. 'I've got paper, paints, pastels, brushes, ink, anything you like. Helen, you might be about to save my bacon.'

Helen followed her into the office which looked out on to the courtyard, catching every bit of the morning sun. In contrast to the traditional farmhouse style of the other rooms, this one was done out in grey plastic shelves and cupboards, with a word processor and a laser printer on the desk. Mireille had all the latest equipment. She took down a sheaf of papers held together with a crisscross of elastic bands.

'This is a copy of the typescript that he's supposed to be illustrating. It's in French of course, so I'm afraid it might take a little while for you to digest before you can get started.'

'Do you know the number of times I've read a book to my children when they were little and found that the illustrator hadn't read the words? Even if it says someone wore a green jumper and they're wearing a blue one, that spoils it. Children notice things like that.'

At first Helen went out into the garden with a second cup of coffee and a tube of sunblock, but she soon found that reading a typescript out of doors was much too difficult. Everything blew about and the sun was too bright for her eyes. So she went up to her bedroom, with its view over a wooded hillside. This part of the house had once been the hayloft and it still seemed to have the fragrance of ages past, a scent which had soaked into the sun-warmed walls. It was perfectly quiet, except for a bee, bumbling its way through the open window and nuzzling at the flowers on the curtains.

'It's like heaven,' she said aloud, then spread out the white typewritten pages on the bed. She could speak French fluently enough but she wasn't used to the style of children's books and just reading and understanding thoroughly took twice as long as it should have done. By the time she had made some pencilled notes, it was nearly midday.

'Well?' Mireille asked, when she emerged. 'What do you think? Will you be able to knock something up for me before tomorrow?'

'I've got a few ideas, but I don't know if they're very good. I've never done anything like this before.'

'I've got to go down to the village,' Mireille said. 'Hop in the car and we'll talk about it as we go.'

Helen worked with pen and ink all afternoon and well into

the evening. Drawing always calmed her; it was her eternal antidote.

At seven thirty, Mireille brought up a tray garnished with a steak and some haricot beans. Instead of wine, there was a glass of milk.

'It's to boost your blood sugar,' she explained.

Helen offered to show her progress, but Mireille waved her away.

'Wait until you've finished. No good interrupting the train of thought. Good luck!'

She tiptoed out and Helen heard the low buzz of the television downstairs. It was not until about eleven o'clock that she was satisfied with what she had done.

'They're great!' Mireille enthused, holding out the sheets of paper to view them from a distance. 'Just perfect. You know exactly how children of nine or ten tick. Something loony, a bit surreal. Heavens, Helen, haven't you ever thought of doing anything like this for a living?'

Helen looked thoughtful. 'Yes, I suppose I have, a very long time ago. But not lately. I'm not even sure who illustrators are. People who work for publishers, I suppose. In London, Paris, New York.'

'Well that's where you're dead wrong, you know. Most of them are freelance, working at home in the bedroom. They don't have glamorous jobs. Most of them are people just like you.'

'I expect they have qualifications.'

'You don't need qualifications, you only need to be able to draw.'

Mireille put the half-dozen drawings lovingly into a folder, ready for tomorrow's trip.

'They don't have a waste-paper basket full of their rejects either.'

Mireille was sceptical. 'Don't you believe it! Listen, I must get to bed. I'm up at six to catch the train. If you want anything tomorrow, just help yourself. I'll be back the day after tomorrow.'

The next day Helen slept in until late, then spent a few hours pottering round the garden, pulling up weeds and cutting back a hedge Mireille had been complaining about. In the house the answering machine and the fax whirred busily by themselves.

In the late afternoon she set off up the hillside behind the house, following a stream which rushed over mossy stones. She found a wild tortoise in the grass, saw a bird of prey hovering above her head, then swooping for the kill. There was nobody else. In England a place like this would have been overrun with people, even during the week.

While she was watching television, Mireille called.

'They loved the drawings,' she said, 'and they want another half-dozen of the same. We might not use them all, of course, but you'll get paid whatever happens.'

'Paid? You mean they're going to pay me?'

'Of course. What did you imagine? They offer a very good rate.'

She named a sum, which to Helen seemed rather high and she wondered if she had misheard. The line wasn't too clear and she had never been very good at French numbers, certainly not those over sixty when they started adding on tens.

'Where are you staying?' she asked. 'Are you ringing from the hotel?'

'I have an arrangement with a friend,' Mireille replied pointedly. 'A very good friend. See you tomorrow, *chérie*.'

Helen put down the phone and shivered. It was cooler tonight and a breeze was blowing through the kitchen window. Outside the empty darkness seemed to be pressing in on her. Hurriedly she slipped on a sweater, then went to lock up and pull down the blind. She made herself a cup of herb tea and took it up to bed, along with Mireille's portable radio to keep her company.

In the daytime and the sunlight it was a beautiful house, a house that could have been a film set. But by night it creaked and groaned quietly, like an old woman's bones. On the surface Mireille had a wonderful life; an exciting career with no ties; a lover up in town. But she was still alone here when she went to bed, listening to the silence.

10 ∫

The taxi from the station backed up on to the drive, pop music blaring from its radio.

'Money in advance,' Mireille announced, putting down her briefcase and slipping a cheque into Helen's hand. 'You can't go home now – not until you've finished the job.'

Helen stared at the cheque and tried to do the conversions in her head.

'I didn't know I was doing it for money. It was just a favour to you.'

'Don't be ridiculous. I shall need some real work out of you during the next couple of days.'

'How was Paris?'

'Very profitable, but I'm glad to be back.'

She glanced around the kitchen, noticing the housewifely touches supplied by Helen.

'I suppose you made that cake yourself? Can't you get out of the habit of cooking all the time?'

'I'm used to feeding huge appetites. It just comes naturally.'

Mireille went to the fax machine and looked at the last sheet which had fallen into the tray. She glanced up at Helen sharply.

'Have you seen this?' she asked.

Helen shook her head.

'No. It's been chuntering away on and off all morning. I never took any notice of it. Why, what's the matter?'

'Oh, nothing.' Mireille folded the paper carefully and slipped it into the pocket of her cream-coloured Paris suit. 'Anything been happening here while I've been away?'

'Not a thing.'

'Great. Helen, I'm dying for a shower. Will lunch wait ten minutes?'

Later, when they had cleared the table, Mireille said, 'You know there's something I've never shown you. Come and look at this.'

She went to the bookshelves set into the alcove by the fireplace and took down an old photograph album held together by a red tasselled cord. The black pages were interleaved with tissue-thin paper in a spider's web design.

'What is it?'

Helen bent over the photograph that Mireille was indicating with her index finger. The picture was in black and white, taken at night, enlarged to almost the size of the whole page. A young man was being manhandled by a couple of riot policemen, his face towards the camera, shouting taunts. It was unmistakably Nico.

'Do you remember those photos of mine? I sold this to one of the American news magazines. Got a nice price for it too. It bought us a bed for our first flat. Otherwise we'd have been sleeping on the floor again like we were in Paris. So you see I do have something to thank Nico for.'

'It's very good. Didn't you ever consider photography as a career?'

Mireille closed the album ruefully. She preferred not to think about lost chances.

'Yes, but I never did it. This picture represents the zenith of my achievements. I framed the cheque though. It's still on the wall half-way up the stairs. Have a look, next time you go past.'

As she thought about her younger self she shook her head in disbelief.

'Oh Helen, I was all upside down in those days. I should have forgotten about babies and gone for it while I had the chance. We both should.'

'I tried, believe me I did,' Helen replied. 'But fate always seemed to have other ideas.'

After university she had taken Nico's advice and made up her mind to fight for what she wanted. It had only been a third-class

degree but she didn't care. All she wanted to do was get a job –
any job at all – so that she could save up the money finally to
go to art college.

The week after she graduated she started work in a sanitary
towel factory; not glamorous, and not the sort of job you wanted
to tell your friends about, but someone had to do it and no brain
work was required. All she cared about was the money in her
pay envelope on a Friday afternoon.

It was boring, but very soon she struck up a friendship with
Daisy Munro and together, every dinner time, dressed in their
skimpy green-and-white overalls and their little white caps, they
found they had an ambition in common. Daisy was a potter and
she was at the factory to scrape together a couple of hundred
pounds to make a start with. Together they devised a scheme
for a craft workshop, with Daisy making the pots and Helen
painting them.

'It'd be great,' Helen ruminated, 'but we'd have to hire a
workshop and we wouldn't be earning enough to pay the rent
until we'd sold something. It's catch 22.'

But Daisy had got their accommodation all worked out.

'My father's got a friend who owns a house in the Yorkshire
dales and he'd be happy to let us live in it for nothing. He's
abroad with the RAF and the house is a sort of investment.
He's only keeping it in the hope that property prices will rise
enough for him to make a profit. All we'd have to do is keep
the place habitable.'

'Have you seen it?'

'Only a photo, but it looks OK. And I've already been in touch
with another potter nearby who'd be willing to fire the stuff in
his kiln. The countryside's lovely round there.'

It all sounded ideal. They would sell the end product at
local craft fairs and tourist shops and it could all be done on
a shoestring.

'There's just one snag,' Daisy said slowly, as she toyed with
the remains of her shepherd's pie.

'What's that?'

'I like girls better than boys, if you know what I mean.'

Lesbianism wasn't a subject people talked about in those days
but Helen didn't see Daisy's sexual orientation as a drawback.

The plan offered escape from sanitary towels into the world of art, and she was eager to take the chance. Renoir had started out painting plates, so why not Helen Butcher?

'I don't care, but I should tell you that I prefer blokes myself.'

Daisy giggled and her bosom shook. She was a buxom sort of a girl with twinkling eyes.

'I just thought I'd get things straight. But don't worry, you're not my type.'

The house, a tiny middle terrace on the outskirts of a small market town, was genuinely eighteenth century, with no heating except for an old black range, but it was September when they arrived so it didn't seem to matter much at first. There was precious little furniture, but they made a round of the local auctions and bought a table and chairs and a sturdy oak bedroom suite for next to nothing. Victorian furniture was still considered junk. Now those chairs were in Helen's dining room and an antique dealer had valued them at £150 each. But it was then that they had needed the money.

As the autumn came on they realised how cold it was going to be. The outhouse where Daisy worked was bitter on winter mornings and even in the kitchen Helen painted wearing gloves with no fingers in them. Away from the range they needed copious sweaters and scarves to keep the chill at bay. To save on coal they went searching for wood in the nearby lanes and brought it home in a wheelbarrow, but neither of them minded; life was fun.

For warmth they went to the pub down the road and the landlord gave them bar work for a few hours a week, to eke out their savings until there were enough plates and mugs and egg-cups and vases to sell. In any case there wouldn't be much trade until after Easter, when the tourists started to venture out of town in their Ford Anglias and their Triumph Heralds. In the pub they became a talking point among the locals – hippies who didn't even have a television.

Helen loved the freedom of that winter. They were both full of energy and the work was original. The plates and vases Daisy turned out were chunky and solid, ideal for Helen's swirls of deep bold colour depicting exotic flowers and birds. There was nothing delicate, nothing wishy-washy in either of their techniques.

'Looks like something from South America,' the landlord of the White Hart commented. 'Sort of ethnic like.'

And ethnic was becoming all the rage.

Kicker wrote from London, where she was at teacher training college, with tales of a bedsit like a box looking out over a bus depot and a gas fire that gobbled up the shillings. Helen infinitely preferred her wood-burning range and the view of frost-covered fields from the kitchen window.

Her parents came for a visit and even her father seemed to have mellowed. Or perhaps Marion had told him to keep his opinions to himself. After all, the girl was over twenty-one. And Daisy seemed a nice, jolly girl.

'Steady,' her mother had said, when they were in the car going home. 'A nice steady girl.'

They had brought her bike from home, together with some extra blankets and a ginger kitten called Biscuit, who soon settled down to catching the country mice.

Towards that first Christmas, when she buckled her bicycle wheel in a fall and took it to be repaired, Helen met Malone, the owner of the local garage. It was a rundown place with a yard heaped high with rusting scrap metal and a thicket of brambles, but Malone was beautiful, with shoulder-length black hair and green eyes and a low, lazy voice.

'A painter are you?' he asked, giving her bike the once-over. 'One of them flower children who drop out and love in, like California?'

'It's too bloody cold to be like California,' Helen protested with a laugh.

He looked up languidly from removing the damaged wheel to take in her man's trench coat tied in a tight knot at the waist and the beret pulled down over her long hair.

'There's the Christmas barn dance in the church hall tonight. Want to come?'

He was slow, but he was never backward in coming forward, as they said round there.

Helen didn't hesitate. 'Yes, why not? It sounds like fun.'

Malone was a man of hidden talents. He introduced them to

macrobiotic foods and taught them to make wholemeal bread in the oven of the range. When he wasn't potholing further up the dale – the passion of his life – he found time to help Helen plan a vegetable garden and offered to teach her to drive. Eventually they started sleeping together sometimes on Saturday nights. It wasn't a commitment, just a pleasure.

'I thought you might have been like her at first,' he said, referring to Daisy, as they lay in bed that first night. 'It'd have been a terrible waste.'

He nuzzled her gently, kissed her slowly. There was none of the constant movement, the frenetic activity of Nico. Malone had no interest in what went on beyond the confines of his own little part of the world.

When spring came, Malone and Sally, his border collie, took the two of them in his old Ford van to try and sell their pots in the new craft shops and galleries which were beginning to burgeon in the more picturesque villages.

They didn't make a lot of money, but it was enough. There was no rent, no gas or phone bills. The electricity didn't cost a lot, since they didn't even have a fridge. The only electrical appliances they owned were an iron and an ancient Hoover that sounded like a Harley-Davidson.

All around the house the painted plates lay waiting to be sold, away from the ravages of Biscuit. On the window-sill they grew bell peppers; from the rafters hung strings of onions. The peace was interspersed with rowdy folk music evenings at the pub, days at craft fairs, nights with Malone. For almost the first time in her life Helen was living in the present.

The idea gradually germinated that perhaps they could make a life of this, perhaps rent a shop of their own. The money saved for art school – never very much – began to dwindle as other horizons presented themselves, but it didn't seem to matter. She was starting to put down tiny roots.

It was during the second winter that life started to come adrift. A storm blew some slates off the roof and they couldn't afford to have them properly repaired, so that rain began to seep in and damp patches appeared on the walls. Keeping the place in reasonable shape had been part of the compact, but they hadn't realised how expensive it would be. Their clothes were covered in mildew and the pages of their books began to yellow and curl. Once more the kitchen was the only room that didn't freeze them to the marrow. Somehow, during the summer, they had forgotten that.

What was worse, Daisy had fallen in love. The object of her affection was a farmer's wife called Eve who lived a couple of miles away down the dale and the only time they could be together was during the day when Eve's husband was out of the house and her children were at school. The icy workshop was neglected more and more.

Yet they hung on for a second summer. When she had run out of plates to paint, Helen made bead necklaces and muslin shawls with fringes, anything that was fashionable. She and Malone went into Bradford and bought joss sticks and scented candles wholesale which they resold to the tourists at a hefty mark-up. The vegetable garden saw them through when money was really tight.

But when October came around again, Daisy caved in. Her lover had cast her off and the story of it was all over town. One evening Helen came home to find her on her knees by the range sobbing, beating her fists on the floor, tearing furiously at her clothes. Around her were the shattered remains of plates and cups where she had smashed them against the wall.

That night, Helen could hear her through the bedroom wall, walking up and down and crying. It was well into the next day before she was coherent.

'Everyone's gossiping about me, in the pub, even in the fish and chip shop. They can't take it, not out here. And the clay's lost its charm somehow. You can be creative when you're in love, but things change. It's time I was moving on, girl.'

'Can't you stick it out just a few months more?' Helen begged. 'We haven't sold as much this season, but there are new boutiques opening up all over the place. People can afford our stuff like never before. Come on, Daisy, one more season. They won't care tuppence about you when they get used to the idea.'

But Daisy was resigned, enthusiasm spent.

'It's not just that. I've had a letter from my father. Our landlord's having second thoughts about tenants that don't pay rent. Tourism's rising in this neck of the woods. He's thinking of turning the place into a holiday home. Central heating, all mod cons. Roses in the garden instead of Malone's spuds. Colour TV. It's the modern world, Helen. We've done our opting out.'

'But I've been making plans. There's a shop to rent in the high street. It would be ideal . . . Or we could go somewhere else entirely, where they don't know you.'

'And wait for it all to start up again in a year or two? Why should I drag you round after me like that? I'm sorry, Helen. I know you can't work without me, but there are other potters. Or perhaps you'd rather stay. You and Malone could get hitched.'

She liked Malone, but she had never looked on him as a permanent fixture.

'Live above his dirty old workshop and be a potholing widow for the rest of my life? Not likely!'

'You're right. The hippy life doesn't last for ever. Malone'll still be festering here in twenty years time, unless he kills himself in one of those underground caves of his. So will Eve. People don't change, Helen, not really. They wish they could, but they can't.'

Where was she now? Helen sometimes wondered. Was she an art teacher in some comprehensive school, still small and plump, her wispy blonde hair streaked with grey, still with long floating skirts and sandals that made the children laugh behind her back?

They had never even exchanged addresses. Daisy had spoken about going up to Scotland to visit her parents for a bit. She didn't want any of the furniture. She didn't want anything. On the day the builders arrived to pull out the old range and the original front door and replace them with a white enamel cooker and a mock Georgian porch, Helen hired a van and headed south with Biscuit in a cat-box and the rest of her belongings in the back.

Sally was sitting outside the garage as she went past, but her master was nowhere to be seen. There would be no more searching for firewood among the bluebells and wild garlic; no more pulling pints at the White Hart; no more snuggling up to Malone to keep the draughts away. She had exactly eleven pounds in the bank.

After Christmas at home she found a temporary job in a

university library. Jobs were still no problem, if you weren't fussy. It wasn't what she wanted but something would turn up. She started to work on a proper portfolio and meanwhile she wrote around for other jobs – anything to do with design – but she didn't stir any interest. Everyone wanted experience or qualifications; two years painting pots in the back of beyond didn't count. Before she knew it she was beginning to drift again.

That was when she had found Dave – on the rebound from the artistic life. When all the fun was over.

The light in the bedroom was definitely the best for drawing, so they dragged a table up there and Helen sat by the window until almost sundown. The window looked out on to the garden and to the wood beyond but nothing passed by all day except the postman's van and a peasant with his dog plodding up the lane. The atmosphere reminded her a little of her days in Yorkshire, except that it was warmer.

Her pen flew over the page. During the past day or so she had had a few more ideas as the project crystallised in her mind and she added to the original drawings or redrew them as her thoughts matured. While she was working a calm seemed to descend on her and she felt as loose as an old sock. Nico might have his own opinions, but to Helen this was the real essence of what life was about. It was only when she stopped work that her tranquillity deserted her again.

It was all so very different from home. There her thoughts were constantly punctured by demands and questions; her brain was always half absent, bogged down with day-to-day minutiae about what to have for dinner, dental appointments, parents' evenings, swimming rotas, her mother's prescriptions, the MOT, holiday dates, finding a babysitter, washing games kit, buying rabbit food, stocking up the freezer in case the children brought friends home – a never-ending shopping list.

Her whole year was a round of events that never seemed to change, starting with the New Year's Eve party they'd always had with couples whose children were the same ages as theirs; people, she'd realised long ago, they had absolutely nothing in common with. At February half-term they normally visited

Dave's sister; at Easter it was the conference season, so while Dave was away she usually entertained a foreign student in memory of her own time in another country; at the beginning of May she helped organise a musical weekend with the university wives' group; in June she was one of the prime movers of the inter-schools swimming gala; in July it was the barbecue they always held for other members of the department; in the summer holidays it was the cottage; at autumn half-term she'd fallen into the habit of taking her mother on a coach tour. Then back to Christmas.

How did she get into all that, lurching from one to the other, on and on and on? Sometimes she felt she was drowning in it. But here she was joyfully free of the whole lot.

Nothing had absorbed her so much for a long time, but she wasn't accustomed to solid concentration and by evening she was tired out with the effort of it. While they were sitting on the sofa drinking mugs of hot chocolate before bed, Mireille kept glancing anxiously at the clock.

'What's the matter with you?' Helen asked. 'You're awfully fidgety. Are you expecting someone?'

Mireille stuttered. 'A phone call, that's all. I think I'd better stay up and wait for it – just in case.'

'Your gentleman?'

'Not exactly. Helen, if you hear anything later on, don't take any notice, will you?'

But in the night Helen was woken by what seemed to be a vaguely familiar noise. A car engine that she knew; a handbrake jammed on in the silence; somebody knocking softly at the front door. The luminous hands of her wristwatch said ten to one. Another of Mireille's lovers? Surely not.

For five minutes she dozed again. The night was warm and Mireille had provided her with a light quilted coverlet which she only pulled up as far as her waist. It was a luxury to spread herself across the bed, arms flung far and wide.

Then suddenly she heard footsteps on the stairs and her bedroom door swung open. Helen stiffened.

'Nico?' she murmured. How had he managed to find her? Surely he didn't know Mireille's address? She didn't know how she was going to face him all over again.

'Helen, is that you? Mireille's only just told me . . .'

The light clicked on and Helen sat bolt upright in bed. She had taken out her contact lenses, but she knew her own husband. The relief that it wasn't Nico almost wiped away the shock.

'Dave,' she almost yelled, 'what are you doing here?'

'Shh . . . keep your voice down! I might ask you the same question. I thought you were at the other end of the country.'

'Yes, I was supposed to be.'

He was wearing his best suit, although it was creased and the tie had been pulled loose. He looked all in from driving.

'I've been down to Nice.'

'You? *You've* been? I don't understand. What on earth for?'

'I thought I'd look into this European Union set-up. Just to be on the safe side. I've got to keep my options open.'

Of course he couldn't contemplate staying on in the department if somebody else got the Chair.

'Did Mireille know you were coming?'

'I sent her a fax yesterday morning, asking if I could stay the night. It's been a long day and I could do with a proper bed. Didn't she tell you?'

'Not a word.'

So that was who she had been waiting for, the rat. Dave pulled off his tie and jacket and began to unbutton his shirt.

'Well she didn't tell me you were here until a minute ago either. She said I oughtn't to wake you at this time of night, but it seemed silly for her to make up another bed when you were here already.'

At least, Helen reflected, she had attempted to be tactful in her treachery.

'I tried to ring you,' Dave went on. 'I got the number from the school, but I couldn't make head or tail of what Malcolm Booth was blethering about.'

So it was all over. He knew everything. He might even have seen Nico.

'What have you done with Tim? You haven't left him to the tender mercies of Emma and Oliver?'

'Don't panic. Your mother's still got him. She didn't seem to mind.'

'Too hot for pyjamas,' he continued, and climbed into bed

naked. Helen recoiled at the sight of his bare flesh invading what had become her own private space and looked away.

'We'll talk about it all in the morning,' she said rather wearily, thinking of yesterday's idyllic afternoon, pleasing herself, doing her own thing – over all too quickly.

'All right by me. Move over, love. I'm exhausted.'

For a split second before the light went out his eyes came to rest on what she was wearing: short sleeved in cream satin with embroidery on the collar – the sort of thing Joan Crawford wore in the black-and-white films of the 1930s.

'Are those new pyjamas?'

Any other time he wouldn't even have noticed. Helen silently staked her claim to the coverlet by pulling it up to her neck and didn't answer.

So there they were again, as usual, lying side by side, his body familiar, yet somehow threatening. The bliss of being alone was over. Unless, of course, she decided otherwise.

Dave was still sleeping when she woke. Quietly she slipped out of bed and took her clothes into the bathroom to dress, while all he did was grunt and turn over. Mireille still hadn't come down, so Helen put some coffee on the stove and made the five-minute journey down into the village to fetch some bread. Sitting in the van in the village square, two warm crusty baguettes on the familiar seat beside her, she remembered how easy it had been just to take to the open road. But this time it was only for a split second. Fleeing was melodramatic, but it didn't solve the problem.

When she arrived back at the house Mireille was in the garden watering the geraniums and a bank of yellow alyssum.

'I thought you'd done another bunk,' she said cheerfully, replacing the battered metal watering-can in the shade of the water-butt and following Helen into the kitchen.

Helen put the bread down on the table.

'I nearly did,' she replied. 'Why on earth didn't you tell me he was coming?'

'Because you two have things to talk about.'

'He thought I was miles away.'

'Well you're not, you're here. And so is he. Don't run out

on him now or I might take it as a signal that he's fair game.
I like those academic men who think a lot. They're always so
enthusiastic and they still look like little boys.'

Enthusiastic? Yes, he had been, once.

'I thought you had your own interests up in Paris.'

'So I have, but I'm not getting any younger. One day he's
going to realise that I dye my hair and that I can't read the
newspaper without glasses. At our age we have to take every
chance we can.'

She looked as slim as she had done at twenty, in a pair of
hip-hugging blue trousers and an immaculately white t-shirt.
To Helen she hardly seemed any different from the day they
had met, but soon, inevitably, there would be the tell-tale signs
– the scraggy neck, the sagging chin – when it would be too late
to pretend they weren't middle-aged.

'At our age I wonder why we bother with men at all,' Helen
said, wielding the bread knife expressively, 'whether it's a new
one or the one we've always had. Biologically, it's virtually too
late. And if they want to go scattering their seed elsewhere, good
luck to them.'

'Unfortunately, it's hard to get out of the habit,' Mireille said,
pouring the coffee into small square white cups on a tablecloth
as yellow as buttercups. Everything in Mireille's house looked
like a still-life.

'Besides, I know that one day I'll be bloody lonely,' she
said, staring at the framed photograph of her daughter in
the room beyond. 'I'm just going to put it off for as long
as I can.'

Dave loaded butter and jam on to a slice of the French bread.
Helen sat in the corner of the kitchen staring out of the open
door, her sketch pad on her knee, pretending to draw. They
were alone, Mireille having tactfully withdrawn into the office
on the pretext of making a phone call.

'When are you planning to go?' she asked him in a flat voice
that scarcely seemed to expect an answer.

'I ought to be off as soon as I can, but I was driving
for two solid days to get down here and it's at least eighteen hours more to get back, so I could do with a bit of a

rest. Mireille's invited me to stay another night if I want to.'

'And do you want to?'

He looked up and caught her profile against the white wall. There was something strange about her that he didn't understand.

'Why not?'

He would expect her to go home with him, but she had already decided to refuse.

'Why didn't you fly down?' she asked.

'There are only two flights a week to Nice from the midlands and they were booked up for bank holiday. Besides I was down in Devon. I took the ferry from Plymouth to Roscoff, but never again. It was a hell of a journey.'

'So all this happened on the spur of the moment?'

'It was Reg who suggested it.'

'Reg? Why? Does he know something you don't?'

She meant about the Chair.

'Of course not,' Dave answered irritably. 'But what they're setting up in Nice is very similar to what we're already doing at the Earth Studies Centre. As well as anything else he wanted me to suss out the situation.'

'You might have discussed it with me first! How can we possibly live in France? There's the children's education, for starters. And there's my mother. I can't leave her all alone at her age. It's really not on, Dave.'

She had mentioned her mother and her children, but had neglected to mention herself. The idea had taken her very much by surprise.

'I couldn't really discuss it with you when you weren't there, could I?' he retorted.

'It never even entered your head until Nico mentioned it.'

She knew that if Dave had met Nico in Nice then the game would certainly be up. But perhaps, in the long run, it would be for the best.

'Actually, it's a bit more complicated than that . . .' he began to say, rather defensively, but then obviously decided it wasn't worth trying to reason with her while she was in a mood. He wiped his mouth with the napkin.

'It's no good discussing anything until we know something concrete, is it?'

There was some sense in that but she still resented the fact that he hadn't even mentioned it. He must have been thinking about it all last week. And she sensed that he was still keeping something from her.

'Did you see Nico down there, by any chance?' she asked, getting it over with.

Dave stood up and she noticed idly that his arm had a graze all along it as if someone had scratched him.

'Never set eyes on him,' he said.

'Well, did you talk?' Mireille wanted to know, when Dave had gone out to the van. Apparently the engine had developed some sort of noise and he needed to make an in-depth investigation.

'No, but I will.'

'When?'

'I don't know. When Dave gets under that van there won't be any sign of him for hours.'

'When?' Mireille insisted. 'Helen you've got to, you really have.'

'I will, I promise.'

But there were her drawings to finish and she went up to the bedroom while Dave spent an hour tinkering outside. When he came up to wash the grease off and change into clean clothes neither of them spoke, but she was aware of him watching her in the mirror.

'Pen and ink drawings? That's new isn't it?'

'I'm doing some work for Mireille.'

'What sort of work?' he asked in surprise.

'Illustrations for a book.'

'One of the books she produces? What made her ask you?'

'Because she liked what I do, why do you think?' she replied rather tartly. It was as though he had forgotten all her old ambitions. 'They'll take a couple more days at least.'

'So you're not coming back with me tomorrow?'

'Probably not. I'll catch the train, I expect.'

'Is that how you got here?'

'Mireille met me at the station,' she admitted, not untruthfully.

For a minute or two he ranged round the room aimlessly and Helen grew impatient.

'Dave, be still, will you? I'm trying to work.'

'Never mind that. I think we should go for a walk. Talk this thing through properly.'

She looked up. The tone of his voice meant that he wouldn't take no for an answer and it was a tone he didn't use very often. She acquiesced with a nod of the head.

A few minutes later they were sauntering up the lane in silence, then out from the dark shade of the trees into the bright sunlight of a meadow where sheep were grazing: those funny Mediterranean sheep, with long ears, that looked like goats. The heat haze of afternoon had not yet gathered and they could see right across the valley to the next village, with its medieval turrets, perched on the opposite rise. Nothing here seemed to have anything to do with her real life. Helen almost expected to see a half-naked shepherd boy sitting on a rock, playing the Pan pipes.

'You didn't go on the French exchange at all, did you?' Dave asked at last.

'Got it in one.'

'So what on earth are you doing here?'

'I just wanted to get away. From school, from the children, from you bawling them out all the time, from the Chair, from the cottage.'

'You love the cottage!'

'No I don't, I hate the bloody place.'

He turned on her angrily.

'Helen, what the hell's got into you? I got a phone call from Mrs Rose on Friday afternoon wondering if you'd be in after half-term. She was quite upset that you weren't bringing your paintings to the Summer Fayre and she said you acted very strangely when you left. I hadn't the remotest idea what to say to her. She seems to have got the impression that you weren't ever coming back.'

Her face was impassive. 'No, that's right. I'm not.'

'You mean you've given up your job? At a time like this?'

'What do you mean at a time like this? In case you don't get the Chair and you want to give up *your* job.'

He ignored this insinuation.

'I'm hardly on a telephone number salary am I? We can't afford for you not to work.'

'I am working,' she pointed out. 'I'm working for Mireille. I've got the cheque in my bag, if you want to see it.'

'But this French exchange business – I don't understand. Why did you make up a thing like that? Are you ill or something?'

She could guess what he was thinking: women of her age – depression – you read about it. Or possibly he was imagining something worse.

'Of course I'm not ill,' she snapped. 'Do you think I've gone dotty or something? Most of all I feel angry. Just so damned angry.'

'Angry? What about?'

She sat down on the grass, her back against a rock, while Dave stood still, his hands in his pockets, looking rather baffled, waiting for her to explain.

'My job to start with. But that's done with. I told Mrs Rose to look for someone else, though evidently she didn't believe me. Then there's you and me, you and work, you and Oliver, you and Ianthe. Which one would you like me to start with?'

She knew that Ianthe was only part of the problem; the visible fraction of the iceberg.

He seemed startled. 'Ianthe? What's she got to do with it?'

'You should know!' she exclaimed, looking straight up into his face. 'I didn't think you'd ever do a thing like that, Dave. Getting mixed up with a student! You're old enough to be her father, do you realise that? And don't bother to deny it either. Do you think I don't know you? All those messages, the whispering, the smirking. Going down to the cottage together, just the two of you. I hope my ghost haunted you there, by God I do. I hope you never had a minute's peace. And now you come down here after a job you don't even consult me about!'

'You weren't there for me to consult, were you? Anyway I don't want the job, not really . . .'

Of course she knew that. He wanted his Chair, that was all.

'. . . and as for Ianthe . . .'

Helen took a crumpled piece of paper out of her pocket and flourished it in front of his nose. At last she had her proof.

'You don't need to deny it. I found this on the floor of the van this morning. Do you want me to read it to you?'

She smoothed it out. It was a letter written on French notepaper which he must have bought specially.

'"My dear Ianthe, I have been thinking about what happened on Saturday night and I just want to say . . ." That's all. I suppose this was the first draft, but I'd be very interested to hear what you wrote in the final version.'

'Look, I can explain all that . . .'

'There's no need. It's all very plain. And while we're on the subject, perhaps you ought to know that I drove down here with Nico. He was coming to the interview, so he gave me a lift.'

What was the point of revenge if he didn't know anything about it? Besides she didn't want him to feel sorry for her.

'So that's it.'

That was all he said, his head bent, that mop of fuzzy hair concealing his expression. Had it always been like that? For the life of her she could scarcely remember what he looked like when they first met. But, she supposed, neither of them were the same people now as they had been then, not physically, not even mentally. If Tim's science book was correct, every cell in their bodies had changed. Rationally, it was a wonder they had lasted as long as they had.

Still he didn't look at her.

'I think I'll get going,' he said, suddenly. 'The van's fixed. It doesn't seem worth hanging around.'

Just as she thought they were going to have a good old row, he was deciding not to discuss it.

'I thought you were staying until tomorrow.'

'There doesn't seem much point now, does there?'

'Dave, we've got to sort this out . . .'

But he had started walking, quickly and purposefully, with long strides, his face set in a scowl, back towards the house. Helen followed, almost jogging behind him to keep up, but he didn't stop. She didn't catch him until they were nearly back in the garden.

'Dave, I said we've got to sort things out . . .'

Slowly, during the morning, it had probably been dawning on him what was coming, but he hadn't devised an answer to it.

'You seem to have decided everything already. Just tell me what you're going to do.'

Helen swallowed hard and told him. 'I want to be in control of my own life and I'm not. That's the bottom line. So I think we ought to get a divorce.'

He didn't even slacken his pace. 'If you're going to go on acting like you have been doing, it seems like a good idea.'

Right in front of them Mireille was standing by the kitchen door, her hand raised to attract their attention, and she was listening to every word they said.

11

'Is that all you've got to say?' Helen demanded.

His calmness stung her, his sang-froid. Perversely, she thought he might at least have made a token protest. They were already further apart than she had realised.

It took her several seconds to tear her thoughts away from him to realise that Mireille was standing there because she was waiting for them.

'I'm sorry to break up the quarrel, my friends,' Mireille said, stepping forward with rather a forced smile. For once she spoke in English for Dave's benefit. 'But there seems to be some trouble. I just got an e-mail message from England.'

'Oh, the wonders of the information superhighway!' Helen muttered under her breath.

'It's for you,' Mireille continued. 'For both of you. Come, I'll show you.'

They saw from her face that it was serious and, uncomprehending, they followed her through into the study where all three of them stared at the message displayed on the green computer screen.

Mireille, do you know where Mum and Dad are? Both of them are in France but I can't get hold of them. I'm putting out an all-points bulletin in the hopes that they'll get the message somewhere. Oliver's gone missing, with just a note saying don't try to find him. I don't know what to do. Let me know if you've seen them, love Emma.

'I realised this morning that the phone was off the hook,' Mireille interjected apologetically. 'She may have been trying to get in touch that way. Sorry to be the bringer of bad news.'

'Oliver's gone missing?' Dave repeated, rather vacantly. 'I don't believe it. He's probably just gone round to Ben's. After all, it's half-term. She's over-reacting, isn't she, sending international e-mail messages here, there and everywhere?'

'It's certainly not something I'd have considered myself,' Mireille admitted, 'but young people take high tech in their stride.'

Helen hesitated. She was trying to consider the situation in a detached manner, but inside her heart was pounding. She hadn't expected this.

'Yes, it's half-term all right, but come Monday morning he's got a maths exam. Oh, heavens, why did he have to do this now, of all times?'

It was a cry from the bottom of her heart. She had enough on her mind at the moment without Oliver rocking the boat.

'I'll give Emma a ring. Do you mind, Mireille?'

'Be my guest.'

She refrained from remarking that two people in the same family leaving home in a hurry seemed rather more than a coincidence.

'If the little blighter's skiving off his exams . . .' Dave began, but Helen jumped in before he could finish getting the words out. She couldn't endure his hectoring when Oliver wasn't even there. What was the point of getting angry at this long distance?

'Don't start on him, Dave, not until you know the facts! You've spent the last few months lecturing him without listening to his point of view. Perhaps this is his way of answering back.'

Dave held his tongue while she dialled their home number. By the tricks of modern technology Emma sounded closer than she did when she was phoning for a lift home from town.

'Mum, where are you? I've been trying to contact you through Mr Booth but he didn't seem to have any idea. And Dad's gone down to Nice for a job interview. Did you get my message?'

'Dad's here with me. We're both at Mireille's. What's happened, love? Where's Oliver?'

'Gone. He didn't come home last night. And there's a rucksack and a sleeping-bag missing from the utility room cupboard. I rang round some of his friends but they haven't seen him.'

'Any clothes missing?'

'I dunno, I can't tell, but he's left his room tidy, and there was a note by the phone asking me to feed his rabbit and not to try and find him.'

Dave, who was trying to catch the gist of the conversation, impatiently grabbed the receiver from Helen's hand.

'Emma, this is Dad. Have you called the police?'

'No, I didn't like to. After all, he's gone of his own accord. It isn't like he's been abducted or anything.'

'But he's only sixteen. You can't leave home at sixteen.'

'Plenty of kids do, Dad.'

But not my kid, that's what they were both thinking. It was every parent's worst fear.

'So, what are you saying?' Emma asked. 'Do you want me to call the police or what?'

'Yes ... that is ... no, you'd better not, not until we get home.'

They could both hear the first question the police would ask. And were your children here alone, Dr Croft, while you and your wife were somewhere in France where they couldn't even contact you?

There was another tussle with the receiver and Helen wrenched it back.

'Emma, look, we'll be home as soon as we can. In the meantime, if you remember any more of his friends, try to get in touch with them, will you? Do you know if Oliver had any money?'

'Just what he earned from his Saturday job, I suppose. But he usually spent that as soon as he got it. Mum, I'm so sorry. I never thought he'd do anything like this. I wish I'd been here.'

Helen was amazed. Normally she regarded her brother with scarcely disguised loathing.

'It's not your fault. I expect he waited until you were safely out of the way.'

Helen heard someone talking in the background, the faint rhythm of pop music. 'Is there someone with you?'

'It's Jake. We went looking for Oliver last night. Out on Higdon Heath. We didn't get back until about two.'

So Jake was there supporting her, doing his bit, while they were both away living their own lives.

'That's good of him,' she acknowledged. 'Say we're very grateful. We'll be home soon, Emma. Tomorrow sometime, I suppose. Are you revising? Just try and get on with it as usual. We'll take care of things when we get back.'

'Come home quick, Mum.'

She sounded scared, not like the usual capable Emma. She wasn't quite so grown-up as she pretended.

'Yes, love, I will.'

She put down the receiver.

'Right,' said Dave, trying to quash any emotion he might be feeling. 'I'd better put my stuff in the van. The stupid little idiot! What did he want to go and pull a stunt like this for? I'm certainly not relishing the thought of driving another eight hundred miles for his sake.'

'Don't be silly,' Helen said. 'We'll both go. I'll drive half. If we set off now, we could be home in the early hours.'

'I thought you'd be staying here. I imagined you'd have another rendezvous with that boyfriend of yours.'

His sarcasm cut her, on top of this bombshell about Oliver.

'Are you mad? Do you think I'd let you leave me here when my son's gone missing?'

Mireille intervened, trying to keep the peace.

'You should hear yourselves! Just get your bags packed up and I'll find some food for you to take on the journey.'

'Mireille – the drawings . . .'

'Don't worry about them,' she said reassuringly. 'You've done half of them and I can wait a few days longer for the rest. Oliver's more important. It's better you get home as soon as you can. Children, eh? What would we do without them?'

Suddenly they had been forced to put their own problems to the back of their minds. Gathering up their belongings as quickly as they could, they tossed the luggage into the back of the camper van, together with some sandwiches and a flask that Mireille hastily prepared for them. Within half an hour they were ready to leave, though if they had stopped to think about the situation they would have realised that they didn't have a clue what they were going to do about it.

'Thanks for everything, *chérie*,' Helen said to Mireille, giving her a hug. 'I'll be in touch. I'm sorry about all this.'

Mireille shook Dave's hand. 'Let me know what happens, won't you? Take care.'

She stood waving to them as the van lurched out of the yard and on to the dusty track which led down to the village. Looking back, Helen saw her white t-shirt framed against the golden stone of the house, the scarlet splash of geraniums at her shoulder. It was a wrench to leave. For a few days the old farmhouse had been a blessed retreat.

Dave said nothing, his mouth set firm, his eyes doggedly on the road ahead. Helen fastened her seat-belt and opened the window, rolling up her shirt sleeves and bracing herself for yet another dash through France. It was a hot day, far too sticky to be motoring.

And now that the first shock and annoyance were starting to wear off, the fears of where Oliver might have gone started to mount, and the frightening possibilities rushed through her head. The cardboard box, the squat. Drugs and rent boys. Squalor and destitution. She'd seen the programmes they had on TV of mothers appealing for their children to come home. Normal mothers with normal teenagers who had never shown any signs of disappearing. They weren't all from deprived backgrounds or broken homes, just ordinary children who didn't think.

Yet somehow they were alien, brought up in a world so utterly different from that of their parents. Sometimes she felt a million miles away from them – her own children. Perhaps her father had felt the same way about her, about her freedom and her ambitions that were so unlike his own pre-war world. She had been alien to him once, too, with her different anxieties, different certainties. But they were anxieties and certainties she knew and understood. She didn't understand Emma's or Oliver's and never really could.

When she was young, everyone believed there would be another war. She thought her husband would get called up, because her own father had been in a war and so had the generation before that. When Dave was forty she actually thought, 'Now he's too old for conscription', even though she knew perfectly well that there would never be anything like World War II again. Thermonuclear conflict didn't need foot-slogging infantrymen. But what did her children have fixed in their heads from childhood? Ecological disaster and perpetual unemployment? Anarchy and disease? Those all bothered her, but not the way they did the young.

'Did you ever run away?' she asked Dave, breaking their tense silence.

'I did when I was twelve. I stayed out in a tent and came home in the morning, frozen stiff.'

'It's different at sixteen. It's serious.'

'If you'd have been there he might not have gone.'

His insinuation shocked her.

'You mean it was my fault? Do you think I can look inside his head any better than you can?'

'You've never left the children before. Any of them. You'd have noticed what was going on.'

'You were there when I was. Why didn't *you* notice?'

'That's different!'

'No, it isn't. It's just a cop-out. Mothers aren't robots. They can't spend every moment of their lives thinking exclusively about their children any more than fathers can. They'd go mad. They do go mad, Dave.'

He looked at her sideways. 'Is that what you've done, gone mad?'

'For want of a better adjective, it probably is.'

They didn't speak any more, except for occasional curt little phrases on the best route to take, every time they came to a crossroads. Time passed. Helen felt like bursting into tears.

Slowly, as they left the *midi*, the countryside was changing, with the olive trees and the scent of lavender giving way to the rolling green landscapes of the north, but it was still as hot. Helen mopped her brow, then fumbled for the sandwiches Mireille had packed up and offered Dave a drink from the flask. It was weak, French tea, not the sort of stuff to sustain you in a crisis. Dave tasted some of it, wet his mouth, then flicked most of it out of the window.

'There's some bottled water if you want some,' she offered,

but he shook his head wordlessly. The motorway stretched ahead and Helen took over at the wheel. There were hundreds of miles of silence between them still to come before they got to Calais.

It hadn't always been so. When they first met they told each other everything. Or so it seemed, from this distance. Helen had decided that jumping into bed first and thinking afterwards wasn't the best basis for a relationship and she wanted to take it more slowly, set the pace herself. Canoodling was a word that was already going out of fashion and now it was probably extinct, but she had liked it. She liked Dave's grey eyes and his curly hair, his finely chiselled features. He understood things she didn't, like relativity and computer chips. If he had a problem he worked it out logically; he didn't live by the seat of his pants like Nico or in the slow, deliberate couldn't-care-less way of Malone.

It had even been conventionally romantic. They met at a bowling alley and she won; or at least he let her win. The next week, on Sunday afternoon, they went to the pictures. On the way home he bought her a bunch of flowers from the shop next to the infirmary that was open for hospital visitors. Great orange tiger lilies they had been and she put them in one of Daisy's vases that had been salvaged from that other life of hers.

Looking back, she realised she had never had a mutually serious relationship before. Nobody had ever come up to scratch in her eyes except Danny and he was well in the past. And perhaps she had that idea that women had always had and probably still had: that if she found the right person then they would look after each other and everything would be all right. Girls were still brought up on Cinderella and they wanted to believe it, against all odds.

At that time Dave was doing research into river pollution and every weekend he would dash up to Derbyshire to take water samples from specified sections of various rivers. While he was busy with his equipment she would sit on the grass and sketch the limestone crags and the ruined watermills, overgrown lushly with vegetation, which abounded there. Once Dave had exchanged a couple of angry punches with a farmer who accused them of trespassing, and such macho behaviour had obviously impressed her. That night was the first time they ever slept together.

In those days he had been happy to nurture all her artistic endeavours. He even let her do a painting of him in the nude, full-frontal, which her flatmates thought was pornographic when they found out what she was doing. Helen preferred to look on it as semi-erotic; she was as much interested in capturing the expression of his face and the shape of his hands as in depicting his penis. It had meant a lot to both of them, that painting. Or she used to think it did. Now Helen asked herself unmercifully if he had only agreed to pose for it to add a bit of spice to their sex life.

'Do what's important to you,' he urged her then, seeing how bored she was at the library. They used to meet at lunchtime in the stacks, next to the scientific journals. 'Why don't you drop this job and do your art course?'

'I can't afford to. All I've got to my name is some old furniture that isn't worth anything and a few left-over pots. I've tried to save a bit but I wouldn't get a grant now. I've used up all my entitlement.'

'You mean you've got furniture?' he marvelled.

Most of it was in her parents' garage. She was sharing a furnished flat with a social worker and a typist; he was living with his cousin and her husband, but there was a baby on the way and very soon he would be out on the street.

Living together seemed the sensible solution and after knowing each other some five or six months they set up house together, in a tiny two-roomed flat at the top of an old house with her furniture, his map and record collections and Biscuit.

They made a pact: she would pay the rent until he had finished his Ph.D. course; then they would swap over and he would pay it while she went to art college. That way at least they would always have a roof over their heads. It seemed so simple. She didn't even dream of anything going wrong.

James Butcher had hung on for years longer than anyone had expected, but eventually he got too much for Marion to cope with and the local authority found him a place in a nursing home. After that he slid downhill fast and only a few months later the matron of the home rang to say that he had died peacefully in his sleep.

'I'll drive you home,' Dave offered.

He was in the middle of writing up his thesis, so he couldn't stay long but he came back for the funeral. Marion put him in the spare room but when she hoped her mother was asleep Helen crept along the dark landing to join him, finding solace in his firm body with the familiar smell she had grown so used to.

'How are you feeling?' he asked, gently stroking her hair. 'You've hardly said a thing all day.'

It was a single bed and she entwined her legs in his, attempting to find a comfortable position.

'It sounds awful, Dave, but I don't care, do you know that? I just don't care. At first I was shocked, when I heard the news, and now I'm home I miss him sitting in the same old chair, but that's all. I ought to feel more than that, oughtn't I? I'm not normal. I'm just thankful *I'm* alive . . . me myself. But I just hate myself for it.'

'I don't,' said Dave, kissing her. 'You mustn't forget he's been ill for years. You've expected this for a long time.'

He didn't know her father so he tried to convince her that such feelings weren't unnatural and Helen struggled to accept that he might be right.

'I never told you what came the morning I heard the news. If it hadn't been for him, we could have gone out for a celebration and now we can't. That's all I can think of.'

'Why, what came?'

'A letter from the art college accepting me on a course starting in September. It means I'm on my way; that is if your thesis is written and they offer you the lecturer's job.'

'Of course they will. It's just about in the bag already. That's great news, Lenny. I knew they'd have you when they saw your portfolio.'

'I'd been keeping a bottle of sparkling wine for this and now look at us!'

No champagne, just the traditional ham salad of the funeral tea, though she hadn't eaten any of it. To save her mother work she had spent most of her time serving food and washing up in the kitchen.

She could feel him smiling through the darkness. 'It's no problem – we can celebrate here. We don't need champagne. I've got something better.'

'Stupid!' she giggled rather shrilly, forgetting about her mother sleeping not far away. It felt rather irreverent, but making love worked better than champagne for blocking out unpleasant thoughts.

However, in her haste to come back home she had forgotten her packet of pills. By the time September came and Dave's confirmation of a lectureship was through, she found that she was pregnant.

It was almost six o'clock the next morning when they turned the van into their own drive. There was no other traffic yet; the sun was shining and nothing stirred, except some sparrows squabbling in the hedge. The roses had come into full bloom since Helen had been away. It seemed a long, long time ago.

They recognised Jake's motorbike parked squarely up against the garage doors.

'So the boyfriend from hell's in residence, is he?' Dave remarked.

Helen glowered at him. 'Don't take it out on them, Dave. We've got enough on our plates already. At least he hasn't got a ring through his nose. If you can't be civil to them, let me do the talking.'

They were lying fast asleep on the settee together, fully dressed with their arms around each other, Jake's hair covering Emma's face. On the floor were the remains of some hamburgers and a couple of beer cans. The TV screen was blank but the video was still switched on and there was a digital message instructing them to rewind the tape.

Emma stirred as Dave opened the curtains and a shaft of sunlight fell across her face. She rubbed her eyes and Jake mumbled something in his sleep.

'Mum, is that you? Dad? Oh thank goodness you're both here! It hasn't taken you long.'

'You shouldn't have waited up for us,' Helen scolded mildly. 'We might have been hours yet. I'll put the kettle on and then you can tell us everything.'

She made tea and toast and they all sat round the kitchen table while Emma repeated what she knew. It wasn't much more than she had told them on the phone.

'I've tried all his friends and they don't know anything. He went round to Gran's to try and cadge some money, dropped hints all over the place, but she didn't give him anything.'

'I should hope not. She's only got her pension.'

'It's not as though he's short of cash anyway. He's got all his pay from the garage and Ben told me he was flogging cassette tapes at school before half-term.'

'So this isn't something sudden? He's been planning it for a while.'

'Looks like it.'

Dave could have said plenty, but Helen noticed that he tried to bite his tongue while Jake was there. He looked rather out of his depth.

'Emma, he's not into drugs of any sort, is he?' Helen asked. That was what worried her most of all, but Emma shook her head emphatically.

'No, I'm pretty sure he isn't. He's had a spliff occasionally, I think, but never anything serious.'

'A spliff? What's that?'

'It's a joint – cannabis,' Jake intervened. He was obviously amused at her ignorance, but Emma wanted to skate over that.

'Mr Vernon – you know Gran's boyfriend – went down town last night and asked at the night shelter in Dover Street and the one under All Saints' Church but they'd never heard of him.'

'Mr Vernon went? That was kind of him. He shouldn't be going to places like that at his age. But he's not exactly her boyfriend.'

'You haven't seem them lately. They seem pretty friendly.'

'He's cool,' Jake said, 'for an old guy. I told him it could be dangerous down there but he said he'd been in the jungle in Burma, so he wasn't worried about a few down-and-outs.'

Helen shivered, thinking of Oliver in the midst of that.

'Jake and I had a look under the railway arches too, just in case,' Emma went on. 'But he wasn't there at midnight. In any case he wouldn't stay around here for us to find him. The first thing he'd do is head out, isn't it? That's what I'd do.'

'Why has he gone?' Dave asked, speaking for the first time. 'That's what I'd like to know. He's got everything he wants here, hasn't he?'

Helen sensed that he was trying to keep the cap on his resentment, but like her he couldn't help viewing his son's flight somehow as a rejection. The same question was running through both their heads – where did we go wrong?

'That depends on what he wants,' Jake said simply. He looked at his watch. 'Look, I've got to head off too. My mother'll be getting up for work soon and wonder why the bike's not there.'

Unselfconsciously he kissed Emma on the mouth and she caressed his long hair from around his face.

'You look a fright. I'll see you later.'

Helen accompanied him to the front door where he fastened on his motorcycle helmet which had been hanging up in the hall.

'You've been marvellous, Jake,' she said, making sure Dave was out of earshot, 'helping Emma like this. I'm really grateful. *We're* really grateful. I'm . . . I'm sorry if you haven't felt very comfortable here in the past.'

'He's a bit heavy, Emma's dad,' Jake agreed with a grin, though it obviously didn't bother him in the least.

'We didn't really know you, I suppose, and it was a bit of a shock at first. But . . . well, you understand what I'm trying to say. You're welcome whenever you want to come.'

'No problem. You know, you look all in. Why don't you get some sleep? Emma's been panicking but nothing's going to happen to Ollie that won't keep for a few hours.'

It was wise advice and Helen decided to take it. Teenagers were always so polite and caring when they weren't talking to their own parents; it was only then that they seemed to turn into monsters. She felt guilty that people she hardly knew had been out looking for Oliver when it was their own responsibility.

She went back to the kitchen and on the spur of the moment prepared some of her favourite comfort food – a large sandwich with dark muscovado sugar in the middle. The sweetness of it soothed her somewhat, though she still didn't know what they were going to do.

Dave was tired out and he went to bed for a few hours but in the end Helen decided not to join him; people who were getting a divorce shouldn't be sharing the same bed. Instead she took a shower, put on clean clothes, filed her nails, put some clothes in the washing-machine. After she had tidied round and looked at the backlog of post, she sat on the settee for a long time trying to get up the courage to go into Oliver's room to find out what was missing.

She didn't want to. It was like admitting that he was gone and up to now she didn't really believe it. Yet it was real enough, the note saying, 'Dear Emma, Don't come looking for me, I'll be OK. Please feed Patch for me, love Oliver.'

At last she went upstairs, stopping for a moment outside his bedroom. He was only a child, really – he still had his own little nameplate on his door – but who knew what was going on inside his head?

He seemed to have taken his Walkman and some cassettes, a couple of pairs of jeans and some t-shirts. She couldn't find his bank book for his savings account either and there should have been over a hundred pounds in that, perhaps more because his birthday was only a couple of months ago.

She wracked her brains to think where he might head for. Dave's sister in Reading? Not very likely; he knew she wouldn't keep it secret. Both Dave's parents were dead and there were no other near relations. Surely he wouldn't go where he had never been before.

She felt Dave watching her, framed in the doorway. It was already after midday.

'Any clues?' he asked, looking round. 'I must say the place is abnormally tidy.'

'He's not such a bad boy, Dave. Just thoughtless. He can't have realised how we'd feel. After all, neither of us was here.'

Dave's initial anger seemed to have subsided now that they were home. He hadn't shaved for over twenty-four hours and he looked haggard; no wonder with hardly a decent sleep in days. Helen felt weighed down by a profound sadness. Normally they would have been able to comfort each other but that was impossible now. The barrier of hostility was well and truly closed between them.

'I'll have a wash and then I think I'll go to the police station,' he said, at last. 'Want to come?'

She nodded. 'Then I'll go to Mother's to collect Tim.'

At least she would have one son home.

The police station was a chastening experience that made Helen feel very small. The police were far from cooperative. In their eyes if a young person left home and there was no suspicion of foul play or fear that he was mixed up in anything illegal they couldn't pursue the matter.

'Otherwise, Dr Croft, we'd spend all our time looking for lost kids. Most of them turn up at home again sooner or later anyway. Has he ever been in trouble with the law?'

'Of course he hasn't!' Helen flared, incensed that he should only address Dave and not her, the way men always did. 'What do you think he is? A car thief, or something?'

'I beg your pardon, madam, but usually it's the parents who are the last to know. We have them in here every day of the week, protesting the innocence of some little shoplifter or glue-sniffer or burglar.'

They made it sound as if it was all their faults, hers and Dave's. Eventually the officer promised to make a note of it, take down a description of him and so on, just in case.

In case of what? Helen wondered. In case they found a body under a hedge – an unnamed accident victim – so that he could be eliminated? They spoke in their own peculiarly formal jargon, talking of 'perpetrators' and 'incidents'. Oliver was just another statistic to them.

'There's the Salvation Army,' one of the WPCs mentioned, just as they were leaving. 'They try, but they haven't the resources to do as much as they'd like. I think there's a helpline too that gives advice. It's someone to talk to, isn't it?'

Next they called at the garage where Oliver worked on Saturdays, washing and valeting cars.

'He was here last week,' his boss told them, crawling out from under a truck. 'Didn't seem any different from usual. He was due a bit of extra money though, for working a couple of evenings. We had a rush job with some wedding cars.'

'So how much did you pay him altogether do you think, Sandy?'

'Forty quid, near on. He's a hard worker. Give him a job any time.'

He nodded towards the glass-fronted forecourt building where his wife was serving at the till.

'Ask Maureen if he said anything to her. I'm sorry he's gone. I shall have to look round for somebody else if he doesn't turn up again, silly young sod.'

With that he returned to his inspection pit. Maureen didn't remember anything either, though she said what a nice boy he was. Everyone thought that, it seemed, all except Dave.

'While you're at your mother's I've got to go in to work,' he said when they were back in the car. 'There's something I have to discuss with Reg, PDQ. Will you drop me off?'

'What, now? Can't it wait a bit?'

Though she couldn't say she was surprised. His job had always come top of the list.

'No. I wish it could, but I've been away for nearly a week and this is urgent.'

She was bewildered. In spite of everything she needed him just now.

'But what about Oliver? What are we going to do?'

'We'll talk about it tonight. I won't be late.'

'You'd better not be,' she murmured, trusting he would hear.

After she had dropped him off at the university she continued along the ring road to Rivergreen House. Tim was playing on his bike in the visitors' car park and came rushing straight into her arms with a whoop of delight.

'Mummy, where's Oliver gone? Are you going to find him?' he asked excitedly.

She hugged him tight and promised that they'd try. Seemingly reassured, he skipped ahead of her into her mother's flat where Helen was surprised to find some changes had taken place during the last few days. There was a large empty space on one wall and Marion was sitting at a shining new keyboard, picking out a tune.

'Where's the piano?' Helen asked when she had given her mother a kiss on the cheek.

Marion got up in that unhurried way of hers, taking off her apron as she always did when visitors called.

'I saw an advert in the paper for someone who did house clearances.'

'You mean you've sold it? Mother, that piano was a hundred years old!'

Marion shrugged it off amiably, as though she sold cherished furniture every day of the week.

'So it may have been, but people don't want that sort of thing any more.' She patted the new acquisition with obvious pleasure. 'And this keyboard saves so much space. What do you think of it?'

'When did you get it?'

'Frank took me down to town a couple of days ago.'

In her mind Helen compared the lovely old walnut piano with this squat electronic appliance in plastic, but she could hardly complain. She had never had the patience to learn to play.

'On the bus?' she asked, rather pettishly. 'I could have gone with you and brought it back in the car.'

'We're not quite helpless, you know.'

Her voice sounded mildly scathing and Helen wasn't used to it. She never thought of her mother as being independent. When James Butcher had been alive she had always seemed just like a puppet: Marion – marionette. But she reminded herself sternly, not for the first time, that it wasn't up to her to run her mother's life.

'But never mind that; I'm just glad you're back. I've been so worried. Where's Dave?'

Helen scowled. 'Called in at the department. He's got a hot date with Prof. Bannister.'

Marion couldn't help but notice her sarcastic tone, but she passed over it for the time being.

'What are you going to do about Ollie?'

'We've been to the police station, but as far as they're concerned it's up to us if he isn't in any sort of trouble.'

'Something criminal, you mean?'

'I suppose so.'

Marion sat down in one of the armchairs and motioned to her daughter to do the same.

'You hear such awful things, don't you? So are you going to look for him yourselves?'

The thought had crossed Helen's mind, though it was a daunting prospect. She threw out her hands in a gesture of helplessness.

'The trouble is we don't know where to start.'

'They go to London, a lot of them, don't they? It's anonymous, I suppose, and they can easily disappear if they want to. There was a programme on television recently about children who run away from home. Some of them fall into terrible company.'

'We could go to London if it would do any good,' Helen said, with visions of searching the sleazy areas around King's Cross, and perhaps Piccadilly Circus where the drug pushers were supposed to hang out. 'But he doesn't like cities. He's always moaning how awful it is where we live and it's a nice leafy suburb. Pollution, industry, he hates all that. He's got a poster in his bedroom with a power station on it and a skull and crossbones underneath.'

'You used to have Elvis Presley. Do you remember?' Marion mused, forgetting, at this distance, what a worry Helen had been in her time.

'I think it's more likely he's gone off camping somewhere. We've established that he must have had a couple of hundred pounds on him. It's enough to take him quite a long way, unless he hitchhiked, of course. Then he wouldn't need to spend a thing.'

'Oh, surely he hasn't gone hitchhiking? I always think it's so risky doing that.'

'We hitchhiked, Mother, when we were Oliver's age,' Helen said, to try and comfort her, though it wasn't quite true. Apart from coming back from Paris with Mireille and Xavier, the only time she had ever hitchhiked was with Kicker and she had always made sure that Kicker was sitting firmly between herself and the driver. Kicker was her own personal self-defence.

'What about you, Tim,' she asked, realising that her other son was listening to everything they said. 'Do you remember Oliver saying anything about going away?'

Tim shook his head. 'He doesn't talk to me much. Only if I touch his computer or his radio or something and then he gets cross.'

'Or doing anything suspicious? Try and remember, darling.'

'He was looking through Daddy's maps in the study,' he volunteered after a moment.

'What, you mean those maps in the cabinet?'

Being a geography lecturer, maps were Dave's hobby and he had a cupboard full of them, some antique and fairly rare so they were strictly out of bounds to the children. But there was also a full set of Ordnance Surveys for the whole of the British Isles.

'I went in there and he told me to clear off.'

'When was this exactly?'

Tim shrugged. 'The day before you went to France, I think. I can't really remember.'

It was the very first clue they had had.

'I'll have a look when we go home,' Helen said. 'See if he's taken one of them. At least it might narrow the field. Tim, why don't you go and get your things together? We'll have to make a move in a minute.'

'And now,' her mother said, when Tim had gone into the bedroom, 'what about you? Have you and Dave fallen out, or are you just fighting about Ollie?'

Helen hesitated. She couldn't bring herself to tell her mother yet. She would say how much Dave was like a son to her, and start worrying about how it would affect the children. In reply Helen could hear herself vowing that there would be nothing acrimonious – the children would always come first – but of course it would be a lie. For once she wanted to come first. It was selfish and it made her feel uncomfortable but it was true. And why should her mother have any sympathy for her? She had been forced to put up with her husband and she probably thought Helen should do the same.

She shook her head. 'It's nothing. Just that he puts his job before everything else in life, but that's nothing new.'

'Well I'm glad to hear it, because I'm thinking of taking the plunge myself.'

Her voice was suddenly full of coy excitement, like a girl, and Helen looked up in astonishment.

'The plunge?'

'I mean Frank has asked me to marry him.'

'Mr Vernon?'

Marion's eyes twinkled and she laughed, proud of her surprise. 'Yes. I'm sorry to have such good news when you're so worried about Oliver.'

'That isn't your fault.' Helen's face broke into a smile. There was always something endearing about elderly romance. 'Mother, I'm so pleased for you! I don't know him very well but Emma and Jake certainly think he's great.'

'You don't think I'm too old?'

'Not if Frank doesn't.'

'Do you remember what you were saying about Paul Valentine the other day?' Marion asked, glancing at her shyly. 'Well I took it to heart. I said we ought to go to bed together before we decided.'

'Heavens, did you?'

'Don't you think I should have done?' She was obviously taking pleasure in her daughter's startled face. 'But it's so much easier now, what with not worrying about getting pregnant or anything. I suppose I'm a funny shape, but he doesn't seem to mind.'

After such a revelation there was nothing to be done but go up to Mr Vernon's flat to congratulate him in person. He lived on the first floor, so there was a small balcony which blossomed with an array of plant life all growing up from pots. Clinging to a trellis on one wall was a clematis in full bloom and on the other side was a vine. In the window-boxes grew petunias and blue and white trailing lobelia and on a table in the middle stood a tray of lettuces. Mr Vernon stepped from amidst his home-made jungle and tipped his old trilby politely.

'Helen, how good to see you! Is there any news of Oliver? I know Marion's worried to death.'

'Not yet, but we think we might have a lead. It was very good of you to go out looking for him. Some of those places aren't very savoury.'

'Oh, I've seen worse. And I wouldn't worry too much, you know. When I was Oliver's age I'd been working for nearly two years. You were a man then, once you were earning. But these days there's no chance to prove yourself in that way, and school doesn't count, at least not with boys. I walked from Newcastle to London at his age. No money, you see. They're too molly-coddled now. Not that I'm blaming you, of course, it's just the system. Anyway I hope you have some good news soon.'

'Thank you,' Helen said gratefully. 'And I hear congratulations are in order.'

He grinned, showing a row of fine teeth which were all his own. 'Yes. Do you think I ought to have asked for her hand more formally? After all you are her next of kin.'

He was a charming sprite of a man, full of life, though she supposed he must be well over seventy. Whatever his age he looked good for a few more years yet. And it was one load off her mind. In any plans she made for the future at least now she wouldn't have her mother to worry about.

When Dave came home he searched through the map cabinet to see if anything was missing.

'There seem to be a couple of maps gone,' he reported. 'The north-west and the Lake District. Perhaps that's where he's making for. I can't think why, he's never even been there.'

'Yes, he has, Dad,' Emma put in. 'He went to an outdoor centre in the Lake District with the school in year 6. Don't you remember? He talked about it for ages afterwards.'

Helen remembered too. It was the first time he had been away from home and he'd insisted on taking his teddy even though he was eleven years old.

'He really loved it there,' she recalled. 'They climbed, sailed, everything.'

'He could do that at the cottage, but he never bothers.'

'That's because we take him to the cottage. The Lake District is something he discovered for himself.'

'So you really believe he's gone there?'

'I suppose it's possible. And it's our only lead.'

Dave pondered. 'At least the population density there's a bit lower than it is in London. It shouldn't be so hard to track him down.'

It sounded as though he had already made up his mind to mount a search, though they both realised it would be a huge undertaking. On the other hand they couldn't just let him go without doing all that was in their power to find him again.

'We'll get going in the morning,' Helen said, reading his mind.

'Do you want to come too? I don't know how long it'll take. I shouldn't be taking any time off really. I'll have finals papers to mark any minute. And what about Tim?'

'I'll look after Tim, Dad,' Emma said unexpectedly. She had always objected to babysitting in the past, but this crisis seemed to be bringing out the best in everyone. 'You go, Mum.'

She turned to her little brother. 'We'll be OK, won't we Tim? We'll go shopping together and you can choose anything you like for tea.'

'Are you sure you can cope?' Helen asked. 'Your exams start in earnest next week. But I don't want to impose on Gran any more either.'

'That's OK, I'm at home anyway, between times. I've got all day to revise while he's at school. Just so long as you leave me some housekeeping money and have the Mini filled up with petrol.'

Trying to avoid her husband, Helen decided to sleep in Oliver's bed, but she couldn't settle properly and she woke at three to find that she was trembling. She had to put her hands over her ears to keep the noise out. In her head she could hear a baby crying but she was sure it wasn't hers. Her first baby had never cried.

Perspiration was dripping down her back and she got up to patrol the landing, listening outside Tim's door to make sure he was still breathing, as she always did when he was tiny. How old were they all before she dared stop doing that? It had always been such a secure contented feeling to know that all three children were at home and asleep in their own beds. But now there was one missing everything seemed upside down. There were some responsibilities you could never get away from.

12 ∫

They were at the cottage when she told Dave she was pregnant and immediately he did the decent thing and asked her to marry him. People might live together, but they were still expected to get married if there was a baby on the way.

'You mustn't ask me unless you really want to,' she protested.

'Of course I want to. Why shouldn't I?'

'It's like I'm forcing you. It's not fair.'

'It wouldn't be fair on you if I didn't. It's my baby too. And we would have got married anyway.'

He seemed to take it all in his stride, but Helen was devastated. She wasn't sure she was ready for any of this. She had only just got used to being one half of a couple for the first time. And the course would have to be given up. With a baby to care for in the spring, art school was out of the question, her last chance gone.

But Dave was determined to do everything properly and he bought her an antique engagement ring out of his first pay packet, a garnet surrounded by tiny seed pearls. He didn't really understand.

'There'll be another opportunity,' he said, trying to boost her spirits; but time was passing and Helen wondered if there really would be.

'I want to get rid of it.'

Had she said those words, or had she merely thought them? Whichever it was, she knew she couldn't really bring herself to do it. For other women she could rationalise it, but for herself it didn't seem right. She couldn't kill it for her own convenience. And being an only child, she had always felt attracted to big families. The timing was wrong, that was all.

Yet as the weeks passed it felt as though her whole body had turned against her, with its swollen breasts and queasy stomach. Just the sight of food revolted her and often she felt too lethargic even to get out of bed in the morning. Everything had become an effort. But Dave was delighted. For some reason she had forgotten, he always referred to the baby as Perkins. 'Perkins is growing nicely', he would say playfully. 'Is Perkins sitting comfortably?' But it was difficult not to bite his head off when she felt so awful.

They had a quiet wedding in a registry office with Helen wearing a short, high-waisted dress and jacket in ivory wool that her mother made for her. It was November, and a biting north-east wind was blowing, with intermittent sleet. She couldn't manage any of the food at the reception, though she tried to act as normally as possible because they hadn't broken the news of the pregnancy to Dave's parents yet. Kicker told her she looked like death warmed up. When nobody was watching she crept away to be sick in the ladies, feeling like a freak and anything but bridal.

A few days in Dublin were supposed to cheer her up, though it didn't feel much like a honeymoon. She sent Dave out to sample the bars on his own while she lay in a warm bath trying to distract herself with a romantic novel. Later, all she could remember about the hotel was that enormous cast-iron bath and the Victorian toilet with rosebuds round the bowl.

Although everyone told her it was bound to stop after about twelve weeks, the sickness went on and on. She was absent from work one day out of two and her boss suggested tactfully that she should leave early, so after Christmas she was cooped up in the flat all day alone. It wasn't even a question of maternity leave; having a baby meant leaving work and never going back.

It seemed like the end of the world, that dark dreary January. At the clinic they prodded and poked and asked her if the baby kicked her much. It didn't seem to, but then she had never had a baby before and didn't know what to expect. They glowered at her ignorance, and she felt humiliated, as if she was back at school and had done badly in a test. Eventually they gave her a chart where she was supposed to record every movement the baby made. In the days before ultra-sound scans were common, low-tech methods were still in favour.

'Does everyone have to do it?' Dave asked.

'I don't know.'

'What about the other women at the ante-natal class?'

'They didn't mention it.'

She seemed normal in every other way. Her blood pressure was as it should be, her ankles didn't swell up, she had hardly put on any weight. By this time she was resigned to the idea of a baby and she had started to talk to it, like Dave did. At least it was something to look forward to. As time passed she even managed to embroider a cot quilt, though she was still overcome with unbearable lassitude. When she mentioned to the doctor that she often couldn't drag herself out of bed until lunch time, he said it was good to rest.

The hospital where she went for her routine checks was two bus-rides away, with a wait of up to two hours in a draughty, high-vaulted waiting-room that must have dated from the time of Florence Nightingale. When it was her turn she had to strip down to her knickers and put on a voluminous gown. Then a nurse would make her lie on the bed and a cotton blanket would be decorously arranged across her abdomen, ready for the appearance of the doctor, who studied her chart and did some more prodding.

'I'd like to admit you, Mrs Croft, so that we can have a better look.'

He was staring assiduously at his notes and didn't meet her eyes.

'Why, is something the matter?'

'Baby doesn't seem to be moving about much, but we'll know more when we've done some tests.'

Why did he have to talk in that ridiculous way? For a moment she was more irritated than apprehensive.

'I'll get nurse to take you to the ward. The consultant will be up to examine you as soon as he's free.'

His face showed no emotion, but Helen could tell by the eyes of the young nurse that all was not well. She didn't look at the other women like that; she smiled and made jolly remarks about their bumps.

It was almost a relief. To Helen it had felt wrong from the beginning, and now perhaps they would stop all their cosy reassurance and tell her the brutal truth at last.

'It's dead, isn't it?' she blurted out. Twenty-five weeks, all come to nothing.

'How are we going to tackle it?' Helen asked as they hurtled up the M6, on the road again. They were going because they had to do something, not because they were convinced that it would lead to finding him.

'We'll go to camp sites, youth hostels, that sort of thing.'

'Don't you have to be a member of the youth hostel association to go there?'

'I haven't a clue, but it's worth a try. Then there are the job centres. He'll have to get a job eventually and with the tourist season just starting it shouldn't be too difficult. Though I suppose they want to know your National Insurance number or something.'

'He's got one. They all get a plastic card these days as soon as they're old enough to work.'

'Do they? So Big Brother's alive and well and nobody cares?'

'And he's tall. He could pass for eighteen at a pinch. We could go to pubs too, tonight. He's bound to try to get to know people.'

It was all very matter of fact and they both tried to keep it on that level, but the Lake District was a big place. In reality their chances of finding him were probably negligible.

'Did you phone Reg?' she queried briefly.

'He said to take as long as I needed, but I've been away for a week already. I don't want this to spin out more than we can help.'

'Doesn't the Senate meet next week?'

'Yes.'

He ventured no more information and she didn't ask. If they divorced, his job wouldn't be anything to do with her any more. She imagined they would sell the house and divide the money up. That seemed the most sensible. There was nothing she particularly wanted except the furniture she had brought down from Yorkshire and a few other personal pieces, like her art deco tea service and that modern landscape, in minimalist greys and black, that Dave hated. She had bought it years ago when she won a couple of hundred on a premium bond. Some books, of course, perhaps the Indian rug in the dining room. Otherwise he could have the lot. She didn't want half a dinner service, or a duvet cover without the matching sheets. All that was just downright petty.

She was determined to keep it on a rational level and it all ran through her mind quite logically as though she was thinking about another person. Her emotions were all used up worrying over Oliver.

As they drove she let her mind wander over the possibilities. It would be strange, living in a little flat again, all on her own except for Tim. (If Tim chose her. She would give him the choice.) And she would need space for Emma to stay in the vacations. Then again, Tim really needed a garden. The money would probably run to a little terrace house, but only in one of the poorer parts of town and that would mean taking Tim away from his school. She didn't want to do that. When they got home she would start to approach a few estate agents.

They left the motorway at Kendal but going straight on, the signs told her, would have taken them to Carlisle. This was the way she should have come to Kicker's funeral. But her son, the living, was more important now.

In a lay-by she heated up some soup but they drank without even tasting it and in twenty minutes they were pressing on. By now they had entered the national park and as the road dipped and rose again they caught a glimpse of blue water with the hills beyond. Sheep were grazing beside the unfenced roads.

'I once came here on a school trip myself,' Helen said. 'We went to Wordsworth's house. It must have been a lonely place then, back at the beginning of the nineteenth century.'

'We are on speaking terms then, are we?' Dave asked. It was the first time they had spoken about anything but Oliver.

'Why wouldn't we be?'

'You should know. You dreamed up the idea of a divorce. Helen, we've got to talk about it. We can't go on like this.'

'Careful!' she called out, as he took his eye off the road and they nearly ended up in the bracken. 'We'll talk about it when this is over. When we've found Ollie.'

'What if we don't find him?'

'We will, of course we will. Eventually.'

Whatever it takes we've got to find him.

She had lost one son, she couldn't lose another. But what if the worst came to the worst and they couldn't find him? By the time he decided to come home they might have sold the house and he wouldn't know where they were. The thought niggled her, though on another level she knew it was idiotic. Perhaps she was going dotty after all.

Glancing at Dave she noticed he was wearing an old jumper she had once knitted for him, worn and shapeless now but still serviceable. She couldn't have managed this alone. Whatever he had done, she still needed a friend – someone who would be on her side. There were ties that bound them together that were beyond even love.

The campsite where Oliver had been with the junior school was down by the lake between Windermere and Ambleside, and they bounced over the bumpy track through mature beech trees to find it.

Helen took out a photo of Oliver for the first of – how many? – times. She had brought a supply of stickers too – the sort with an address and telephone number for putting at the top of letters or on the backs of envelopes – crossing out their names and putting in Oliver's, then sticking them on to pieces of card. If she gave them out to everyone who might possibly see him then it might jog their memories if he did turn up. It was a pity they didn't have more photographs of him, but Oliver always made himself scarce if anyone got their camera out.

Not surprisingly, the campsite proprietor hadn't seen him. Neither had the people at the couple of employment agencies they tried or at the youth hostels, though they all promised to keep a look out.

'He's young,' the man at the job centre told them. 'We'd notice him if he came looking for work. They're all on youth training nowadays. There aren't many sixteen-year-olds any more. Still,' he agreed cheerfully, 'I'll keep my eyes peeled.'

The tourist information centre provided a list of local campsites and they began to visit them, one by one. After all, he must stay somewhere and though he hadn't got a tent, he probably had enough money to buy a small one, perhaps second-hand. That suggested other leads to try: camping shops, small ads in shop windows. The list seemed endless.

It started to rain, that fine Lakeland rain that soaked right through to the bone, and they carried on in cagoules and wellingtons, often leaving the van to trudge down unmetalled lanes and muddy farm tracks. Seven campsites they tried; no Oliver. It was only a scratch at the surface.

In a village post office the old woman behind the counter thought she recognised the photograph, then changed her mind.

'We get so many in here, you understand,' she said apologetically over the top of her half-moon spectacles.

'There are always a few of them every summer,' the assistant in a camping shop commented lugubriously. 'You're not the first parents we've had in here. I don't know if they ever turn up, stupid young buggers.' He handed the photo back to Helen. 'I hope it's you that finds him and not the mountain rescue.'

As evening came on, the tourist pubs began to fill up with walkers back from a day on the fells. It was the last Saturday of half-term and there were plenty of young people among them, but those of Oliver's age were all with their parents in noisy family parties, munching crisps and sparring with their siblings. The boys in student groups were older, swilling down lager and acting the fool to impress the girls.

Already Helen had shown Oliver's picture countless times. It was getting easier to know what to say; her little spiel was ready. The students shook their heads, but promised to keep a look out. They all said that.

The light was slowly starting to fade, which in early June meant it was almost ten o'clock, and they had been on the road since eight that morning.

'Let's forget about a proper campsite tonight,' Dave said. 'We'll just dive down one of these side roads and park where we can. We can be gone first thing and nobody will be any the wiser.'

While he mixed instant mashed potato and fried sausages on the tiny gas ring, Helen dragged bedding from the cupboard. When the meal was finished they would remove the table top and the seats would be dismantled to make a sleeping place. It was no good suggesting separate beds in a tiny space like this; they would have to sleep alongside each other whether they wanted to or not.

'You know,' Dave said, as they cleared up later, 'we've been doing this all wrong. Those little cards with the stickers on will only end up in the bin. Why don't we photocopy his picture on to A4 paper, then write something eye-catching at the top – 'Have you seen this boy?' or something like that – with our name and phone number underneath. Like a wanted poster. Then we can divide the map up into a grid with squares of a certain size and distribute one poster per square. That way we'd know we'd got an even coverage. We can pin it up on noticeboards, in shop windows, even on telegraph poles. Surely nobody could object to that.'

Helen smiled in spite of herself. This was a glimpse of the Dave she used to love and admire: someone with brains, even in a crisis; someone who wasn't stuck in the rut of the department to the detriment of all else. If she was honest with herself she didn't really want to divorce him at all. What she wanted was for that Dave and that Helen who had once existed to come back again. How long ago had that been? She wasn't sure. If it was only a matter of sex, she could even forgive him, but she was afraid it wasn't. He probably had more in common with Ianthe than with her now. Somewhere along the way they seemed to have lost each other.

'Brilliant! It's a pity we didn't think of it at home. We could have made a more professional job of it. But I think there are some felt tips in the cupboard. I suppose they'll have to do.'

The van was equipped to deal with most emergencies; everything from paracetamol to string.

'So all we've got to do is find a place that does photocopying. I don't suppose there's much call for that sort of thing round here.'

'There's bound to be somewhere. Come on, we'd better get some sleep. We'll have to move out early before someone comes to complain about us stopping at the roadside.'

She opened the window for a snatch of fresh air. The rain had stopped and there was absolute silence except for the occasional bleating of a sheep. Streetlights were nonexistent and there wasn't even a moon, so that the blackness seemed to stretch for ever. All day they had been busy, with no time to think; now, suddenly, there was nothing else to do. They settled down, arranging the sleeping-bag around them, all the time avoiding each other's eyes, then turned away from each other and tried to get some rest.

But Helen slept fitfully again and at five, when the sun was already well up, she pulled on jeans and a short-sleeved jumper and slipped out of the van to stretch her legs.

The sky was clear and the world seemed bright and newly washed. Below her, across the field spread a little tarn, its black waters like a mirror. Around the edge was a reed bed sheltered by a stand of ancient beeches and beyond the fell rose up steeply, its slope covered with new green shoots of bracken. In the distance a mountain peak stood out starkly in the morning air.

For a long time Helen sat on the stile at the side of the road and watched, letting the peace of the place flood into her soul.

'Couldn't you sleep either?' she asked, feeling Dave at her side, still wearing his pyjamas.

'Not very well. It's not exactly the Ritz.'

'The Ritz couldn't top the view, though. I could stay here for ever and ever. It's like the cottage used to be, remember? You could wake up early in the morning and watch the sea and be absolutely alone. It was like the beginning of the world. Now all we get is transistor radios with heavy rock.'

She had said it dozens of times but he still hadn't taken the hint, so his reply surprised her.

'I know. The cottage has got out of hand recently. The students all think it's university property.'

'Yes, and treat it accordingly.'

'They don't value old things at that age. It's a shame we ever dreamt up the idea of students staying there in the first place. It just seemed a good idea at the time.'

'It shouldn't be all your responsibility. There should be a proper warden who's paid to look after the place.'

He turned the suggestion over in his mind. 'Good idea. Why didn't you ever mention it before?'

She grinned. 'I never thought of it before. It's this place. Sitting quietly does you the world of good.'

'You've got goose-pimples,' he commented. 'I'll put the kettle on, then we can get started.'

'I've been thinking something else too.'

'What's that?'

'What if we find Oliver and he refuses to come home?'

'He's got to come,' Dave said reasonably. 'He's too young to leave home. What's he going to do? Sponge off the state? They don't give kids his age unemployment benefit any more.'

'Dave, you mustn't do anything to pressure him. He won't take it. That's what made him run away in the first place.'

'Because I pressured him?'

'Yes, if you want to know the truth.' She was tired of pussyfooting around the point. 'You never let up with all your high-flown expectations of him. He's got the right to decide what he does with his own life.'

'Yes, but he doesn't know.'

'I don't suppose you've ever asked him.'

'Yes, I have. Of course I have.'

That was what exasperated her. He didn't even realise what he was doing.

'No you haven't. When did you last have a proper conversation with him? You've been working late at the department for months.'

'I've been working on the book. You have to publish these days, or you've no chance of getting on. You know that.'

'And then at Easter you were on the conference trail as usual. February was Kuala Lumpur touting for students. You never see the children.'

Now it was her turn to lay the blame. She had been trying for months to persuade him to speak to Oliver about girls and about sexual responsibility, also without success.

'So this is all my fault, is that what you're saying?'

'No, not exactly. I should have listened to him myself, way back when he was choosing his subjects for GCSE. We should have asked him what he wanted, not told him what he had to do. I know what I'm talking about, Dave. My father didn't want me to do art. He thought it was rubbish and I've never really forgiven him. Not even now, to this very day.'

'So let's get this straight. If we find him working as a waiter or something, we've got to let him get on with it?'

It would be hard, but as far as she was concerned that was just what they were going to have to do.

After breakfast Dave went searching through the cupboard for the felt tip pens. It was still early, but newsagents often had photocopying machines and they ought to be open by about seven.

'What's this?' he asked, bringing out an old exercise book covered in wrinkled brown paper. Helen glanced up.

'It's Father's diary. Something he wrote in the war.'

'You never mentioned it before.'

'I didn't even know it existed until a couple of weeks ago. Mother made me have it. I couldn't very well refuse.'

'What did your father do in the war?'

'Don't ask me. He was with Monty at one stage. In the desert I suppose. He used to rabbit on about it when I was little, but I never listened. Only one pint of water a day, and you had to use some of that to shave in. You know the sort of stuff.'

Dave laughed. 'When you said that you sounded just like Oliver.'

'Did I?'

'Don't you think you're a bit childish about your father, after all these years?'

She pounced on his words angrily.

'Childish? What do you mean?'

'I mean it's time you stopped being so hostile every time he's mentioned. There you go calling him "Father" all the time. Didn't you ever call him "Dad"?'

At fifteen or sixteen she had made a conscious decision always to call him Father. To distance him. Besides, 'Daddy' didn't suit him.

'Not since I was old enough to think about it.'

'You preach at me about how to handle Oliver when your own relationship with your father was the pits.'

'Yes, and that's exactly the reason why I want you to be more understanding.'

'Yet *you* never tried to understand *him*. I bet you're not even going to read this, are you?'

'I meant to. That's why I brought it. But I probably shan't.'

'You know, you're fairly level-headed most of the time. But when it comes down to your father, you just flip. You act as though you're still twelve years old.'

'I feel twelve years old.'

She turned away, pretending to be busy, trying to end the conversation, but Dave wouldn't leave it at that.

'What will you tell your mother when she asks if you've read it?'

'Lie, I suppose. Look, Dave, what does it matter? I didn't like my father, but it isn't something unique in the universe. There's no need to give me a hard time about it. We've got more important things on our minds.'

He opened the diary and flicked idly through the pages. 'Mind if I read it?'

'Go ahead, but it's just snippets. No proper narrative or a journal or anything. He wasn't an educated man.'

'The war was his education. Don't knock it. I think this sort of stuff's fascinating.'

He scanned the first page. 'It seems to start in January 1943. Listen. *Fourth year of war. Almost three years since I sailed. Two years, eleven months and ten days to be exact. I wonder if we'll be out of here this year?* Mustn't it have been hell, never knowing when you could get on with your life?'

Helen thought it sounded rather like them.

He went on: '*Terrible day, rain at night, sandstorm during day. Jerry digging himself in at Zemzem. No mail for a week. One razor blade between six of us.*'

'You see! It's just gossip.'

'He must have been in the battle of El Alamein. Wasn't that the year before? He was quite old in the Second World War, wasn't he? Don't I remember you saying he was born in 1900? I supposed he just missed the first lot.'

Helen had no idea and cared less. 'Dave, we're supposed to be looking for Oliver,' she said impatiently. 'Let's just get on with it, shall we?'

So they set about the business of the day. With the help of a photocopier and the felt pens they produced a reasonably fair 'wanted' poster with Oliver's picture in the middle, smiling out at them, and their address and telephone number below. It was his school photograph, but his tie was loose and his hair untidy. It was a good likeness.

The weather had taken a turn for the better and it was

pleasantly warm as they careered along narrow roads, seeking out pubs and church noticeboards, the lakes calm, the hills without the caps of mist they had been wearing yesterday, but the splendour of the countryside was lost on them. Their short truce of early morning seemed to be over and neither of them spoke very much except to give directions, each one taking turns to drive the van while the other fumbled with boxes of drawing pins.

All day Helen wrathfully remembered Dave's words. How dare he accuse her of not understanding? What was there to understand? Her father wasn't a sympathetic man, that was all there was to it. It was the reason she had tried so desperately always to sympathise with whatever her children did, always tried to be like a friend. And look where it had landed her. Pinning up posters in shop windows and in cafés, at campsites and in bus shelters. Two hundred of them in all. Well, she had warned Dave how it would be, but he had taken no notice.

In the evening they ate in a pub and turned in early, but not before Dave had regaled her with more extracts from the diary. *The ship has to zigzag to avoid torpedoes . . . Spent the night on Southampton station waiting for a train. Freezing cold, didn't get to London until midday.* He was only doing it to annoy her.

By the third day half-term was over and most of the tourists had metamorphosed into middle-aged couples who could come away when they pleased, all correctly dressed in Aran sweaters, red socks and knee breeches. They looked like the sort of people who would call the mountain rescue on their mobile phones. There was nobody left of Oliver's age and they were no nearer finding him now than they had been on Saturday.

'We ought to ring home,' Helen said. 'Let them know what's going on.'

'Nothing is going on.'

'No, but I don't want Mother to worry that we're lost too. I saw a telephone box in that last village. Did you notice how they still have the old red ones here? Everything for the tourists.'

She knew perfectly well he had seen it. He had been on the phone morning and evening ever since they came away, but when she tackled him he said he was ringing Professor Bannister.

'Heavens, twice a day?' she asked, but he had a retort all ready.

'Unlike you I don't give my job up at a moment's notice without a word to anyone. How can I? I've got five people to support, four of whom obviously don't even give a toss where the money comes from.'

She flinched, knowing he was right, and didn't mention it again.

She dialled their home number, but all she got was the answering machine. Then she tried Rivergreen House.

'Hello, Mother, it's me. There's no news, I'm afraid. I think we've just about exhausted the possibilities, but we've left posters everywhere. If he's in the vicinity, someone's bound to put two and two together.'

'Listen, dear, we've some news this end. Ollie isn't in the Lake District by the looks of it. Frank saw him on television last night. At least he was ninety-nine per cent sure it was him.'

Helen was perplexed. 'Saw him on television? How?'

'It was on the news. They're wanting to build a motorway up in Yorkshire and there are protests. They're going to cut down a wood or something. Oliver was there.'

'What, protesting?'

'He was sitting in a field with a placard in his hand.'

'Where was this exactly?'

'Just a minute. I've got it written down. Frank put it on a scrap of paper. I can never remember names. Hang on, dear, I'm just putting my glasses on.'

Helen wrote down the name her mother gave her.

'And you're absolutely sure it was Oliver?'

'It's the sort of thing he'd do, isn't it? And it's a lead. I expect it's worth a try.'

Anything, Helen felt, at this stage was worth a try.

13

They didn't even allow her to walk up to the ward. Two porters came to wheel her away, just as she was, in the gown that fitted like a parachute, starched and sparkling white. After some mumbled discussion with the sister they spirited her into a side ward, away from all the other pregnant women, and the curtains were drawn around her. Suddenly she had to be hidden away.

'I want to ring my husband,' she kept repeating.

'I'll do it for you,' the nurse said briskly as she set about the usual routine: pulse, blood pressure, temperature. 'Just give me his number.'

But Helen wouldn't have it.

'I want to do it myself,' she insisted and eventually a telephone on wheels was brought to her bedside. Only then did they leave her alone.

Her voice trembled as she spoke down the phone. 'They're keeping me in,' she said. 'You've got to come.'

He didn't understand at first.

'I've got a lecture in a few minutes.'

'It doesn't matter. I need you. You've got to come, as quick as you can.'

'Honestly, I don't know if I can get away . . .'

The tears were running down her cheeks.

'Dave, just get here! Please, just get here.'

The phone went down and she lay back numbly on the bed. What was going to happen now? How were they going to get rid of it, this dead lump inside her that wasn't a baby any more? They hadn't told her that.

In about three-quarters of an hour Dave put his face around the curtain.

'Here you are. I've searched this wretched hospital from top to bottom.'

'Have you spoken to anyone?'

'Not really. The doctor rang me just after you phoned, but he didn't explain what's happened.'

Helen groped for his hand. She had meant to be brave for his sake, but just the relief of seeing him made her break down in sobs.

A little later the consultant, aloof and matter of fact, came to talk to them, using the euphemisms of his profession. Even then they could scarcely take it in, but when he had gone a nurse began to connect Helen up to a drip.

'Why do you have to do that?' Dave demanded.

'It's to induce labour. Didn't Mr Sutherby explain?'

Neither of them asked how long it would take. The hospital had already imprisoned them, swallowing them up in its own huge mechanism. They seemed to have lost all freedom of choice and did exactly as they were told without question.

Dave tried to bring her coffee from the machine down the corridor but the nurse confiscated it with a frown.

'She can't have that. She mustn't eat or drink.'

'But it'll be hours, won't it?'

'Water, that's all she's allowed.'

He felt small and inadequate, sipping on his own coffee – warm dish water in a paper cup. They didn't know how to discuss it without grazing all those sensibilities that felt so raw. Helen remembered the beginning when she had hated this intruder in her body. Now she wanted it more than anything else in the world.

'It was my fault, I didn't love it enough,' she whispered, when the silence between them seemed suffocatingly long.

Over in the day room they could hear the music of a familiar children's programme on the television. Life was going on as normal but they weren't part of it any more.

Dave held her hand tightly. 'It wasn't that. There must have been something else. We'll find out . . . after it . . . afterwards.'

We were only kids ourselves, Helen thought when it was all

long over. We'd never had much to do with birth and death. Her father had died, but he was an old man. That was a natural progression; this was nature gone horribly awry.

When the contractions started in earnest later in the evening, the time came for her to be wheeled down to the labour ward and Dave was told to go and wait outside.

Helen hadn't expected this. She didn't know how to go through it on her own.

'No!' she shouted. 'You can't send him away. I want him here.'

It made the doctor look uneasy. This baby was only twenty-five weeks old and even a living child of that age was usually too small to be viable then. To him it wasn't a baby at all, merely a foetus. It was a difficult time for everyone and he didn't welcome too much emotion. A woman alone would grit her teeth and get on with it.

'I want to stay,' Dave affirmed, taking his cue from Helen's face.

So to avoid any fuss the doctor reluctantly agreed that he should stay until the end of the first stage of labour. They gave him a green gown and a little hat made from disposable fabric like a dishcloth, though afterwards he didn't remember much about it except Helen's face dripping wet and the way she yelled.

She never uttered more than a moan when she had the other three, but with that one she did. She screamed at the top of her voice. During the second stage, when it was time for her to start pushing, they insisted that he left, almost manhandling him out of the door, even though she swore loudly at them. She had never behaved so badly in public before or since. Afterwards she supposed that it was her own way of coping.

She never saw the baby. It was wrapped up and bundled away out of sight. Only later did they learn that it was a boy but nobody would have mentioned that if Helen hadn't insisted. What happened to it they didn't know. The hospital chaplain came and muttered something about everything being done properly and Helen was too upset to ask any more.

It was in the early hours of the morning when she was deposited in the post-natal ward. Dave hadn't come back so she supposed he had been sent home, but she daren't get out of bed to look for the phone. They would disapprove of patients making phone calls in the middle of the night and she already had a bad enough reputation with the nurses.

The sister brought her a cup of tea and instructed her to sleep but she couldn't. Even though she was exhausted she stayed wide awake all night, hearing every movement in the ward, seeing every light that went on and off. She felt violated, weighed down with guilt and failure. And all around her was the sound of other babies, crying somewhere in the darkness.

For weeks afterwards she was constantly in tears. The doctor offered tranquillisers but she refused them angrily. Pills couldn't mend what she was feeling, even though she didn't know what would. Everything she ever tried she seemed to fail at.

For days on end she didn't leave the house. Sometimes she would still be lying in bed when Dave came home from work, but then she would get up and watch television until the close-down late at night. Often she didn't even bother to get dressed but hung around all day in dressing-gown and slippers. And throughout it all Dave looked on helplessly, not knowing what to say or do to comfort her.

On her good days, which were few at first, she walked over to the university library where she used to work and poured over articles on obstetrics in the medical journals, trying to find out what she had done wrong. All else, including art, had lost its relevance.

They said it was bad to smoke so she threw away her cigarettes and never touched another; they emphasised the need for good food and exercise even before conception, so she bought multi-vitamins and drank fortified milk, gave up alcohol and ate fruit and liver. Nearly every day she went to the swimming baths. It was almost an obsession, but the only way to make her feel like a proper woman again was to produce another baby, and this time she was determined that it would be perfect.

Very gradually the crying stopped, but never completely. It never really stopped until she was pregnant again and until she couldn't read in bed without the baby kicking the book right off her stomach.

*   *   *

'Shall we go, or is it just another wild-goose chase?' Helen asked as they walked back towards the van.

'We've done all we can in this area,' Dave said with a non-committal look. 'What do you think? I suppose we've nothing to lose.'

They had drawn a blank, but the posters were in position and they might as well move on, though they had certainly never heard Oliver complaining about motorways before.

'It was probably a spur of the moment thing,' Helen suggested. 'And you soon make friends at a demo.'

Dave made a face. 'Well you should know. It must run in the family. Secretly I believe you're rather glad he's doing this.'

She studiously ignored the intended jibe, though he had guessed correctly. If young people didn't protest about the world, who would? When Nico railed against complacency he was absolutely right.

'If he is doing it. Have you ever heard of the place?'

'Look at the road map. Where a motorway's in the course of construction they put a dotted line. It shouldn't be too difficult to find.'

They spent a quarter of an hour examining maps; then it was back to the nearest village where Helen stocked up with food at the corner shop while Dave filled up with petrol. By the time evening was coming on they were on the move again, heading south-east with the hills behind them.

'We mustn't get our hopes up,' Dave cautioned. 'Frank might have been mistaken. He must only have been on the screen for a split second.'

But Helen couldn't help but get her hopes up. Everything she had touched recently seemed to have turned sour; she was due for a change of luck.

It was too late to drive the whole distance tonight, so they found a small campsite on high ground just off the main road; a farmer's field, set about with dry stone walls and open to the cold wind that blew across the Pennines. Even on a sunny June evening it felt like the middle of nowhere.

'I'll light the barbecue,' Dave offered, seeing her pull on a thick jumper. 'It'll keep us warm after we've eaten. What a life, eh?

On the move, living out of tins and packets. Makes you think, doesn't it?'

Don't say it, Dave. Don't say we don't know how lucky we are. A new place every night, not caring about what doesn't really matter; there were worse ways of living.

'It's probably doing him good, you know,' she said. 'Kids these days get everything handed to them on a plate. Time was when people had children to support them in their old age, but it's not like that any more. We seem to work to keep them, not the other way round, and it's not natural. They need to do something for themselves. Perhaps that's what Ollie's doing.'

When the charcoal was hot enough Dave put chicken pieces to cook alongside tomatoes and courgettes while Helen cut bread and butter. The sun was going down as they ate, casting a golden sheen over the sparse countryside and when Dave suggested turning in, Helen lingered in spite of the chill. She still dreaded the intimacy of the double sleeping-bag even after several nights of it. All they did was go through the motions, like strangers, and she was beginning to feel the strain. She didn't think they could keep it up much longer, trying to be polite to one another, with all those unspoken thoughts bubbling to the surface which had to be drowned again until they got home. It was like suffocating, like slowly turning into a zombie.

Next morning they didn't have much trouble finding the place they wanted. There were notices by the roadside for miles around: 'Ban the motorway extension', and 'Save our countryside' hand-painted crudely on boards, or nailed to fences. Someone had risked life and limb to spray 'No to the Mway' in red on nearly every bridge in the vicinity.

They stopped in the nearby village to ask directions from an old man out walking his dog.

'Oh, yes, you can't miss them,' he said. 'They're camped up in Brandon Woods. A pack of idlers most of them are. You know the sort; old buses, lots of litter, scrawny old dogs. New-age wottsits.'

'Travellers?' Helen supplied obligingly.

'Aye, that'll be right. They come down to collect their giros at the post office once a week. Life of Riley, that is.'

'Are there many of them?'

'About fifty, give or take, I should think.'

'And what about the locals? What do you think about it all?'

The man took off his cap and smoothed his hair down. They and their van looked too respectable for protesters, but perhaps they were journalists or from the radio or something.

'Some are for it, some aren't. They spend their money in the village. And those woods are a nice bit of countryside. Good luck to them, I say. Why should the government get all its own way? They never do aught for us.'

One moment he was cursing them as layabouts, the next he was praising them. Helen guessed that he didn't really know much about them on a personal level. He was just repeating what he'd heard, a little proud, a little ashamed.

They said goodbye after he had pointed out the best way to get to the camp. Dave parked the van opposite a pretty church, which seemed to have escaped the ravages of Victorian restoration. There was a row of stone cottages fronting the main street with a few fifties' council houses behind it and some up-market barn conversions on the other side of the road. Besides the post office and general store there was an ivy-clad pub with restaurant attached, a garage and a couple of pretentious second-hand shops selling what Helen liked to call 'junque'. All their trade would probably be lost when the road was built.

The two of them set off on foot up a farm track and over a stone bridge which crossed a stream. The next field was a yellow mass of buttercups. Helen stopped momentarily to run her hand over the moss on the old masonry of the bridge and look down into the sparkling water.

'Fancy running a motorway through all this!'

'They have enquiries into these things,' Dave replied, rather testily. 'If they've been through the proper procedures, then nobody has any business trying to stop it. As the old boy says, they're just a lot of idlers.'

Helen held her tongue. In the past Dave had had sharp words to say about motorway builders himself, but all these days on the road hadn't helped his temper. And perhaps their hopes of finding Oliver were going to be dashed again. In truth they were no further forward than they had been when they started out.

After a quarter of a mile they could see ahead of them a small encampment of tents and caravans on the edge of the wood. There was smoke rising from a fire and people moving about. The way to it lay across a field but as Helen put her hand on the gate, suddenly, from above, they heard a shout.

'Freeze!'

A teenage boy slid down a rope from an oak tree right into their path and stood facing them from the other side of the gate, legs apart.

'My God, they've been watching old Robin Hood movies!' Dave groaned, staring at the youth who was wearing military-style camouflage trousers, and, incongruously, a t-shirt with the message 'Fuck the Department of Transport' emblazoned across it. 'What the hell do you think you're doing?'

'We can't have just anybody up here. Where are you going?'

Helen scowled at Dave. She didn't want him messing it up before they'd even started.

'We're not doing any harm,' she said. 'We're looking for someone, that's all. We thought he might be here.'

'Why d'you think that?'

'Someone saw him on television. It was here, wasn't it? They were filming you a few days ago?'

'That's right.'

'His name's Oliver. Oliver Croft. Is he here with you?'

'Who wants to know?' the young man asked suspiciously.

'We're his parents,' Dave interrupted, exasperated at his attitude. He was used to having the upper hand with lads like this, the same age as his students. 'And as far as I know we've as much right to walk this way as you have.'

'Shut up, Dave. Let's just be civil, eh?'

Helen turned back to Robin Hood.

'Is he here or not?' she asked.

'He's old enough to do as he likes. He doesn't want you poking your noses into his life.'

Helen's heart turned over. It seemed that Frank had been right.

Dave took a step forward. 'So he is here?'

'Maybe.'

'Look,' Helen said, 'we don't mean you any harm. All we want to do is see Oliver. Won't you just take us to him? We don't want to make trouble.'

'Speak for yourself,' Dave said under his breath.

They eyed each other with suspicion. 'We don't let just anyone into the camp. For all we know you've come from the police or from the road people.'

'Of course we haven't,' Dave snapped, in no mood for games. 'We've told you, we're Oliver's parents.'

'If you won't take us to him,' Helen suggested, 'why don't you go and tell him that we're here. We just want a talk, that's all. We're not cross.'

She glanced sidelong at Dave's thunderous face.

'We're not cross,' she repeated. 'Can you tell him that? We'll wait here, OK?'

Her voice seemed to be getting louder and her words simpler, as though he hardly understood English, but eventually he seemed to get the message. He agreed to go and find Oliver so long as they didn't come inside the field.

'If you do,' he said, 'there's dogs up there. Fierce ones.'

Then he plodded off in the direction of the group of tents.

'Arrogant sod!' Dave exploded. 'What right has he to start telling us what to do?'

'None, probably, but why antagonise them? And remember, Dave, no shouting at Oliver. We agreed.'

'You agreed.' He leaned his back against the gate, his hands in the pockets of his trousers. 'All right, we agreed. I'll do my best, but I warn you, my best might not be good enough.'

Helen strained her eyes to catch a glimpse of the encampment.

'It's not such a mess as I thought it would be. I bet that man in the village has never been up here. There's no litter, just a few sheets of polythene wafting about.'

'Yeah, but what do these people live on? I'll bet the village shop has to lock up its doors and windows with this lot in residence.'

'Oliver's got quite a bit of money. He doesn't need to steal. Anyway, he wouldn't.'

'Who knows what he'd do when he's with people like Little John there? In fact I wouldn't be surprised if they made him give them all his money.'

'Oh, surely not!'

They waited patiently by the gate. Helen hadn't expected it to be like this. There was some yapping of dogs and some children shouting in the distance but on the whole it was a peaceful scene in the English countryside. Perhaps no developments were expected today, no police, no confrontation with the road builders. She was glad there were children, because that meant women, and they would be a counterbalance to the male aggression which was bound to spark as soon as there was trouble. Further up the track they appeared to have built a barricade out of boulders from the dry stone wall and some old farm machinery, and in the wood beyond she could just make out tree houses; shelters built high up in the branches. They had their strategy all ready.

'At least there are no police. I imagined some sort of guard on the place. I'm amazed they haven't been evicted before now.'

Eventually the youth sauntered back to them over the field.

'Doesn't want to see you,' he said laconically.

'What!'

'That's what he said. Don't blame me, chum. I'm only the messenger.'

'But he's got to see us,' Helen insisted.

'Can't see why.'

'Then we'll go and see him ourselves,' Dave said, but the gate was between them and the young man had no intention of letting them open it. Helen pulled on Dave's sleeve in a little gesture of restraint, fearing the worst. These past few days, he had been unnaturally calm about the situation, but now they knew Oliver was all right she could sense his fury mounting. All he wanted to do was get the affair over with, preferably by dragging Oliver back home with them kicking and screaming. But Helen didn't believe it would be as easy as that.

'Will you at least take him a note?' she pleaded, fumbling in her bag for something to write with. 'We won't disturb you, but at least take him a note. We're in our van down in the village. Tell him to come and see us there, if he doesn't want to meet us in the camp. We're not here to force him to come home. We just want to make sure he's all right. Will you tell him that?'

She scribbled something similar on the paper and pushed it into his hand.

'Please,' she begged again, and eventually he agreed.

'All right. But don't blame me if he doesn't want to see you.'

'Come on,' she said to Dave, after they had watched him retracing his steps towards the group of tents. 'Now it's just a case of waiting.'

'Waiting! It's ridiculous! Our own son won't even speak to us! How long are we going to have to hang around until he comes to his senses?'

'He'll come eventually. He doesn't want to talk to us in front of his pals, does he? He's only been here a few days and it'd be losing face. Anyway we've got this far. We don't want to blow it now.'

When they were back in the village, Dave made a beeline for the telephone box while Helen went to the shop to buy some bread and milk. The vicar was there chatting to the man behind the counter and she questioned them about the protesters. It appeared that there was quite a lot of local support, particularly from a mushroom farmer who was afraid the pollution from the motorway would ruin his crop. Some of the more militant of the Women's Institute had taken an interest too.

'England's green and pleasant land, you know,' another customer said. 'We must save some of it for our grandchildren.'

'The vicar says we can leave the van in the lane beside the church as long as we like,' she reported back to Dave. 'And use the loo in the church hall when it's open, but that's not all the time nowadays. He's scared of vandalism from the protesters. The church is locked up except for services. People seem to understand what they're trying to do up at the camp, but no one welcomes the influx of strangers and all the attendant publicity. What have you been doing?'

'Giving Reg a ring. I'm getting a mobile phone as soon as we get back. It's ridiculous combing the countryside for phone boxes. I really can't stay much longer, you know. They'll give me the sack, never mind the Chair.'

'He'll come. Tonight probably. They'll all be down in the Queen's Head for a drink, I dare say.'

'And what are we going to do until then?'

Helen emptied her string bag and opened up the tiny cupboards to put away the shopping.

'I'm having a strong cup of coffee and then I thought I'd do some sketching in the churchyard. What about you?'

He shrugged. He hadn't thought of bringing anything to do.

'I'll look at the paper and there's still the diary to finish. It'll pass the time, I suppose. What about lunch?'

'Go to the pub. I don't want anything. If Ollie comes I can see the van from the churchyard.'

It was a strange day and they passed it as best they could. The churchyard was on elevated ground and Helen, sitting on the grass sketching an elaborate gravestone topped by an angel with a three-foot wing-span, could see what was happening up and down the village street. Dave went to the pub at lunchtime and stayed nearly an hour. Then he slipped over to the phone box again to make a call. Ianthe? Reg, again? She was past caring. Or so she told herself.

Eventually, by mid-afternoon a breeze started to get up and the grass where she was sitting began to feel damp. Gathering up her equipment she went back to the van. Dave was sitting with his legs stretched out across the front seat reading.

'Who was Peggy?' he asked, after a mumbled greeting.

'Peggy? I don't know. Is that in the diary?'

'It's June 1944. He was at the D-Day landings, your dad. Nearly didn't make it off the beach. The two fellows on each side of him were killed.'

'Were they? I knew he was there, but he never went into details. What's that got to do with Peggy?'

'This is D-Day plus 7. Listen. *In among the bodies was a girl about 18. Only a kid. Nearly blubbed when I saw her, she was so like Peggy. We dug a trench in the garden to bury them.*'

It didn't sound anything like the father she remembered. 'Some girlfriend of his, perhaps.'

'It was grim what they went through, wasn't it? We never did the war at school so I only know what happened from old films, but it wasn't quite so glamorous in reality.'

'He always made out the war was the best time of his life.'

'Kidding himself, by the sounds of it.'

He could see she didn't want to talk about it and changed the subject.

'Well, no sign of him.' This time he meant Oliver.

'He'll come. I'll make extra food tonight just in case. Corned beef hash is one of his favourites.'

They were both sick of convenience food, but Dave said the bar meals at the Queen's Head weren't up to much either. Anyway they couldn't leave the van, just in case.

But Helen knew her son all right. Just about six, the time when they normally ate at home, the corned beef hash was almost ready and they heard footsteps outside in the lane.

'Mum!'

'Oliver, are you all right?'

Helen pulled back the door to look at him. She had only seen him a few days ago but even so she was sure he had grown. His shorts and t-shirt were grubby but otherwise he was looking tanned and rather healthy from his outdoor life. He made no objection to her giving him a kiss, but he didn't look at Dave.

'I'm fine. Anything to eat?'

'Nothing fancy, I'm afraid. Can you squeeze in?'

He climbed up into the van and was forced to come face to face with his father whom he decided to acknowledge.

'Hi, Dad.'

'Hello, Oliver. I must say you've led us a merry dance.'

He saw Helen shake her head and decided to play it her way. He turned his attention to the hash.

'Sit down,' he said. 'This is ready to dish up.'

Oliver readily accepted his ample plateful. 'How did you know where I was?' he asked.

'The wonders of modern science. Mr Vernon saw you on television.'

'What, Gran's Mr Vernon?'

'We thought you'd headed up to Cumbria at first. Dad realised some of the maps were missing. We've been up there looking for you.'

'Sherlock Holmes eat your heart out!'

While Dave sat in the driver's seat, Oliver and Helen sat at the tiny table and they all started to eat, Oliver very heartily. After the first few mouthfuls had assuaged his initial hunger, he said: 'I'm not coming home, if that's what you think. I've made up my mind about that.'

'No,' Helen agreed steadily, praying that Dave wouldn't interrupt, 'I didn't think you would. But we had to come to make sure you were all right. We've been worried sick. You could at least have left a note to say where you were going.'

'I didn't know where I was going,' he said, reasonably enough. 'I only heard about this from a lorry driver I got a lift from. I didn't think you'd make such a fuss.'

'Oliver, when your child leaves home with nowhere to go and hardly any money, it's natural to make a fuss,' Dave said, resorting to sarcasm.

'I didn't think you'd care. You were always hassling me.'

'Only because I wanted you to make something of yourself.'

'Yes, well, your idea of making something of myself is different from mine. I'm not into school, like Emma. I never have been.'

Helen remembered when he was little and the tantrums they had always had on the first day of term. Usually she had to drag him bodily to the car, push him out at the school gate and then wait to make sure he didn't do a runner. Little? He didn't grow out of that until he was at secondary school.

'You don't seem to realise what you've done,' Dave said. 'Going off in the middle of exams while nobody was at home. Unsettling the whole family. Emma and Jake have been out in the middle of the night searching for you. She summoned us back from France on the Internet, for heaven's sake. We've even had to involve the police. Mr Vernon went down town looking for you in night shelters.'

'He's a goer, isn't he?' Oliver said with a grin.

Dave ignored him. 'And to cap it all when I rang the school to tell them you'd disappeared, they told me that if you didn't turn up for the exams we'd have to pay some enormous sum to compensate them for the money they've wasted entering you.'

Oliver's grin turned into a sneer. 'Now we come down to it, don't we? Money's the only thing you ever think of, Dad.'

'Money comes in quite useful, believe it or not. You can't go through life sponging off the state, like your pals up at the camp.'

'I'm not sponging off anybody.'

'Not yet you're not. But remember, the government doesn't part with social security for people your age nowadays.'

'I know that. I can work. I've worked at the garage for ages, I've done a paper round, I cut people's lawns all last summer holidays. And they're not all layabouts up there. One of them's a solicitor, but he's given it up. He thinks this is more important.'

'At least he's got something to go back to. You haven't got anything. And that's another thing. Don't you realise that you're breaking the law?'

'No we're not. The farmer doesn't mind us using the field and the road company have had an injunction slapped on them. They're the ones who are breaking the law.'

'I very much doubt that.'

But as usual, Oliver had no compunction about contradicting him. 'You would doubt it, but you don't know anything about it, do you? You're jumping to conclusions like you always do.'

'And when this is over – as it very soon will be, because these protests never come to anything – what do you think you're going to do then? Go on to the next demo, and then the next?'

'Why not? It's something worth doing, and I'm not thinking of settling down with a wife and a mortgage yet, am I?'

As Helen had feared, they were just going round in circles.

'Oliver,' she intervened, 'your dad and I want you to come home. Don't go back to school if you don't want to, but at least think about doing some sort of a course next term. At the tech perhaps. You need it, love, you really do.'

'No, thanks. I'm not coming home for him to start on at me again. You shouldn't have come, Mum. I'm all right.'

'You're only sixteen!'

'So what?'

There was nothing so guaranteed to wind Dave up as a teenager's careless 'so what?' Helen glanced at him with a shudder. She knew the signs, but Oliver didn't care.

'They were fighting in the trenches in the First World War when they were sixteen and nobody complained.'

'Yes, that's Mr Vernon's attitude. Or something very like it. But it's a different world now, Ollie.'

Oliver was mopping round his plate with a piece of bread and wasn't really listening.

'Any more of this?' he asked hopefully.

'Have you been eating properly?' she asked. 'I suppose you're in a tent, not out in the open?'

'People bring us food a lot of the time. Sort of well-wishers. Since we were on the news people have heard about us. Someone even brought us some strawberries yesterday. Otherwise we all pay our whack and everybody takes turns at cooking. It's all right. I brought my own tent with me. I saw it advertised in the paper. It only cost £30. I bought it ages ago.'

'And you didn't tell us?'

'You'd have stopped me, wouldn't you?'

Inside Dave something snapped. He couldn't bear any more conciliatory talk like this.

'Yes, and now we're going to stop you again.'

Without any warning he turned the key in the ignition and the van shuddered into life, but Oliver, quick as a flash, realised what he was trying to do and sprang to his feet.

'Hey, you're not kidnapping me, if that's what you think.'

He swung back the heavy door of the van, ready to jump out.

'Dave!' Helen yelled. 'Don't be such a bloody idiot. Do you want to kill him?'

Dave put his foot on the accelerator and the van jolted down the lane, but as he was about to pull out on to the main road a milk tanker lorry came from nowhere and he had to slam on the brakes. Oliver leapt down, landing on his knees in the grass.

'Ollie, no! Come back,' Helen shouted, but Oliver didn't look round. He was running down the road like a rabbit, back towards the farm track that led to the encampment. In a frenzy, Dave was about to do a three-point turn and follow him but Helen shouted even louder.

'Stop it. Stop it! Don't you ever put your brain in gear before you do anything? Calm down, damn you! Now he'll never come back.'

Their eyes met. At that moment her husband's face had the same look as her own father's on the night he found out about Danny, and for the first time she realised how much defeat was there as well as anger.

14 ∫

For a time they both sat in absolute silence, Dave with his hands still on the steering wheel, Helen staring out of the open door of the van where Oliver had jumped. The engine was still running.

Helen was the first to move, pulling on her cardigan against the cooler evening air and slinging her bag over her shoulder. Dave pulled the key out of the ignition. He guessed where she was going.

'What's the point of following him?'

'I'm going to give it one more try. I've lost one child in my life, I'm damned if I'm going to part with this one. If I don't leave on good terms with him, I don't see how I can leave him at all.'

'Do you want me to come?'

She gave him a withering look. 'Don't you dare. You've done more harm than good. Now I'll handle it my way.'

He nodded resignedly and she started out up the village street with a feeling of desperation. Apart from that first terrible experience, being a mother was what she had succeeded at more than anything else in her life. If she failed now, what on earth was she fit for?

In the past it was always Emma they had feared for, never Oliver. Dave had been baffled by Emma: all those stages that young teenage girls go through, like the pop star posters on the wall, the giggling sleep-over parties, the brash makeup and the revealing clothes that horrify fathers who think in terms of latent sexuality, not innocent fashion. Helen had done all that so she had never been fazed by it, but she realised where it could lead. Oliver, on the other hand, had never seemed very complicated. He had never been as rude and argumentative as his sister, at least not until recently. But boys locked up their feelings, taking refuge in sullen silences, running away from reality. Perhaps that was more dangerous after all.

The lane was deserted now – even the lookout had abandoned his post – so she started walking purposefully across the field towards the camp, along the dried-out ruts the caravans had made. The camp-fire was alight and the sound of a voice accompanying a guitar drifted towards her, mingled with the smell of wood smoke. She envied them that, at least – the camaraderie of youth, so soon over in the compulsory stampede to pair off into couples.

Someone saw her approach and came out to meet her some twenty yards from the first of the little forest of tents. This time it was a different man, with a baby sleeping in his arms. His beard and neat shoulder-length hair reminded Helen of one of the disciples, but still she wondered if this image of a big peace-loving family living in harmony would hold out when the chips were down. Oliver knew nothing about these people or their motives.

'Oliver doesn't want to see you,' the man said at once, knowing who she was.

'We're going home tomorrow. I only want to say goodbye.'

'We can't all live in posh houses and pass exams, but that doesn't make us scum,' he replied, thinking he could read her mind.

'I never thought you were.'

'Haven't you ever felt that you ought to protest about something? Like it was the right thing to do?'

'As a matter of fact I have.'

'What, you've been on a demo?'

Helen nodded.

His face was expressionless. 'Good on you. Look, I'll see what I can do.'

She waited, standing awkwardly in the middle of the field and eventually she saw Oliver venturing out towards her. Meeting her half-way.

'Where's Dad?' he asked.

This bickering was all so pointless. Oliver was much more like Dave than either father or son cared to acknowledge. The work of the Earth Studies Centre, with its emphasis on conservation of the environment, had made an impression, even if it was only an invisible one. Most sixteen-year-olds didn't leave home to protest about a motorway.

'He's back at the van. He realises what he did was stupid. To be honest he's confused. This has all been so unexpected. He doesn't really understand what's going on.'

'And you do?'

'You'd be surprised. And I certainly know that running away never solved anything.'

But Oliver didn't see running away as negative; it was a positive affirmation of his independence. He stood his ground.

'Look, Mum, what do you want? I'm not coming home and that's final.'

'Yes I know. But what happens when the bulldozers come in? They will come, you know. It's big business and the law's on their side. You might get hurt if there's any sort of set-to, even arrested. It'll be no holds barred.'

'We're all prepared for that.'

'Just so long as you're going into it with your eyes open.'

He wasn't, not really. There would be violence and that would shock him. He still had a lot of growing up to do, but his mother couldn't protect him all his life. She opened her bag and took out a plastic card.

'This is a phonecard that can only be used for our home number. I got it for Emma for university but you can have it. I want you to call at least once a month to let us know where you are and that you're all right. If you're in trouble of any sort we'll come and bail you out.'

'Oh yeah?'

'We will, Oliver, I promise. We don't want you ending up jail. There's one more thing. Tomorrow morning I'll go to the post office in the village and deposit fifty pounds in a savings account in your name so that if you want to come home at any time you'll have the train fare. OK?'

He nodded. 'Thanks.'

'You can collect the savings book when you go down there. And you know where we are. Your bedroom's waiting for you any time you like.'

She glanced up at him. 'Give us a kiss?'

He put his arms around her and she hugged him tight, scared she was going to burst into tears. To stop herself she tried to make a joke of it, encircling his throat with her hands. 'I could strangle you, Oliver Croft . . .'

He grinned for the first time. 'I'll be all right.'

Of course he would. He was sixteen.

'I'll get going then. Take care.'

'You too.'

He put the phone card in his pocket. 'Thanks for this. Bye Mum.'

'Bye, love.'

She turned and picked her way back across the grass. It was the loveliest of June evenings, still and clear, the light muted. The trees in the lane were motionless, the undergrowth in dark shade, but the middle of the track where she was walking was bright and her own shadow stretched out before her, lengthening as the sun edged towards the horizon.

He would come home eventually; her head told her so, though her heart wasn't so sure. It was the same pain she had felt leaving the hospital with no baby, the same sadness she thought she had forgotten floating up from her unconscious mind, however much she told herself that this was different. Oliver she had brought up; Oliver was alive. And now it was time to let him go. She would have to be satisfied with that.

Dave wasn't in the van when she got back and she supposed he had gone to the pub – that last refuge of the man who doesn't want to talk. For a moment she thought of joining him – a couple of whiskies could do her the world of good – but the idea of the smoky bar and Dave's glum face put her off. Besides, people might be talking about the protesters and let slip something to start her worrying again. When she left she wanted to go with optimism.

So she lit the gas and boiled some milk to make hot chocolate. It was still light outside, but she drew the curtains and changed into her night clothes, sipping on the comforting hot drink. With nothing else to do she went to bed.

At about ten thirty she heard footsteps on the road and guessed it was Dave. The van wasn't hooked up to the electricity supply, but he took the torch from the dashboard, shining it down to see if she was asleep, and she made the mistake of opening her eyes.

'The pub's got a very tasty guest beer,' he remarked, then accidentally caught the kettle with his sleeve. 'Damn it, I wish we'd got a proper light in here.'

'How much have you been drinking?' she demanded accusingly.

'Only a pint.'

'And you've been there all this time?'

'Two halves. I made them spin out. What's wrong with that? It's hardly a crime.'

She was in no mood for bandying words.

'You know very well. Aren't you going to ask how I got on with Oliver?'

'How *did* you get on with Oliver?' he asked, perching on the front seat to try and get undressed in the tiny space that was available. He didn't think it was worth suggesting a night-cap for himself. 'Pass my pyjamas, would you?'

Helen leaned across to the cupboard and pulled them out.

'I made him promise to ring us every month and I'm going to give him fifty pounds so that he can get home if he ever wants to. I just hope he doesn't have it all stolen.'

Apart from the violence, that was what bothered her most.

'And that was it, was it? Talk about selfish!'

'He thinks it's us who are being selfish. And in the end we can't force him to do anything. At least he isn't in London living in a cardboard box.'

'We should be thankful for small mercies, should we? What are we going to tell people, I wonder? How did your son get on in his GCSEs? Well actually he didn't sit any of them. He's left home and he's living with a pack of new-age travellers. We'll be lucky if we ever see him again.'

'You don't bring up children just so they can get straight A's in their exam results,' Helen replied coldly.

'Yes, OK. Sorry.'

He realised he had gone too far and continued to get undressed in silence. Helen flattened herself into her side of the sleeping-bag to make enough room for him. At least tomorrow they would be at home and they wouldn't have to go through this farce of sleeping in the same bed any more. She turned over, burying her head in the pillow.

Dave climbed in beside her and lay on his back with his hands behind his head. That was usually a sign that he wanted to talk, so Helen waited, though she didn't expect what came next.

'Do you ever think about our first baby?' he asked, after a while. 'We called him Perkins, do you remember? He never even had a proper name.'

Helen's face flushed in the darkness. 'I don't think there's a day goes by when I don't think about him,' she said slowly.

'Isn't there? I thought you must have forgotten. You've never mentioned him for years – not until this evening.'

So he had noticed that. In the past she had been careful not to say anything. Over time she had come to think of it as her memory, not his.

'Neither have you. Even after it happened, you would never talk about him. In the end I gave up, I suppose.'

'You were so upset, I just wanted to distract you. For months it was like walking on egg-shells. I was so relieved when Emma was safely on the way and we could put it all behind us.'

'You can't put a thing like that behind you, Dave. It's there with you for the rest of your life. I never could enjoy being pregnant with any of the other three. Every day was just one more to tick off out of 280.'

'Is that how many there are?'

'In forty weeks, yes.'

'I didn't realise you did that.'

She still had a little weep on his birthday, too. It wasn't until she had got that January anniversary over that she could start to look forward to the rest of the year.

'Once the others were born I felt guilty, still feeling that there was one missing. But I thought you wanted to put it out of your mind.'

'I did. I felt pretty inadequate and left out, I suppose. Everyone was worried about you. Nobody much cared what I was thinking.'

She turned towards him and put her hand on his arm. 'Sorry. I didn't think it affected you so very much.'

'I came home from the hospital feeling dreadful. As if I'd been punched in the stomach, that's the only way to describe it.' He put his hand over hers and held it. 'I feel just the same now, actually.'

'What, about Oliver?'

'I know I've overdone the heavy father, but somehow in my mind he was going to be the replacement for little Perkins. I never felt like that with Emma because she was a girl, but Oliver was going to be everything he wasn't able to be. Whereas I suppose I should have just let him be himself. At least that's what I managed to figure out just now, sitting over my beer in the pub. I'm not very good at amateur psychology.'

'If only I'd known what I know now, I wouldn't have let it happen like that,' Helen said. 'I've read so much about it since. We ought to have held him, given him a name, had a funeral service. That's what happens these days. They even take photographs.'

'Of stillborn babies?' Dave asked, hardly believing it.

She nodded. 'And they never even let me see him. They just whipped him away like a piece of rubbish . . .'

The old memory, mixed with her parting from Oliver, was too much and she started to sob. Dave pulled her into his arms, hesitantly at first, wondering if she would object, but she didn't.

'Don't, Lenny,' he said, trying to comfort her. 'You'll set me off too. It was nature's way, the doctor said, and I've always tried to believe it. There must have been something wrong. Don't you remember how sick you were? You were never ill like that with any of the others. Besides what's the use of torturing ourselves about it after all this time?'

He paused, still cradling her, while she dried her tears on his pyjamas. 'Bloody awful parents we've turned out to be, haven't we?' he said at last.

'Emma's all right. Her heart's in the right place, whatever you say. And Tim's going to be fine.'

'Two out of four. Not a wonderful total.'

'Oliver's only young. He'll get over it. Most kids who run away come home sooner or later, that's what the police said.'

Helen lay back with her head on his shoulder, in her old place. 'Dave?'

'Mm?'

'Thanks for mentioning Perkins. We should have talked about it before – years ago – instead of clamming up.'

He kissed her gently on the cheek, then the mouth and she responded. She yearned for some physical contact and there was no one else who could ever console her in the same way. Dave, his body warm and beautifully familiar, was one person she didn't need to put up a front for. There had been times, after the children were born, when neither of them had been very interested in sex, but when they had eventually come together it had always been good. In spite of all the years, the spark was still there, as well as the tenderness. And tonight, after their conversation, it was as though something had been laid to rest at last.

In the morning Dave wasn't sure if they were supposed to be reconciled or not, so he didn't say much over breakfast, but whistled to himself as he checked under the bonnet.

'Home by midday if we get a move on,' he said genially. 'All set?'

'Not quite. I've got to call in at the post office to set up Oliver's account first, so we can't go until after nine.'

She tried to speak impassively. Perhaps he thought it had all been put right, but it was the past they had straightened out, not the present. She wasn't going to be bulldozed into changing her mind about anything. In any case the thought of going home and leaving Oliver here was too much for her to feel light-hearted.

In the end it was nearly ten before they set off with Helen behind the wheel. Driving was one skill she knew she was good at and sitting in the driving seat always boosted her confidence. She needed that at the moment. Now she came to think of it, this was the countryside she had learnt in. A wayside milestone, miraculously preserved in the age of motorways, told her that it was only thirteen miles to that little Dales town where she too had been a hippy, and for a rash moment she flirted with the idea of making a detour to see if Malone was still running the garage and if another Sally was still stretched out patiently in the back of his van amidst the potholing gear. But the prospect of witnessing Malone's Grecian features gone to seed made her keep to the main road. Her memory might have been playing tricks again and anyway there was real life to be faced up to once they were back home.

'I was talking to a fellow in the pub last night,' Dave said, breaking in on her reverie. 'About your dad.'

He didn't know if it was the right time to embark on this – he wasn't sure how she would take it – but a long journey with no distractions was ideal for a talk. There were no escape routes.

Helen blinked. 'Whatever for?'

'He was a bit of an authority on the war. Amateur enthusiast, you know the type. I was telling him about the diary. He said your father's regiment was the one that liberated Belsen.'

He glanced sideways, to gauge her reaction.

'Belsen? You meant the concentration camp?'

Of course there was no other Belsen he could mean. The word was inextricably linked to the flickering black-and-white images of wide suffering eyes and skeletal bodies that hardly seemed to be human beings any more. Of rows of shrunken corpses piled high. You wanted to turn away, to switch off, but you couldn't because you felt it was your duty to know and to remember. And afterwards it stayed uncomfortably long in the mind's eye. Could her father possibly have seen that?

'But it couldn't have been,' she objected. 'Surely he would have mentioned it – wouldn't he?'

'I don't know. How can you broach a subject like that? Particularly to your daughter.'

She knew from experience how much fathers always strived to preserve their daughters' innocence, doubly so in those days after the war. It was going to be a better world where such horrors couldn't happen. In any case he had never told her anything directly. All she knew about his war she had learned by a kind of osmosis; it was there in the background and she had taken it in almost unconsciously.

'But he loved the war – at least he always gave that impression. Dave, I just don't believe it. He couldn't have kept quiet about something like that – it was too horrible. What does the diary say?'

'Nothing, that's the puzzle. It's only sporadic anyway, after D-Day. I suppose there wasn't much time for writing. The last entry's on the 12th of April 1945. They'd heard reports that the Allies had crossed the Elbe and joined up with the Russians coming the other way, so the war was just about over. He seems to have had a lot of time for the Russians.'

'Yes, that's true,' Helen said, searching deep into her memory. 'He hated the Germans but he always said the Russian people were all right, even when Khrushchev was installing nuclear bases in Cuba.'

'Perhaps that memory of victory over the Germans was the one he wanted to keep, not the one of the camps,' Dave said, trying to find an explanation. 'Perhaps he blocked it out, pretended it didn't happen, by making the decision not even to write it in his diary. Not surprising really if he did. It would be enough to give you nightmares for the rest of your life.'

He had read somewhere how the suicide rate rose for men of that age when wartime anniversaries came around. Decades later they still hadn't come to terms with their experiences.

'And this man in the pub – he was absolutely sure it was the same regiment?'

'Oh, yes. He knew all about it. I'm pretty sure he was right.'

The diary was still on the dashboard where he had left it and Helen put out her hand to touch it. Young people of her generation, never having been called upon to fight themselves, had arrogantly despised war, while taking for granted their parents' sacrifices. And children could only know what their parents chose to tell them. There was plenty about her life that Emma and Oliver had never dreamt of. If he had remembered the good times and not the bad, then it was only human nature. He was no different from her.

'Memories do get distorted over time,' she admitted. 'I'll ask Mother. Surely he must have talked about it to her.'

'Why don't you read the diary? Judge him for yourself. I know there's not much substance in it, just little snapshots, but it shows he was human. I don't believe you've ever thought of him as a person in his own right.'

She frowned, so he took the hint and said no more. It put her on the defensive, these little digs he was always making about her relationship with her father. In her opinion Dave was in no position to judge, but nevertheless he had managed to arouse her curiosity for the first time.

They were joining the motorway sliproad, with those long white arrows pointing to the sky which read 'The South'.

'I might,' she said, mentally calculating the mileage home. That was as far as she was willing to go.

Emma and Tim were at school when they arrived and the house was empty. On the fridge Helen found a parcel addressed to her, postmarked Carlisle, though she didn't recognise the writing. It was a large padded envelope marked fragile and stuck down with layers of brown sticky tape.

'Is that all the post there is?' Dave enquired, dumping bags on the kitchen floor. Helen wondered if he was waiting to hear from France.

'Only the credit card bill and this. I think it must be from Duncan.'

Dave glanced at the clock, seemingly oblivious to what she had said, once he knew there was nothing for him.

'Quarter to two. I've got to ring in. The Senate met this morning. It should be all settled by now.'

So after all these months they were going to find out for sure. Helen wished she felt excited, but she didn't.

He dialled the number while she began to pull away the sticky tape, but the parcel was still impregnable and she had to fetch the scissors from the study to prise away the staples underneath. When she got back Dave was speaking to Reg.

'Yes, it's me, Dave. We're home. How did it go?'

From inside the bag she pulled a water colour which had been framed in plain wood. A card tucked in the corner read: 'Carole would have wanted you to have this. It brought back all her best memories. Hope it brings back yours. All the best, Duncan.'

'And did you explain it all? How did they take it?'

It was a painting of Kicker standing in front of a wire fence wearing a long Indian-type skirt with tassels round the hem and wellington boots. Behind her, on the fence, strands of coloured wool were blowing and beyond that loomed the shapes of men in uniform. Kicker had a plastic rose between her teeth.

Helen, forgetting to listen to what Dave was saying, fingered the glass. She had painted it from a sketch she had done at Greenham Common in the early eighties. Kicker had spent two of her summer holidays there, living for six weeks on end under a polythene sheet even in the driving rain, sitting with the other women round the tiny campfires to protest about the American nuclear missiles that were based there. With her wry sense of humour she used to stick plastic roses in the mud around the shelter for a garden.

Helen had only gone down for a couple of weekends when the sun was shining and when Dave had been able to look after the children – a poor sort of solidarity. But she knew it was no picnic. Every day there had been abuse from the soldiers who patrolled the perimeter fence, from the police, from the locals.

At other times, Kicker told her, they had been sprayed with mud and blood and excrement. They had been evicted and arrested, all their possessions had been taken away, but it hadn't broken their spirits. And sometimes they would weave coloured wool into the wire fence, or decorate it with flowers and balloons, though the soldiers always came to cut them off again. But they never did it properly, so that there were always little strands of colour on the fence, blowing in the breeze or hanging limply – little signals of determination.

It was one of the best paintings she had ever done.

'So they bought it? We can go ahead? . . . Richard George is the choice of course . . . I'd have to think again if it wasn't . . .'

Helen came back to her senses and looked up, startled. Richard George? Surely he hadn't been offered the Chair above Dave? But his face showed no trace of dismay. In fact he had a wide grin on his face.

'Well, that's it then,' he said, replacing the receiver.

'So what happened? Didn't you get it?'

'Oh yes,' he replied nonchalantly. 'But I turned it down.'

Helen was astounded. 'You did *what*?'

'I turned it down,' he repeated.

'I don't believe it! Do you mean to say we've had to go through all these months of uncertainty for *nothing*?'

'It's not what I want, it never has been. I just don't get a buzz out of the department any more.'

The first part was a lie for a start. She knew how much he'd always wanted to be Professor Croft.

'And now something better's in the wind.'

She couldn't comprehend it. 'Surely not the French job?'

Though she supposed in the circumstances perhaps it wouldn't be so bad.

'No, but the French job gave me the idea. We've got a pollution monitoring station at the Earth Studies Centre already, and if the EU are financing something in the Med why shouldn't they do the same for us to monitor pollution in the Channel? Reg has been thinking about a joint venture for enlarging the place for ages, possibly in collaboration with other universities. If we could get an EU grant it could go ahead. Among other things we would run courses on pollution control for people in the oil and petrochemical industries. I would be in charge and be made up to professor. There would be at least one other permanent post and probably other research fellowships.'

Helen noted that she hadn't been wrong about the title.

'Doesn't it take years to get money out of the EU?' she asked, rather bewildered. He had caught her off guard and for a moment she was jubilant. At least he was still capable of being unpredictable.

'That's the trouble, but they seemed very interested when I went down there. You remember that oil spillage off Cornwall a couple of years ago? When they had me on nationwide TV news?'

Of course she remembered. The children had videoed it and people had stopped her in the street to talk about it. Later on he had visited one of the North Sea oil platforms on a fact-finding mission. His fifteen minutes of fame.

'They knew about that – the part the Centre played in monitoring the slick and the aftermath of it all. We reported it in one of the journals. Well, there's a conference on sea pollution coming up in Amsterdam in August – one of those big international jamborees with worldwide coverage – and I'm going to give a paper. If there's money to be handed out, I'll be on the spot. And Reg has arranged everything this end. There'll have to be more discussions, but the Senate were keen. They like the name of their university bandied about.'

'And will there be – money, I mean?'

'Probably. There's a lot of hot air spouted at these dos, protocols drawn up that nobody really wants to sign. Our little scheme's peanuts compared to all the grandiose plans that never come to anything. I should think we're in with a very good chance.'

There seemed to be an awful lot of ifs involved. No wonder he had been on the phone morning, noon and night. But if it all came to nothing, where would he be then?

'Dave,' she exclaimed, 'why didn't you tell me all this?'

'You weren't even here when it started,' he said, rather evasively. 'Besides, we've had other things on our minds.'

'We've been together almost constantly for days! Didn't you even trust me enough to tell me something as important as this?'

So suddenly the tension was back, and they were arguing again. The armistice hadn't lasted long.

'That's a bit rich, after what you did! Running off to France with that slimeball, telling me a pack of lies!'

She supposed he was referring to Nico.

'You really don't know why I went to France—' she began, but he didn't let her finish.

'I've got a pretty good idea. In fact I told Reg I'd resign if Jones was appointed.'

'That would have been rather like cutting off your nose to spite your face, wouldn't it? Anyway you can't talk. At least I suppose that if this scheme comes off, some of your research students will be in for a job. Ianthe first on the list, no doubt.'

His eyes hardened. 'She'll certainly be qualified for it when her thesis is finished. Ianthe's a very bright girl.'

'And I suppose she'll be helping you write this paper of yours?'

'She may well be giving me some feedback.'

Helen gave a hollow laugh. 'Feedback! That's a Freudian slip if ever I heard one!'

He was obviously determined not to listen to her any more. 'Term's over in a couple of weeks,' he continued, picking up the bags again to take upstairs. 'Then I was intending to go down to the cottage to work on my paper for the conference. At least that was the original plan. But perhaps in the circumstances it would be better if I went straight away. I can take all the marking with me. Then I'll be out of your hair.'

She bit her lip. He was happy and she was spoiling it, but as usual he was doing just as he liked and she wasn't. She had always been jealous of the way his ambitions were fulfilled and she still was. On top of that, the issue of Ianthe clouded all their arguments.

'I suppose if this all happens, it'll mean living down there permanently?'

'Yes, it will. I take it you don't want to do that?'

Helen looked down at the painting that was still in her hand. Kicker had crammed a lot into her life, always doing what she thought was right. Even dying so young, it could never be called a wasted life. That was what comforted Helen now.

This year there would be no Christmas card, but the question wouldn't go away. There must be no drifting back; she had to finish what she'd started.

'No,' she replied decisively. 'I don't.'

15

During the evening, after he had spent the rest of the day at work, Dave packed up most of his clothes, a box of books and all his computer equipment in the van and quit the house. They didn't exchange a word but Helen imagined he was going to the cottage, though she suspected that he would probably spend a few days on the campus first to do some catching up. Or perhaps he had wangled an invitation to Ianthe's.

'Aren't we going to the cottage in the holidays?' Tim kept asking.

Helen hadn't plucked up courage to tell the children yet, so she was forced to explain that they couldn't go because Daddy was doing some important work for a conference and didn't want to be disturbed. Tim was puzzled.

'So aren't we going on holiday this year?'

'Probably not, but don't worry, we'll find plenty for you to do at home.'

'Carl says I can go on holiday to his caravan if I like. He says it's great. Right next to the beach and everything.'

'Well, I don't see why you shouldn't, if his mum and dad will have you.'

It seemed like a splendid idea, if it meant Tim having some sort of a holiday. Emma had already arranged to go to the Greek islands with a couple of girlfriends in July and after that she was going to be working in a pub preparing bar meals until October, trying to get together some money for university.

Meanwhile, Helen had plenty to occupy herself, straightening out her life. She finished off the drawings for Mireille, and later, when she had sent them off, she began extricating herself from all her various commitments. She cancelled her aerobics night and resigned from the university wives group and from the swimming gala committee. One of the neighbours asked if they needed to borrow some chairs for their barbecue as usual, and she said with relish that there wasn't going to be any barbecue. When the exchange students' agency rang, she told them that she wasn't intending to entertain foreign students ever again.

Then she began writing round to publishers with copies of the illustrations she had drawn for Mireille's book on the off-chance that they would offer her some work. It was a meagre portfolio and probably an overcrowded market, for all she knew, but she didn't want Dave to keep her if she could help it, now that they were living apart. She had never had any illusions about being another David Hockney, but this was art of a sort and it might be a living. Most of all it was what she wanted.

There were still the credit card bills to settle up after her trip to France and that would eat up quite a bit of the money she had stolen from Nico. Apart from that she only had her last month's salary from school and the money Mireille had paid her. Fortunately, while Emma was in the Greek islands, there would only be her and Tim, and the main bills would be debited from their joint account as usual.

Dave had taken the computer and the printer away with him, so she had to dust down her portable typewriter, buy a new ribbon for it and write the letters on that. It didn't look as professional as she would have liked, but then beggars couldn't be choosers. It was sobering to realise how much her standard of living was going to drop without Dave.

When the letters were in the post, the days were spent adding to her portfolio. She started as soon as Tim went off to school, switching on the answering machine and setting herself little targets, so that she wouldn't be tempted to drink coffee or go out to do some gardening. She had to be professional about this. It was no good hoping to be taken seriously if she didn't put the effort in.

June was a beautiful month with long sunny days and warm evenings and life took on a leisurely pattern. When Tim came home they ate outside and played together until his bedtime.

Emma was out most nights as soon as the exams were over, celebrating the end of her school career, so by about nine o'clock Helen was alone.

It was then that she forced herself to think about her father's diary. Her mother had asked her to read it and after what Dave had told her she felt she ought to, so she put it on her bedside table deliberately, so that it would be in her mind.

It was right that she at least tried to understand, but she had to steel herself just to open it. Touching what he had touched made her remember a small girl who had hungered for his approval and never seemed to win it; and so she had been defiant and pretended not to care. Even after a lifetime that still hurt, and it added to all her other hurts. Often she sat in bed with the tears pouring down her cheeks. She could only bring herself to start reading because of her curiousity about Peggy, and at first it took a large gin as well.

'Why wasn't Father in the First World War?' she asked her mother, as they sat drinking tea at Rivergreen House. 'Surely he was old enough?'

It was difficult to get Marion alone these days, but Mr Vernon had slipped upstairs for a few minutes to minister to his tomato plants.

'Yes, he was, but he worked with his father on the farm, so I suppose it might have been a reserved occupation. I think he wanted to go but he was needed at home. That's why he was so keen to join up in 1939, even though he was getting on by then.'

Helen didn't even know he'd lived on a farm.

'I thought his parents owned a grocery shop.'

'I think they did, after the war. I never knew them, you know. His mother died at the end of the thirties and I don't think his father lived much longer.'

'Didn't he have a brother?'

'Bert? He was killed in the blitz.'

'In London? What was he doing there?'

But Marion had no idea. It had all happened long before she had come upon the scene, and by the time they were married he had no family left.

'It was always strange having no in-laws,' she remembered. 'I've never even been to that part of the country. I once suggested that we went back to have a look at the village he was born in, but he wasn't interested.'

'Have you ever heard of Peggy?' Helen ventured at last, unsure of her ground, in case her mother didn't want to be reminded of another woman who was obviously so important to him.

Peggy had featured in the diary several times. She seemed to have haunted him. *All the other chaps have family to send letters to. I wouldn't have had to write this diary if I could have written to Peggy.* And when he had a slight injury and had his finger in plaster: . . . *when she was little, Peg wanted to be a nurse. Anyone would have been cured just looking at her* . . . He seemed to see her everywhere, in every woman he came across, though there weren't many: just occasional glimpses of the girls of north Africa (. . . *the women here have splendid eyes* . . .) to the poor starving women of war-torn Europe (. . . *it's terrible what they'll do for food and mostly it isn't voluntary either, just like my Peg* . . .). As though she had been forced against her will.

But her mother knew at once. 'Peggy? She was his sister. Only about a year younger, I think. She died a long time ago, just after the First War. I know he was very fond of her.'

'What happened to her?'

Marion shook her head, baffled by these sudden questions after all the years of indifference.

'I don't know. I don't think he ever said, but people died young then, didn't they? It wasn't unusual. There's a photograph of her somewhere. I'll see if I can find it for you, if I haven't thrown it out. I might have done. It seems silly to keep photos of people we don't even know.'

Helen had just one more question that she had saved until last.

'Did you know Father was in one of the regiments that liberated Belsen?'

Marion gave a little sigh, almost like a whimper, as though it hurt her. 'Yes, I did know that. It's one reason why I didn't want to read the diary. He only told me once, a couple of days before we got engaged. It was as if he wanted to get it off his chest – so that there wouldn't be any secrets. But he never mentioned it again in all the years we were married.'

To his generation a wife's role was not that of a confidante and he had been brought up to keep his feelings under control. Considering displays of emotion to be unmanly, he had kept quiet or, as Dave had suggested, perhaps he had blocked it out or somehow withdrawn from it emotionally.

'It isn't in the diary. Dave found out about it by accident.'

'He was a secretive sort of man, your father,' Marion pondered. 'Looking back, I think it probably affected him quite deeply. After all he was forty-five by then. An eighteen-year-old might have been able to put it behind him. And he must have seen some harrowing things. But it wasn't done to make a song and dance. He used to have nightmares – scared me to death sometimes – but they didn't have counsellors to help you through a crisis like they do now.'

'Perhaps that's what made him so cynical.'

'He wasn't an easy man to live with,' Marion agreed, still reluctant to criticise. She had never heard of repression. 'I got used to him, but I don't think you ever did.'

She tried to smile, hearing the sound of Mr Vernon tapping at the door. Was it an accident that she had found the very opposite of James Butcher in this benign, affable man? 'Still, what's the point of dwelling on it now? Life goes on, doesn't it?'

'Mum, it's Dad on the phone!' Emma yelled from the kitchen. 'Want a word?'

Tim had answered it first and they had had a good long conversation. It was a relief to Helen that Dave hadn't dumped his children, even when he had moved out. He had rung religiously, twice a week, ever since he left.

'No,' she called back. 'He must have spent a packet already. He's been on over half an hour.'

She heard them saying their goodbyes. Her father was wishing her good luck in Greece.

'What's the matter?' Emma demanded, coming into the sitting room. 'He's been gone nearly a month, and I don't think you've spoken to him once in all that time. Mum, you two haven't split up or anything, have you?'

Emma was never one to mince words when she found it necessary and at least it was an opportunity to discuss it.

'To be honest, I don't know,' Helen confessed. 'It may turn out to be the best solution. He's got his paper to prepare down there. If things work out he'll be in Devon all the time and I'm damned if I'm going to live at the cottage permanently with students milling around the house all day. I want to develop a career of my own, not be dragged round on your father's coat-tails all my life. Besides,' she added, in mitigation, 'Tim has school here.'

'He's only at juniors. He could easily move.'

'That's not the point!'

Emma's face fell. 'So what are you saying? That you're getting divorced?'

'We haven't got round to discussing it properly yet, but it's on the cards.'

'But you can't! What about the house? Will you have to sell it?'

What she really meant, Helen thought with annoyance, is where am I going to spend my holidays?

'I've really no idea. That may not be necessary. The mortgage is nearly paid off and the cottage already belongs to Dad. But I may need the money.'

'But how did it happen? I always thought you were so happy! When other people's parents split, I always swore that you were different. Don't you love him any more?'

She had missed him, there was no doubt about that; they had been friends for a long time and friendship was just as precious as love, perhaps more so. But it wasn't as simple as that. She looked up into her daughter's face.

'I'm sorry, Emma, but these things happen. We've had a good run for our money by today's standards. You're grown up now and it won't really affect you very much.'

'No, but it will Tim!' she exclaimed. 'Mum, I think it stinks!'

And much to Helen's astonishment she burst into tears.

'It's not just me, you know,' Helen started, then gave up. Why did Emma automatically jump to the conclusion that it was her fault? And Tim would probably think the same. He would most likely love to go and live by the seaside. She was the one they would pressurise and put the blame on, not Dave. But perhaps they would understand if they went down there and caught him with his new girlfriend. All of them were going to have to get used to that.

Marion had managed to unearth the photo of Peggy and she made a special journey on the bus to bring it.

'Frank's son has come to visit, so I thought I'd leave them together for a while,' she said. 'I don't think we ought to live in each other's pockets when we're not even married yet. But I've brought the wedding invitations to show you. I want you to tell me if you think they're too fancy. Over the top, as Frank calls it.'

Inevitably they spent some time chatting about the wedding which had been booked for the very end of August. At their time of life it didn't seem worth waiting any longer. But eventually Marion started rooting in her handbag for the photo.

'Here it is. What do you think?'

It was the head-and-shoulders studio portrait of a young girl, of perhaps seventeen or eighteen years old. Her shoulder-length hair was parted down the middle and she was wearing a dress with a crocheted collar and a cheap bead necklace. On the back someone had written 'Peggy, 9th September 1919'. The date was surprisingly exact; perhaps it was her birthday.

'See the resemblance?' her mother asked.

Helen was at a loss. 'What resemblance?'

'Doesn't it strike you? It was the first thing I noticed. I suppose I haven't looked at the photo for so long, perhaps not since you were a child, so I didn't see it before.'

'See what?'

Her mother was exasperated. 'Her hair's a bit darker, but otherwise she's the very image of you.'

After some anxious waiting, Helen got a phone call asking her to go down to London and to bring some of her other work with her. They specified cartoon drawings, the jokey sort that illustrate various kinds of modern school books, and it meant a frantic few days of sitting up in the study until midnight, hoping for inspiration. Working for money wasn't at all like doing it for pleasure; it meant getting it right all the time.

After the publishers she ate a late lunch in a sandwich bar. If she was quick there would be time to go to St Catherine's House before catching the train back home, so she took the tube to Holborn and walked down Kingsway towards the Strand. The office of the Registrar General was a vast place and she hesitated at the entrance, unsure of what to do.

'Births, marriages or deaths?' the attendant enquired, in answer to her plea for help.

'Deaths.'

'This century is it?'

'Just after the First World War, I think. I'm not sure of the date.'

He pointed her in the direction of the banks of shelves, ceiling high, stacked with enormous books.

'Deaths are there, but without the date you'll have to do a bit of searching. If it's a woman don't forget it's the maiden name you want.'

'Oh, yes, I've got the name. It was Peggy Butcher.'

'Peggy? That'd be Margaret. Usually is. What about the place?'

Helen nodded. 'I know that. She was my aunt.'

She surprised herself saying that. She had never thought of Peggy as her aunt before.

'And now the family's dead and you've got curious? That's what usually happens. It's always best to ask when they're alive, before it's too late. And before you have to pay money,' he added with a chuckle.

It was rather a scrum – the middle of the afternoon in the summer holidays and the tourist season to boot. As well as British people on day trips to London, the place was swamped with Canadians, Australians, Americans and others from equally far-flung places, whose ancestors had left England at any time during the past hundred and fifty years. It was hot and the registers were heavy and unwieldy. She almost decided not to bother, but in the end she was glad she did, for it was quite a thrill to find the name she wanted, written in a copperplate hand, together with the date and the place of death.

But this was only the index, not the actual death certificate. That would be forwarded to her later through the post after she had filled in a form and paid her money.

'It's taking a long time at the moment,' she was told as she gave in her cheque. 'Mid-summer rush.'

So it wasn't until quite a while later that the certificate arrived: 'a certified copy of an entry of death pursuant to the Births and Deaths Registration Acts, 1836 to 1874', it said. There they were, the barest of facts. On 30 May 1920, Margaret Ellen Butcher, female, 18 years, had died at School Cottage, Main Road. Under 'Rank or profession' it read 'Spinster, housekeeper, daughter of George Butcher, farmer'. The cause of death was puerperal eclampsia and the informant was Maurice Rogers, her employer, 'in attendance'.

Nobody died of puerperal eclampsia any more, though Helen had heard of it. It was a disease of late pregnancy heralded by a sudden rise in blood pressure, accompanied by convulsions, and usually, in those days, death. The certificate told her most of the sad story; a young girl, pregnant while away from home in service, though at least her employer seemed to have had enough decency not to throw her out. Poor Peggy! Nowadays, there would have been no danger. Her blood pressure would have been constantly monitored all the way through pregnancy and both she and the child would have lived. All those years ago Peggy was probably too ashamed even to go to a doctor, whereas now she would have had that baby and been proud to show it off.

'I thought I'd drive over to Shropshire on Sunday,' she told Emma. Tim had gone away with his friend's parents to their caravan on the Norfolk coast for ten days or so and it seemed an ideal opportunity.

'What on earth for?'

'It's where your grandfather came from. I thought I'd ask Gran to come with me. She's never been there.'

'Will she want to?' Emma asked doubtfully. 'When she's getting married again?'

'What's that got to do with it? I thought she'd enjoy the day out, that's all. I'm just afraid that it's a little bit too far for the Mini, but there isn't time to get it serviced.'

'Why don't you get Jake to check it over for you?'

'Do you think he'd mind?'

'He's very cheap,' Emma grinned. 'Only charges about enough for a night out.'

Helen totted it up. Two cinema tickets with pizzas afterwards and perhaps a couple of Cokes. Jake was very conscientious about not drinking and driving. It was cheap at the price.

'By the way,' Emma said, 'Dad rang while you were out shopping.'

Full marks, Dave, for remembering the date of his daughter's A level results. He could never be disappointed in Emma on that score. She had done just as well as the school had predicted.

'He's in Amsterdam, giving a paper,' she continued, getting no response.

'Yes, how did it go?'

'OK, I think. He's coming home for Gran's wedding. He asked me to take his best suit to the cleaners. I said why didn't he ask you, and he said he didn't think you'd take kindly to going on his errands.'

'He obviously knows me pretty well,' Helen commented wryly, but Emma didn't think it was very funny.

'He also wanted to know if you'd had any visitors.'

'What kind of visitors?'

'I got the impression he meant men.'

'So he's checking up on me now, is he? What a nerve! What did you say?'

'I told him I didn't think you had. You've worn nothing but a stained shirt and those old blue trousers since he went away, and the bedroom's full of canvasses you've hauled down from the loft.'

Emma's astute observation certainly precluded any lapses from the straight and narrow. That was why she'd shoved that nude picture of Dave right underneath the bed.

'Seriously, Mum, when are you going to decide what's going to happen between you two?'

'At the wedding, I expect. If we get a chance.'

It was already less than a fortnight away and during the summer Helen had grown calmer. That first phase of denial, then anger, was starting to pass. She was trying to get on with her life and found she was coping very well. Seeing Dave would only open up old wounds and she wished he was staying away.

'Promise?'

'I'll do my best. But there are two of us, Emma. Don't take it all out on me.'

It was a long straggling village, nearly a mile from one end to the other, with a couple of pubs and not much else. The church was only open for services once a month and the Wesleyan chapel had been turned into an up-market workshop making hand-crafted furniture.

'School Cottage? Yes, it's just up the road next to the Old Schoolhouse there, by the bus shelter,' a woman told them, when they stopped to ask the way. She was selling produce on a stall at the roadside – a sort of mini farm shop.

'Not that we've more than two buses a week these days. Do you want to buy a raffle ticket? The money's going to fight the new development on Butcher's Corner. Executive homes they call them, but nobody round here can afford anything like that.'

'Butcher's Corner, did you say? What's that?'

'It used to be a couple of derelict houses. Shops, in the days when we had shops. They've knocked them down now, of course.'

Marion pulled out her purse and bought a strip of raffle tickets. 'If I win a prize,' she said, 'there's no need to send it on.'

'Do you think it could be where Father's family used to live?' Helen wondered, as they strolled on up the road.

'It could be, I suppose. Names stick. At that time villages had good big grocery shops that sold everything from a pound of butter to a fishing rod. These days they'll all go into Shrewsbury to the supermarket. Now where did she say School Cottage was? That's another name that hasn't changed.'

It turned out to be a typical pre-First World War villa with the date 1900 carved above the door and a bay window on either side. The grubby rendering was in need of a coat of paint. In front there was a pocket-handkerchief-sized garden with a wooden gate and under one of the bays sat a couple of gnomes fishing in a rather slimy pool.

The house next door had been converted many years ago, but it was still recognisable as the old Victorian schoolhouse, built like so many others in the late nineteenth century with a tower where the school bell used to hang. Between the two dwellings was the high wall of what had once been the school yard and let into it was a gate, obviously long unused, for the hinges were rusty and it was almost completely covered by Virginia creeper.

Helen was trying to straighten out the story in her mind. School Cottage must have been the house of the schoolmaster in the days when a schoolmaster was still somebody in the village; next in hierarchy after the vicar and the doctor. Just after the Great War her father's sister Peggy, just eighteen years of age, had been in service here. As the schoolmaster had allowed her to stay until well on in her pregnancy, he must have been unusually benevolent. Or else he was the father.

Was he married? Surely not, otherwise his wife would certainly have thrown her out. Did she go to him willingly, or did he force himself upon her? From her father's diary it was obvious that he believed her to have been cruelly wronged – the angry reaction of a doting brother – but what did he really know about her feelings? Remembering her father, she suspected precious little.

Was the schoolmaster middle-aged, or perhaps a young man not much older than Peggy herself? If he was single, what had prevented them from being married? In any event it had never come to that. She had died – James Butcher's little sister – and he had never forgotten it.

And when, forty-five years later, in May, the anniversary of her death, there had been another teacher and another eighteen-year-old girl who looked just like the first, it had all come back to him. It was history constantly repeating itself.

So like Peggy and yet not Peggy. He had thought the worst the first time, just as he had the second time, and there was no reason to be surprised about it, because that was the sort of man he was – so rigid that he could only ever confide his feelings to a diary. It wasn't just the war he had suppressed.

Helen had wept over that diary for nights on end, like a period of mourning for a father she never wept for when he died. He was capable of a little love, she believed that now, but perhaps after Peggy he hadn't dared to love anyone else so much, not even his own daughter. And when his war had wrung dry any emotions he had left he'd pretended it had all been wonderful. A trace of that, if nothing else, Helen recognised in herself.

Instead of dislike she felt pity for him now – grumpy and cold as he was – now that she knew it wasn't her fault. For with that knowledge had come a tremendous liberation from the guilt she had always carried with her. In that way suddenly she was free of him. It had taken her a long time to grow up.

'Your father probably went to this school,' Marion was saying, peering over the wall to where the old yard was now a smart patio and a shrubbery. 'Doesn't it make a lovely house?'

Helen hung back, still trying to peer into the windows of School Cottage, but the venetian blinds were firmly shut. And nobody could know for certain, so long afterwards, what had happened here.

'Mother, do you mind if we go and have a look in the churchyard? We could see if there are any Butchers buried in it. Perhaps Peggy herself.'

But all the old stones had been flattened or laid against the church wall. The modern ones, in an adjoining plot, only seemed to date from about 1935. There were no other clues. And all they found at Butcher's Corner was a building site with a couple of skips full of rubble. The old garden behind was a forest of fluffy rose-bay willow herb going to seed, waiting for the bulldozer.

'That's why your father wouldn't come back,' Marion remarked. 'His family was gone and things are never quite the same way you remember them. Mustn't it have been quiet here in the twenties? No cars, and probably hardly any buses either. No wonder people used to get het up about girls getting pregnant. They hadn't much else to think about.'

Had it caused ill-feeling – a village feud – one group closing ranks around the schoolmaster, another siding with the girl? Had her family refused to have her home? At this distance it was an impossible question.

They had a pub lunch and sat in the garden at the rear under a striped umbrella eating tagliatelle in a cream sauce with Parmesan cheese and mangetout, washed down with a glass of white wine. Among the other diners was a group of German students on a walking holiday. Times had changed and not always for the worse.

'Do you think the family rejected her?' Helen asked, still musing on the fate of Peggy. She and Peggy had a lot in common.

'People were stricter. You were expected to behave in a certain way and you had to be courageous to step out of line. I certainly wouldn't have done it.'

With a nod, Marion accepted a slice of strawberry flan which the waitress cut for her.

'Not that we knew much, even in my day. I got married to have a nice kitchen all to myself, not for hanky-panky.'

It still amused Helen to hear her mother talk about sex. But with such a large age gap between her parents she had never imagined passion.

'What about children?'

'Of course, but not until well after the wedding. Nine months to a year later, that was the accepted interval. Longer than that and people started asking questions. It wasn't thought right to – well – use anything.'

'So you did it all correctly?' Helen laughed.

'Oh yes. Your father wasn't quite so keen on a baby at first – I suppose it was his age – but he was fond of you in his own way.'

'It never felt that way from where I was.'

'He didn't know how to show it, that's all. People didn't cuddle children then. The books told you it would spoil them.'

Helen had come to realise that this was part of what Mireille called her unfinished business. When the past spilled out of the cupboard it was better to sort it out, not just push it all back in again.

'I always blamed him, you know,' Helen said. 'About art college. About breaking up with Danny.'

'I know that. But after the sacrifices we made to send you to grammar school he thought art was a waste of time. Anyway, it turned out he wasn't well, and you've got to make allowances.'

Marion was a patient woman who had always tried to make the best of what life handed to her. It would never have occurred to her to bear a grudge and she didn't understand those who did.

'Then when I was all set to go the second time, I got pregnant myself.'

'Yes, it was bad luck. But you don't blame Dave for that, so it's no good blaming your father either. You haven't done so badly for yourself, all in all.'

The thought had never struck her before. Blame Dave? For that pact of theirs that was never honoured? She would never have done that.

Or would she? Subconsciously, perhaps she'd blamed him all along. The idea was still niggling her when they left the pub and she didn't say much all the way home.

16

Helen first saw Ianthe in the supermarket car park getting out of a smart little white hatchback, almost new, which made the Mini look even more like a candidate for the scrap yard. Watching the bush of red hair, she hung back, unwilling for them to be thrown together, but she was surprised. From what he had said, she thought Ianthe might have been down at the cottage with Dave all this time.

Inevitably their paths crossed, by the delicatessen counter, where Ianthe was buying cottage cheese and de luxe bean salad. She was in beige shorts and a little black top and her pale complexion was flawless, except for half a dozen freckles on her nose.

By chance their eyes met – or perhaps it wasn't chance at all. Ianthe, looking suspiciously flustered, tried to brazen it out.

'Oh, hello. Mrs Croft, isn't it?'

'Yes, that's right. Ianthe? I'm afraid I don't know your second name.'

'No, I don't suppose you do. How's David?'

'I might ask you the same question. You've probably seen him more recently than I have.'

Ianthe was startled. 'I haven't set eyes on him for more than two months.'

'That does surprise me. I thought he was your tutor.'

It was Helen's turn in the second queue and she asked for six ounces of honey-roast ham. The assistant was serving Ianthe with a tub of black olives.

'He is, but now that I'm writing up I don't need to see him any more.'

She had finished her transactions and attempted to escape, but Helen pressed on regardless.

'I always got the impression that yours was rather more than a professional relationship.'

'You must be joking. You've got nothing to fear on that score, thank you very much.'

'Are you kidding me? What about that weekend you spent down at the cottage together at spring bank holiday? And a quarter of salami. That one at the back.'

The assistant, slicing the salami, was listening intently with a twinkle in her eye and Ianthe began to blush. With her red hair it didn't suit her.

'I don't think this is the time or the place, do you?'

'Let's go over there then,' Helen suggested, unwilling to let her get away so easily. 'In the corner by the lemonade. I'd like to get this straightened out once and for all.'

Obediently Ianthe wheeled her trolley to where Helen indicated.

'Now,' Helen demanded, when no one else seemed to be within earshot. 'Are you or are you not having an affair with my husband?'

'Did he tell you I was?'

'I don't need telling. I've know him long enough. And he didn't deny it when I brought the subject up.'

'That was probably because he was too embarrassed to tell you what really happened.'

This was all very intriguing.

'Well if he won't tell me, why don't you?' she invited.

'I don't really think it's up to me.'

'Come on Ianthe, he might be embarrassed, but I'm not. You went down to the cottage at spring bank holiday with the intention of sleeping with my husband, right?'

'You make it sound so cold-blooded. It wasn't like that at all.'

'Hot-blooded is more the adjective that springs to mind.'

'Look,' she attempted awkwardly, 'we were attracted to each other. He's a nice guy.'

'Yes,' Helen agreed. 'I know he is.'

'He was helping me with my thesis. We were . . . thrown together.'

'Cliché, cliché! I suppose he told you that his wife didn't understand him?'

'No, as a matter of fact he never said anything of the kind. I don't think he ever mentioned you, to be honest.'

Helen didn't know whether this was a good sign or a bad.

'And was the weekend at the cottage the only time you'd been alone together?'

'Yes, of course. At least, we were alone in his office sometimes . . .'

Getting through the preliminaries no doubt, Helen thought.

'Well, let's skip that for now. You got down to the cottage, it was a cool evening and you made up the fire together. He chopped some more logs, while you went out for something to eat. Is that the story so far?'

Ianthe was amazed. 'Yes, actually it is.'

'And then you sat in front of the fire to eat in the twilight? It's so much more romantic if you don't put the lights on.'

'How did you . . .?'

Helen was beginning to enjoy herself.

'I told you, I've known him for a very long time. And then I suppose he suggested you have an early night. Lots to do in the morning?'

She nodded. 'That's the gist of it, though I was the one who had to make the first move. We were pretty pally by then, if you know what I mean, but that's as far as it got. By the time we arrived at the bedroom, he'd got cold feet. Said he wasn't going to sleep with a student. I wasn't much older than his daughter, and anyway he could get the sack if anyone found out. Sexual harassment of students. They've got a code of practice about that sort of thing.'

One of the assistants was filling up the shelves with cartons of fruit juice and they were forced to move along towards the tea and coffee.

'You mean nothing happened between you after all?'

'That's right. He wrote me a letter later, apologising, and I wrote back telling him to get lost. I wasn't particularly pleased at the time. In fact I threw a vase at him. Sorry, I expect it was one of yours.'

Helen began to laugh. If there was anything Dave couldn't abide it was hysterics.

'Not that brown and yellow one with the dried flowers in it? On the shelf above the bed?'

'Yes, that's the one. He was quite cut up about it actually. He tried to gather the pieces up and stick them back together with superglue. Was it an antique or an heirloom or something?'

'No, not exactly. It was the last remaining vase by Munro and Butcher, *circa* 1970. The first flowers Dave ever bought me I put in that vase. He must have a better memory than I thought.'

Ianthe didn't know what she was talking about and was itching to get away.

'Listen, I can't stop any longer. I'm going to an interview this afternoon.'

'Oh, aren't you going to be applying for one of these new jobs at the Earth Studies Centre?'

'Heavens, no.' Ianthe gave Helen a look that cast aspersions on her sanity. 'I'm giving up geography altogether after my degree. I've applied to the Inland Revenue.'

Dave drove up from the cottage early on the morning of the ceremony, arriving just after ten, and Helen came down to meet him in her wedding outfit of skirt and jacket in silver grey: suitably demure for the daughter of the bride. Dave had let himself in with his own key and was rummaging through the post she had left on the hall table.

'Hello,' he said, looking up. 'You look nice. Any chance of a cup of tea?'

He acted as though he had never been away and Helen clenched her fists. Why was it that sometimes she loved him and sometimes she hated him, frequently both at the same time?

'Help yourself, the kettle's just boiled. I've got to round up Tim. It's time he was getting washed.'

'What time do we have to be there?'

'Twelve at the church. There's a wedding car calling for us here at eleven thirty and we're picking up Mother on the way.'

Dave made for the kitchen and at that moment Tim rushed in through the back door from the garden.

'Daddy! I saw the van! Mummy said you wouldn't be here until the last minute.'

Helen winced at his truthfulness and Dave picked him up bodily, swinging him up into the air.

'It is the last minute. Time you were in your best clothes.'

Tim made a face and surveyed his father's jeans which had a patch of oil on them.

'You too.'

'Yes, but I'm having a cup of tea first. Then I'll race you.'

'You go up and start washing your hands and face, Tim,' Helen said. 'I'll be up in a minute for inspection. So will Daddy. Go on, off you go.'

Dave groped in the cupboard for mugs. 'Where's Emma?'

'Gone to Jake's to make sure he's wearing something decent. We're meeting them there.'

'So Jake's coming too, is he? How did he do in his exams?'

'Not so hot as Emma, but he's scraped in. They'll only be twenty miles apart next year.'

'Her exam results were wonderful, weren't they? Two A's and a B. Has she confirmed everything with the university yet?'

Helen told him that it was all fixed up. While they were talking about the children they were managing to stay civil, so she continued.

'Oh by the way, I've had another phone call from Oliver.'

'Still sitting in that blessed field?'

'No, the bulldozers moved in about a month ago. Just after he talked to me last time, in fact. Didn't you see it on the news? There was quite a battle with the police at the end. Oliver was arrested for obstruction, but they released him almost straightaway because of his age.'

Dave opened the biscuit tin and took out two or three ginger nuts which he proceeded to dunk in his tea. Helen didn't understand why she had ever been worried. Having seen the calorie-free contents of Ianthe's shopping trolley, she was confident that they were incompatible on more than one count.

'So they've moved on somewhere else have they? Where's the next battle for freedom taking place?'

'No, the group has split up apparently. Some of them have gone south, to one of those open-air rock festivals. Oliver's got a job on a market garden near York. He's been there for the last two weeks.'

'Christ, the nearest Oliver's ever come to gardening is destroying the delphiniums with his football.'

'Amazing, isn't it? And guess what? He's thinking of taking an agricultural course.'

'What, after two weeks?'

'There's no need to scoff. At least he's actually beginning to think things through.'

Dave glanced at the clock and sipped on the hot tea, trying to drink it as quickly as he could.

'Emma tells me you've been doing some more artistic work,' he continued, straining to make conversation.

'Yes, I've got a commission from a publisher to illustrate an ELT book.'

'ELT?'

'English language teaching. The book's for French kids learning English. I think they only picked me because I'd understand the French in it, but at least I've got a foot in the door. If I can do it properly they may offer me more work. And I've sold all my cats to a greetings card manufacturer. They've got a grotty little factory round the back of the football stadium. It wasn't a fortune, and they're going to put some awful words with them, but it was enough to pay for this outfit and some extras for the wedding.'

There was a shout from Tim that he had finished washing, and Helen yelled back that she was coming.

In a different tone of voice Dave said: 'Emma also told me you'd had someone to value the house. I half expected to see a "For Sale" board up as I came round the corner.'

Helen scowled, annoyed she had let it slip. She had thought Emma safe at work, but she'd come home early complaining of a headache and found a young man in a dark blue suit with a tape measure and a clipboard in the front garden.

'You'll be living at the cottage if your job comes through,' she pointed out, 'and I need the money. I'm intending to buy a little flat with some of my half and spend what's left on a part-time art course. If I can keep myself with some work I shan't need to ask you for anything at all.'

'So you're really going to go for it, this art career?'

'It's what I've always wanted and it's never too late,' she replied, thinking of her mother. 'The estate agent says we'd probably sell the house reasonably easily, with it being so near the university and reasonable schools. It adds a few thousand to the price.'

Dave looked grim. 'You might have told me all this, instead of letting me find out through Emma. I didn't know you were going to go this far.'

'I thought I made it pretty plain before. And it was rather sneaky of you getting Emma to spy on me. Particularly asking if I'd had any visitors. What I do is none of your damned business.'

'What do you expect?' He put on the same sulky face that Oliver often wore. 'I don't want Conrad Jones waltzing round my house, now that I'm not in it very often.'

Helen was aware that she had gone rather far in trying to imply that she and Nico were still interested in each other and it was time he was undeceived. He had behaved treacherously over Ianthe but she was in no position to hold it against him. However much it still hurt, on that score they were probably at least quits. She gave a cynical laugh.

'I don't think Nico's ever done much waltzing, and if he has done, it wasn't here. If he did roll up it would probably be with a couple of policemen. The last time I saw him I stole his wallet and threw his credit cards in the river.'

Dave nearly choked on his tea. 'What did you do that for?'

'He owed me from years back. It's a long story. Look, you ought to be getting changed, or we'll make Mother late.'

When he had gone upstairs, she remembered that she hadn't asked him about his job and she grinned. It would serve him right.

'Couldn't we just have gone in the Mini?' Dave asked, seeing the shiny white limousine resplendent with satin ribbons pulling up outside.

Helen was adjusting her hat in the hall mirror while Tim fidgeted, feeling silly in new blue trousers and a shirt and tie. Dave was wrestling with a safety pin and a white carnation.

'You don't think I'd let my mother go to her wedding in that clapped-out old wreck?' Helen said. 'If I have to give her away, I want to do it properly.'

Dave reflected that she was in that strange mood again, half joking, half deadly serious.

'You're giving her away, are you? Isn't that a man's job?'

Perhaps he had expected to be asked himself, as the senior male member of her family, but Frank had refreshingly modern attitudes towards such traditions.

'This is the end of the twentieth century, Dave, and I'm her only relative except for a couple of nieces and nephews. Come on, Tim, don't keep touching your hair. I know it feels funny but it looks just right.'

With an ill grace Tim did as he was told, but as they were climbing into the back of the car, he said suddenly: 'We couldn't have gone in the Mini, anyway. Mummy's sold it.'

Dave's eyebrows went up. 'Whatever for?'

'Jake says the big end's gone,' Tim informed him. 'We've got a new one now. It's Japanese.'

Dave looked over his head to Helen. 'Is that right?'

She had decided that if she wanted something doing, the best policy was to do it herself. It was what she should have done long ago.

'I didn't think you'd mind. I only got a couple of hundred for it, but Sandy at the garage got me a good deal on this new one. It's four years old but it's in good condition. I sold the Florio to pay for it.'

'That awful black-and-white landscape? I thought it was your favourite.'

'It was, but the car's more practical. And do you know, the price has rocketed. It only cost me two hundred and thirty-five pounds fifteen years ago and now it's worth a few thousand.

'Do you think any of my stuff will ever do that?' she continued, with a sly glance. 'Perhaps I ought to put that old vase at the cottage into an auction. Who knows what it's worth now?'

She paused, relishing the look of horror in Dave's eyes. 'It's just a shame that it had to get smashed.'

'Who said it was smashed?'

'Ianthe told me. In fact she told me everything.' She indicated Tim with a nod of the head. 'Ssh. Big ears. We'll talk about it later.'

'Are you staying here for a bit, Daddy?' Tim wanted to know.

'Or can we come down to the cottage? Haven't you finished your speech yet?'

Dave began to explain to him about the conference, and the paper he had given.

'There were a lot of important people there. I'm waiting to hear whether they're going to give me some money, but there doesn't seem to be much doubt about it now. When they do I'll be living at the cottage all the time.'

'What about us?' Tim asked, perplexed.

'You'd better ask your mother about that.'

'I suppose if all those students are there, there won't be room,' Tim said, rather gloomily, remembering how the students always seemed to commandeer his toys. They were particularly fond of his construction kits and the girls insisted on reading him stories, even though he could read perfectly well for himself. Sometimes they even wanted him to sit on their knees.

'No, the students won't be there, if I have to live there all the time. We'll have to buy a whole new house for student accommodation and for offices. It's going to be quite different.'

'That's good, isn't it Mummy?' Tim demanded.

And Helen was forced to agree that it sounded very good indeed.

The wedding took place in the church just down the road from Rivergreen House. At first, Marion said they would walk and why waste all that money on a proper wedding car, but Helen discovered that nobody had been able to afford a car for her first wedding either, so this time she deserved the VIP treatment.

Her outfit didn't bear much resemblance to that first one either. Instead of a plain costume in sensible grey, she was in apple green and pale pink and wore a broad smile, instead of that nervous little grin Helen always remembered from her childhood. Her mother's face was like a black-and-white photograph suddenly blossoming into colour. Being twenty-one or two might sound agreeable but being properly grown up was better.

Frank certainly wasn't wearing white gloves either and he insisted on holding his bride's hand firmly throughout the whole proceedings.

'Doesn't this bring back happy memories?' Emma whispered

to her mother gushingly, as they came out of the church door into the sunshine to pose for photographs afterwards, but Helen knew what she was up to.

'Not particularly,' she replied. 'When I was married, the weather was atrocious and I felt sick so your father went out without me and came back drunk as a skunk.'

'On your wedding night?' asked Emma, genuinely shocked.

'I'm afraid even in our day wedding nights didn't have quite the connotations they once did.'

Emma teetered on unaccustomed high heels. 'What, you mean you'd already . . .? God, the way Dad goes on at me, I thought you couldn't possibly . . .'

'Shush, Emma. Look at the camera. You're spoiling the shot.'

Her daughter's image of her as a virgin bride was what made Helen smile for the photographer, together with Jake's surreptitious nudge and murmured comment that Frank and Marion were most likely well past anything like that.

'I hate buffets,' Dave grumbled, balancing a glass of champagne in one hand and an asparagus roll in the other, when they happened to bump into each other at the reception, after making the rounds of Frank's relations and a couple of cousins Helen hadn't seen since her father's funeral. There were only about twenty-five guests, including Frank's brother who was in a wheelchair, but who nevertheless had a habit of abstractedly patting Helen's bottom whenever she talked to him.

'I think it's all very tastefully done. Frank's son's in the catering trade, so he arranged it all and Mother did the cake herself. I don't think she's done a wedding cake since ours.'

Dave was on at least his second glass of champagne, and there had been a couple of aperitifs before that. A little alcohol always loosened his tongue.

'Pretty much a fiasco, our wedding, wasn't it?' he murmured.

'Perhaps that's where we went wrong.'

'What, you mean we ought never to have got married in the first place?'

He knit his brow, and one of those silly curls of his bobbed on his forehead. Helen had always been very fond of those curls.

'No,' she said. 'As a matter of fact I don't mean that. Though perhaps we ought to have stopped to think about the next twenty-odd years instead of just the next nine months. Dave, why didn't you tell me about Ianthe?'

'What exactly ought I to have told you?'

'That you and she didn't have an affair after all would have been nice to begin with. On the other hand, I believe the biblical stance is that the thought is as much a sin as the deed.'

'Do we have to go through all this?' Dave asked, looking uneasy, in spite of the champagne. 'I expect she told you what happened. I know how women enjoy pulling men to pieces behind their backs.'

'She's very beautiful, but I don't really think she's your type, do you?'

Dave gave an expressive grimace. 'Probably not. She has some very irritating habits. Even if you put sugar in your tea she makes an issue of it. And she's terribly aggressive. The most innocent remark and she jumps down your throat. She chucked your vase straight at my head.'

'Did you duck?' Helen enquired, suppressing a snigger. Sex was all very well, but it was the little pleasures and irritations of life that made or marred a relationship. And Dave hadn't bargained on the assertiveness of the modern young female. He certainly couldn't cope with a woman doing the seducing.

'I don't know why you think it's so funny.'

'I don't really. I felt the same about Nico. Everything he did annoyed me intensely. I think we've probably both made fools of ourselves.'

Dave drained the champagne from his glass. 'So what are we quarrelling about, for heaven's sake? Can't we just go back to where we were? Lenny, I don't want to get divorced, just over this. We've been together too long. I know I've been stupid, but I really missed you on my own down there. And you don't know how cut up I was thinking about you with Conrad Jones.'

'The trouble is, it's not a question of going back. That means wiping it all out. It's a question of going forward, and I'm still not sure about that.'

Her mother was trying to attract her attention and she left him in order to supervise the cutting of the cake. Afterwards, Frank's son, Jeremy, was to drive the happy couple to the airport, to fly off on honeymoon to Jersey.

'Do you know, Gran's never been in a plane before,' Tim reported to his father in surprise. 'Jake's going to write "Just Married" on the car with Emma's hair mousse, when Jeremy's not looking.'

At last they were away. Frank's relations were all going back to Rivergreen House to make sure the presents were under lock and key. Emma and Jake volunteered to take Helen's London cousins to see the castle and the local sights before they all came back for an obligatory supper, though Dave wasn't very keen on this last idea.

'Do they have to?' he grumbled. 'They won't go home till midnight and they'll probably drink all we've got in the house. I fancied watching a video with an Indian takeaway tonight.'

But his complaints were to no avail. One of the duties of marriage was putting up with each other's relations.

So eventually there were only the three of them left: Helen, Dave and Tim, amidst the debris of the party. The waitresses were all eager to come and clear away and Helen started packing the top tier of the wedding cake into a box to take home.

'We'll have what's left of those quiches too,' she said. 'It's a shame to let them go to waste.'

'Shall I call a taxi?' Dave asked.

'Why bother? The bus goes from just outside. There'll probably be one along in a minute.'

Dave had never heard anything like it. He hadn't been on a bus for years.

'Are you on an economy drive or something? Taking all the food home and catching buses! You haven't drawn a thing out of the joint account since June except for Tim's new school clothes.'

'I wanted to find out if I could do it, that's all, particularly after your lecture about telephone number salaries. Besides I'll have to learn to manage on my own.'

So they went home among the Saturday afternoon shoppers coming back from town and were forced to sit squashed together on the side seat of the bus nursing the big cake box. It wasn't long before Tim embarked on his own campaign for wearing her down.

'Mummy, why can't we go and live at the cottage too?'

'It would mean leaving all your friends behind. You wouldn't like that.'

'I wouldn't mind, except for Carl. I could go to school in the village. It's only up the road. I wouldn't need to get up till really late.'

'Yes, but when you're eleven it would mean going ten miles on the bus.'

'Do you think they play football at that school?'

He would have gone to the ends of the earth if it meant getting away from football.

'I'm afraid they probably do.'

'I could put up with that,' he said stoically, 'if we could get a boat. That'd be great, wouldn't it?'

'It sounds rather dangerous to me.'

'I think it sounds rather exciting,' Dave cut in. 'You could do your art course down there, couldn't you? It's less than half an hour's drive into town. I owe it to you anyway. Remember that agreement we once had? We could afford a full-time course if we sold the house here, though I'd probably need a flat for when I'm visiting the university. Emma could live there in the vacations, so she'd still be near her friends.'

'What about the students?'

'I told you, they're moving out. And it won't matter where you live if you're going to be freelance. We could use the student dormitory ourselves, downstairs as a study for me, upstairs as a studio for you. There's heaps of light, or perhaps we could have an extra window let into the roof.'

'And the village is nothing like it used to be.'

'It's heaving in the school holidays,' he admitted, 'but at the end of June it was idyllic.'

'Please, Mummy,' Tim begged.

'It's going forward, isn't it?' Dave asked, looking at her hard.

The bus lurched round a roundabout and Helen was nearly catapulted into the lap of the man opposite, but Dave grabbed her by the waist and pulled her back. Sitting with their arms around the cake box and almost around each other it was difficult to make a dispassionate argument.

'We can't discuss it properly on a bus,' was the best she could muster, amazed at how easy it was to reach a point where the future included both of them. That's what had come of standing up for herself and getting all the resentment out of her system.

'I've got some time off and there's a few days before Tim starts school. Why don't we go up and visit Oliver and find out what his plans are?' Dave offered. 'Meanwhile we can all be thinking about it.'

'He wanted me to send up some more of his clothes and his ghetto blaster,' she remembered. 'And I'd like to see how he's getting on. But not in the van. Let's be civilised and stay in a hotel for a change. With en suite bathroom and no washing up.'

Dave, who had always begrudged the price of a hotel when they had the van, didn't murmur.

'Sounds great. What do you think, Tim?'

A few days later they were standing together on the medieval walls of York and a fierce wind was blowing out of a leaden sky. It was September and only a couple of days before the start of term, but this time, thankfully, she wouldn't be going back. Tim and Oliver were chasing each other up and down the stone steps. Even Emma had come with them, but she had gone exploring the narrow little shopping streets alone.

Playing at happy families again was proving more successful than Helen had ever dared to hope. She and Dave still had plenty to talk over, including commitment, including forgiveness. They would have to establish new ground rules and she was realistic enough to know that it would take time to build each other's trust again, but three months apart seemed to have done them good. Perhaps every couple ought to try it after a certain number of years.

She leaned against the battlements, looking away over the city towards the massive grey towers of the Minster, which were covered in scaffolding for renovation work.

'Did you ever hear what happened to Nico?' she asked casually. Dave had never asked her any more about her flight to France and she was too discreet to offer a full confession, but she was curious to know what had become of him.

Dave's look was one of contempt. 'He's crawled back into the woodwork, I'm glad to say. I heard he'd landed a minor lectureship somewhere in Belgium. Certainly nothing spectacular.'

'So he didn't get the French job?'

'Not likely. They were very cold about him. It seems he was mixed up in something shady in France in the sixties. They had a photograph of him kicking a policeman. It was on the front of an American news magazine at the time and someone must have remembered seeing it, I suppose. Did you ever hear of anything like that?'

'No. I told you, I only knew him for a couple of months at the most. They obviously didn't consider him for Reg's job either?'

'Not after they found he'd been sacked from his job in Hong Kong.'

'Was he? I wonder what for?' Helen exclaimed, making a good pretence of being shocked.

'Nobody seems to know but I expect it was for faking his results. It happens. Anyway it appears that all his references were forged. No wonder they were so glowing.'

Down below them Tim and Oliver had started to squabble, but Dave was trying valiantly to turn a blind eye. To distract his attention, Helen took his arm and they began to stroll on at a leisurely pace. The thought of sending the two older ones out to the cinema while they had an early night was very enticing, and they kissed, a little flirtatiously.

'How did they find out?'

'That's the strange part about it. Someone sent the vice-chancellor an anonymous fax.'

It could all have been very different. IIis affair with Ianthe might have been real. Or he might have been glad to be rid of her and never come back. Could she have coped with that? She liked to believe so, though she was glad it had turned out the way it had.

'It makes you wonder who'd do a thing like that, doesn't it?' she remarked.

If Dave had his suspicions he kept them to himself. Oliver and Tim had caught them up and they started to make their way back towards the hotel, all together.